THE GENERAL'S RELIC

MAX WINTERSON

Sonny's Big Cat Eyes
Publishing ®

The General's Relic.
Second Edition

Sonny's Big Cat Eyes Publishing®

SonnysBigCatEyes.com

ISBN: 978-0-9985653-7-8

Printed in the United States of America.

To my wife and companion, Shelly,

who has always supported my passion

for Civil War history.

Chapter 1

Jerusalem City, 1862

The crumbling stones that two diggers move with their shovels have ancient symbols on them. Jesak looks up and sees his friend on a slight rise struggling to dig into the hard soil. Here in a shallow ravine the digging is easier. It is towards the end of the Ottoman Empire. Jesak hears hammering and the sound of construction at the new settlement outside the old walls of Jerusalem, a five thousand year old city, full of hidden secrets and unknown treasures. For centuries wars have been started and fought for its possession, causing more turmoil than at any other point on the globe. Both know this and hope to find artifacts and relics they might exchange for food or other goods on the black market.

One of the men, the older one named Jesak, pauses, then brushes dirt from his callused hands. "I found something." His fingers feel the edge of what could be a box of some sort.

He leans closer, sweeps a bit more, then spits. He rubs the edge of the trinket with his robe. It shines like gold in the dull twilight of a hot evening.

He stands up and looks around to make sure no one is watching. He waves to his fellow hunter. "I need your help! Quick before we are spotted!"

The younger man runs as fast as he can over to Jesak. Together they dig the item out of its hidden hold, but when the younger man starts to yelp in anticipation, Jesak cautions that they should load the box before anyone sees them.

Upon reaching his modest home, Jesak places the box on the table, then cleans up, and prepares his supper. Only later, after his evening prayers, does Jesak go to the box and gently work his fingers around the box's edges. Jesak manages to pry the box open and slide the top off to the side. Jesak is surprised to see a strange, bluish, metallic-looking rock.

Jesak sighs. "I bet this old rock will bring a nice price."

Jesak puts the gold box back in the burlap bag. He reaches up and grabs hold of an old wooden ladder with one hand. His other hand tightly grips the burlap bag slung over his shoulder. He places his foot on the bottom rung and grunts as he pulls himself up the ladder to the upper rooms of his house. He takes the box out of the bag and places it on a short table. He hears his son mumble something in his sleep from the adjacent room. Jesak lays on his mat and sleeps.

Deep into the night, Jesak dreamt of a terrible battle. Jesak could vividly see a mighty army arriving on the hills surrounding Jerusalem. The uniforms the army's soldiers wear seem strange. They carry strange weapons of steel strapped to their belts with long, slender steel-tipped spears. They arrive in great metal wagons that make great dust clouds and sound like rolling thunder.

The dream is terrifying. Jesak awakens with a sudden jolt. Jesak is surprised to see the box glowing and that it seems to be humming. Jesak lowers his head back on his pillow and drifts back to sleep.

The following morning Jesak and his son travel to the marketplace. Around midday, after making a few inquiries about selling the item on the black market, Jesak's head throbs, and he becomes dizzy. With his son's help, Jesak stumbles back to their small, humble shack. Jesak hides the box in a chest. He manages to climb up to his sleeping quarters and collapses.

Chapter 2

Captain Lewis Wallace stands atop the battlement wall. He raises his binoculars in front of him and looks out through one of the gaps of the castle parapets in front of him. Off in the distance he sees a group of the bandit nomadic Arabs that constantly raided and pillaged any Jewish settlers caught outside the safety of the walls of Mishkenot Sha'anim, the first Jewish settlement outside of Old Jerusalem.

Captain Wallace lowers his binoculars and lets them hang against his brown frock coat. He puts a hand on the hilt of his sword and speaks to the Jewish soldier next to him. “You better ring the bell for this side of the wall. That group of Arabs is riding this way and they’ll be up to no good.”

Captain Wallace pushes back his maroon fez and dabs sweat from his forehead with a cloth. He looks towards the community’s windmill and sees the founder of Mishkenot Sha'anim arriving in his signature black carriage. A crowd is gathering around the carriage. “Sir Moses Montefiore is arriving on a trip from England I see.”

The Jewish soldier turns to look where Captain Wallace is looking. The air is dry and the sky is brilliant blue. “Yes, he arrived earlier today.”

Captain Wallace looks out over the entire compound. “It is incredible what he has built here with the money from the estate of Jewish New Orleans philanthropist Judah Touro. Sir Moses did a splendid job building this wall around Mishkenot Sha'anim. Without the wall no one would be safe here.”

The Jewish soldier rolls a cigarette and lights it. "You should get some credit for our safety. I am glad that your Confederate Jewish senator Judah Benjamin sent you here. Your network of informants has been a big help in protecting us from the bandits. We probably would not have such good information if it were not for the Confederate Secret Service."

"We're called the Secret Service because our services are a secret. Let's keep it that way. I'll let you in on a secret. I have heard that the plan is to reestablish the Jewish State of Israel and Mishkenot Sha'anim is just the beginning."

A second soldier climbs up to the walls parapet and walks over to Captain Lewis Wallace. "Sir, I have a note for you from one of your scouts in the old city of Jerusalem. He wants to be paid with a gold coin as usual."

Captain Wallace pulls one gold coin out of his haversack. "What is the message?"

"One of the local treasure hunters, a man named Jesak, has discovered a strange gold box that he is looking to sell. Jesak has taken sick. Rumor is he may die."

"I know Jesak. He is a good man. Never finds much but I had better check out this gold box myself."

A doctor arrives late in the afternoon at Jesak's house. Concerned neighbors gather outside. As the doctor leaves, Captain Lewis Wallace approaches the house.

Captain Wallace's scouts watched for men like Jesak. They would gather together in groups of four or less looking at old maps. Then they would go to areas no one else would venture into, burning incense and praying against evil spirits.

Mostly the treasure hunters would find gold coins buried during the decline of the Ottoman Empire.

Captain Wallace approaches four men standing outside the house. “What’s all the commotion about?”

“Jesak lives here. Yesterday he was well. Today he has lesions all over his body.”

“Is it a virus?”

“No one can say. A neighbor says a strange glow came from Jesak’s window last night, and today at the market he was trying to sell a strange box that was warm to the touch. Now he appears to be on his deathbed.”

“Have any of you seen this box?”

The man standing closest to Jesak’s door frowns at Captain Wallace, then turns and looks towards Jesak’s house. “No and I hope not to. An evil spirit is upon us.”

Jesak dies in the night. The next day, the talk around the marketplace is about Jesak’s death. Captain Wallace spots Jesak’s son coming into the marketplace and follows him. The Rebel is curious to see what Jesak’s son knows about the box. Captain Wallace catches up to Jesak’s son a block away from the main market.

“Excuse me! You there!”

“Can I help you?”

“Yes, I am a friend of your father. Well, I was a friend. I’m sorry to hear of his passing.”

“I haven’t seen you before.” The son casts a suspicious look towards Captain Wallace.

“I spoke to your father just a few times. Do you know what may have caused the sickness that befell your father?”

The son walks around to the back of his cart and pulls back a canvas covering. "This! This is what caused my father to fall sick and die. I am going to a man now who will buy this cursed object from me."

The Rebel agent moves his hand near the box.

Jesak's son yells, "Do not open it!"

The agent lowers his hand and bends closer in wonderment. "I won't open it, but if it's okay, I would like to examine the box closer."

The young boy nods his head.

The Confederate Secret Service agent runs his hand close enough to the box to feel its warmth. Bending over the box, he can hear vibrations and humming.

Captain Wallace reaches into his carry bag. "I will double whatever the man in the neighboring town is paying." He pulls out a bag of gold coins.

"It's all yours." The boy grabs the bag of gold and then carefully hands the box to Captain Wallace who secures the box in a large gunnysack.

Sitting on his bed later that night, Captain Wallace, thinks about how the Confederate's possession of the deadly gold box might help the war effort. The able-bodied agent of the Confederacy thinks to himself too about whether it was sheer luck or a blessing from a higher power.

He addresses a letter to Jefferson Davis, the president of the young Confederacy, to let him know of his success and his plan to have the relic transported to the Deep South by way of sailing it to Nassau, Bahama on a large frigate steamship and then transporting it on a blockade-runner to Charleston, South Carolina. He is confident he and the talisman will make it past the Yankee blockade. Unbeknownst to the Yankees, the blockade-runner's success rate in running the gauntlet is at about 80 percent.

Chapter 3
May 1862

Captain Wallace sends word to the Confederate government that to ensure the safe delivery of the gold box, he would like his most trusted fighting companions to join him in transporting the relic. They are officers and cavalrymen in Jeb Stuart's outfit. They are Virginians, born and bred to be loyal patriots. The two have also served on Robert E. Lee's personal staff and are well educated in the knowledge of operations in the Confederate army. Both men also serve in the ranks of the elite Confederate Secret Service. Espionage and operating behind enemy lines are their primary specialty.

Captain Wallace places his CSA decoder on his desk. He drafts the letter to Jeb Stuart, and then concentrates as he encrypts each letter using the encoder.

Brigadier, soon to be major, General Jeb Stuart, commander of Confederate cavalry in the eastern theatre of the Civil War, throws back a tent flap, then proceeds to enter Walt and Henry's tent.

"Walt, Henry, we have an overseas letter from Captain Wallace. They want you two on the next blockade-runner out from Wilmington, North Carolina, heading to the Ottoman Empire, and once there to make your way to New Jerusalem. Captain Wallace has a treasure that he intends to bring to the Confederacy, and he is afraid of bandits robbing him on the way."

Walt takes a puff on his pipe. “That is a long journey. Our fight is here with you, Jeb. The war could be over before we get back to Virginia.”

“Captain Wallace would not ask this of you unless it was important. He knows we need every man in this fight,” Jeb strokes his long reddish beard. “I want you two to pick one other man to go with you. Someone you can trust. Captain Wallace sent the letter encrypted. I want you to read for yourselves how important this could be to our war effort. We do not want this treasure to fall into enemy hands.”

Walt and Henry know just the right man for the job.

When Walt and Henry ride up Captain Malcolm Sloan is sitting atop a huge bolder writing in his journal.

“What are you writing there, Malcolm?”

“I keep a diary of our day-to-day adventures. You can bet folks will want to read this after the war.”

Walt looks over at Henry and then back to Malcolm. “Would you be interested in going overseas on a special mission? Captain Wallace has discovered something. Something the Confederate Government wants brought here. They need a strong detachment of men to safeguard this find on its journey from the Middle East to Charleston.”

Malcolm shakes his head, then nods to his comrades, “You know you two don’t even have to ask. After all the combat we’ve had together I’ll fight alongside y’all anywhere, anytime.”

*

The next morning before the break of dawn, the three Confederate Secret Service agents load onto a small, sleek blockade-runner. No sooner had they hit an even keel did a Yankee shell whistle over their heads.

The captain of the vessel laughed. "You guys are in for a real treat. The Yankees are making it hot for us."

Walt, Henry, and Malcolm take cover as exploding shrapnel rains down in the water.

"Give me everything from the boilers, we are going to put some distance between us and these murdering Yankees!" the captain thundered, as the large Yankee warship fell farther and farther behind.

After arriving in Bermuda, Walt, Henry, and Malcolm board a ship named the *Palmetto Belle* that gets them to their destination in a fortnight.

Near their journey's end, the three gather together towards the front of the ship, ocean spray blowing onto them. The three are decked out in their finest Confederate uniforms, and their staff officer's buttons glisten in the bright afternoon sun. The wind coming off the ocean blows their cavalry capes about them. Their hats are black cavilers with Hardee emblems on the sides and a single feather plume. They also wear red sashes around their waist. Two of the officers are wearing CSA swords with matching CS two-piece belt buckles. Captain Malcolm Sloan's accouterment is a CSA Atlanta-style belt buckle.

Walt steps a black boot upon a box of ammo and takes a puff on his pipe. He leans forward. "Gentlemen, with this relic weaponized we might be able to win this war with one mighty punch."

Malcolm asks, "Do you think this Old World relic is that powerful?"

"You heard what it did to those villagers in the Holy Land who were a little too curious and went and opened the cursed thing." Walt puffs on his pipe. "I don't know about you, but I cannot wait to see the end of this cursed war. Our missions are getting more and more dangerous, and I for one would prefer to not die in the Muslim-controlled Ottoman Empire."

Henry strokes his red beard. "You know, I am with you on that one."

Upon landing in Beirut, Lebanon, the three Confederates visit a partially burned Maronite Christian Church. They pack away their Confederate jackets, capes, and slouch hats, and leave their flashy possessions in a hiding place at the church. Walt, Henry, and Malcolm dress in clothing given to them at the Maronite Church, consisting of a blue, purple robe worn by Walt, a green, red robe worn by Henry, and a solid white robe worn by Malcolm. The robes and turbans are perfect for protecting them from the sand, dust, and heat of the Middle East.

They wear their white cotton shirts, wool pants, and tall cavalry boots under their robes. The robes are perfect for hiding their pistols and swords. Their belts are made of rugged brown leather with CS and CSA buckles holding their accouterments. Each of them carries two loaded pistols in their haversacks.

Walt looks down at his new garb. "These are some fancy robes for touring the desert."

Henry checks to see if Walt and Malcolm's accouterments, guns, and swords are covered up. "We need to blend in. We don't want the Muslims to notice us, if we can avoid it. There has recently been a lot of bloodshed between the Christians and Muslims in these parts."

Malcolm laughs, looks at the ground and then over at Henry. He rolls his eyes. "Recently, huh? There has always been war in these parts, spanning thousands of years and dozens of cultures."

A deadly civil war was fought in 1860 in the district now known as Mount Lebanon Mutasarrifate, resulting in the massacre of tens of thousands of Christians. Peace is now somewhat upon the land, thanks to an international intervention led by France.

The three agents approach a group of Frenchmen standing guard in the archway of a structure the French occupy. They present diplomatic papers for French officials that request the Confederate States of America be recognized as a legitimate government. The papers also include Jefferson Davis's thoughts on the politics of the ongoing French Mexican war. After a day in Beirut, the three travel by a small boat bound for the beautiful Port of Jaffa in Palestine. From there it is a short journey to Jerusalem, where Captain Wallace awaits them.

Upon arriving in Jaffa, the three men secure horses. Walt and Henry pick black stallions, while Malcolm chooses a beautiful white Arabian horse for his mount. Walt pays for the horses with gold coins.

The three take off the next day on the Jaffa Jerusalem road. They pass through the impressive Jaffa gate to begin their journey. The scenery is breathtaking with the big rolling hills and small Middle Eastern settlements dotting the road.

Henry, the most knowledgeable agent, points out the name of the occasional trees. "Those there are mesquite trees. Over yonder, you can see the acacia, almond, and old olive trees. All of these trees are quite common around this area and are old."

"How do you know all of that?" asks Walt.

"Just a hobby of mine. I have always wanted to travel to the Holy Land."

They pass an occasional stagecoach and many people riding camels. Near the settlements, stacked stone walls cross the hills dividing properties.

That night they stay at a two story tavern. Walt carves a masonic symbol on the wall next to their table at dinner that night to let other travelers know the masonic order now travels this road.

Henry notices Walt, with his knife out, carving something on the wall. "What are you doing over there, Walt?"

"Oh just leaving our mark."

"What for?"

"So others will know we were here. Give them fair warning not to mess with us." Walt secures his knife and returns it to his pocket.

The next day, the three get an early start. They arrive in Jerusalem and are greeted by Captain Wallace. He takes them to an inn to get a meal and catch them up on what has transpired.

The men are in one of the inn's courtyards sitting on pillows later that night when Malcolm asks, "How far are we from the Jordan River?"

Henry takes a puff on his pipe. "About twenty miles. I wouldn't mind seeing it. I am feeling a little better about our security. No sign of any trouble so far. I know the history of the area very well. I know of a spot where King David crossed the River Jordan, headed back to Jerusalem, after killing Absalom and crushing the rebellion against his kingdom."

Malcolm gets a serious look on his face. "I remember reading that in the Bible. You know, I haven't been baptized. With the war going on and men losing their lives around us daily, it would be a good idea to have assurance I will make it to heaven in the event my life is taken. I would like to be baptized in the Jordan River, sir."

"Well, Henry here can help you out with that request. As you already know he is an ordained Episcopalian minister."

The three check with Captain Wallace that evening and the trip to the Jordan River is agreed upon.

The next day the weather is beautiful. The cavalrymen are in high spirits. With the humidity being low in the area, it is a delightful change from the climate of the Deep South. Henry baptizes Malcolm Sloan in the River Jordan much to everyone's delight.

"Thank you for doing this for me Henry. It means a lot." Malcolm reaches out his hand towards Henry.

Henry shakes his hand. "It was an honor and a privilege Malcolm."

*

Back in Jerusalem the following day, the relic is carefully put into a crate and loaded onto the stagecoach.

Captain Sloan closes the lid on the crate. "The intricate gold designs on the box by themselves would bring a fortune sold to the right buyer."

Captain Wallace walks over to the three agents. "Walt, if you don't mind, we have a few passengers from the new section of Jerusalem, where Jewish people live. Please forgive them if they seem nervous. They and the driver are concerned about what is in the crate and that you three are escorting the stagecoach. I told them it is a payment for goods and not to worry. I, too, am getting a little concerned. I have heard stories today of bandits attacking along the highway."

Walt puts his large hand on Captain Wallace's shoulder. "Don't worry a bit, we always win in a fight, as you well know. We will protect this stagecoach with our lives and then some."

The stagecoach gets a significant distance away from Jerusalem, well past the Serpentine road. It is getting towards evening, and it would be time to find an inn soon. Walt rides in front of the stagecoach, with Henry and Malcolm side by side in the rear.

As the team comes around a bend in the road, without warning, fifty horsemen appear in battle formation directly over a hill in front of them.

Captain Wallace riding shotgun on the stagecoach shouts, "We are going to die!"

Henry and Malcolm ride to the flanks of the horsemen. Walt takes his horses reins in his teeth. His two pistols materialize as he charges into the bandits.

The horsemen split. Walt rides into the middle of their line dropping five men on his first pass. Ten more men go down as the bandits ride into the trap sprung by Malcolm and Henry circling opposite ends of their flanks.

The three Confederate cavalrymen continue firing into the bewildered bandits, racing around and through the bandits diminishing ranks, throwing down their spent pistols, as they are emptied, and grabbing fully loaded ones from their haversacks. Finally down to only half their original number, the bandits beat a hasty retreat.

Walt rides up to the stagecoach, where the passengers have been watching the action crouched down in the coach. Captain Wallace stands up from his shooting position on top of the stagecoach, pumps his breech carbine in the air and gives out a victorious Rebel yell.

Walt gives Captain Wallace a salute. "Just like I said, the bad guys here run away just as fast as the Yankees do back home!"

Captain Wallace pumps his fist in the air. "The General's Relic will make it to the Confederate States safely with your command on watch."

Walt looks over at Henry. "We had better retrieve our pistols and get moving. We've got a mission to fulfill. I'd like to get the General's Relic to the Confederacy as soon as possible."

Chapter 4
July 1862

The agents complete their mission, escorting the General's Relic out of the Holy Land, through the Federal blockade, arriving safely in the Confederate States of America. The gold box is put under the jurisdiction of the Confederacy's war department.

A small piece of the mysterious material inside of the General's Relic is crushed into a fine powder, loaded into a canister shell, and then detonated by canon over a group of farm animals to determine the effect the General's Relic will have as a weapon of war.

The experiment does not go as planned. The soldiers watch in horror as a flag on the field flickers and without warning turns from the expected direction of the wind, then points towards the battery that has just fired the live round. The dust from the crushed material blows back on to the battery of men, killing them all. Also killed is one of the Confederacy's most promising officers, a lieutenant related to Robert E. Lee.

Observers and scientists in an enclosed safety structure watch the disaster unfold. One of the observers, a good friend of the lieutenant, rushes out of the enclosure with a bandana wrapped over his mouth and nostrils, attempting to save his friend. Small dust particles from the General's Relic find their way into the soldier's lungs, overcoming him as he tries to carry his friend to safety. During the live fire demonstration, the General's Relic manages to kill some of the Confederacy's finest artillerymen.

It is determined that such a deadly weapon can only be used if the army is under complete desperation, and no other alternative for victory can be expected, except for inflicting large, sudden causalities upon the enemy. The destruction of the entire Federal army in one blow would be the outcome, but the complete destruction of the Army of Virginia is also a possible outcome if the wind shifted in the wrong direction. The powers of the General's Relic are secretly kept in reserve and ordained for use only with signed orders from three high-ranking generals and the president of the Confederacy.

The Confederacy carries the relic onto the battlefields where some of the most famous Civil War battles are fought. Robert E. Lee and Stonewall Jackson acquire their greatest victories together, keeping the General's Relic in reserve, hesitant to use the deadly weapon. Only a few officers know of the existence of the General's Relic. The agents charged with handling the gold box disguise it by placing it in an ammo box on an ordinance wagon. A lock is kept on the ammo box. The officers tell the drivers of the wagon that the generals want to keep a wagon loaded with ammunition in reserve in case all of the other ammunition is exhausted. The wagon drivers become suspicious of what the wagon caisson might contain.

"Ned, how come the general never asks us to pull our ordinance to the front?"

"It does seem strange. I'm getting tired of staying in the rear on guard duty while our comrades are dying on the frontlines."

"Why don't we break the lock? I bet we are carrying a shipment of gold."

"No, we've got our orders, and we cannot go second guessing why the generals do what they do. Captain Sloan might have us shot if we disobey his orders."

Later in the evening, against strict orders, Ned decides that one peek at what they're guarding won't hurt anything. He slips over to the wagon, pulls out a piece of stiff wire with an L-shaped bend in it, and picks the lock open on the ammo caisson. Ned raises the lid of the ammo box. His eyes grow wide when he sees a gold box with intricate designs on it.

"I knew we were guarding gold. I just knew it." Ned raises the lid on the gold box and sees a large rock glowing pinkish red.

Ned runs over to his mate. Jim sluggishly waves Ned off. Ned puts his hand on Jim's arm. "Come on. You won't be able to see it in the morning with the other soldiers around."

Jim begins to doze off. "Let me sleep, Ned. I'll see it tomorrow."

Ned empties his haversack, and then scoops the glowing rock into his haversack. He walks over to Jim, feeling lightheaded as he does. Jim rises up from his sleep.

"What is it?"

"This is what we have been guarding." Ned brings out a reddish glowing rock.

Jim's eyes get wide. "Ned, your face is blistering! Get that thing away from us!"

The rock glowed stronger. Jim looks down, and his exposed hands are blistering.

"Jim, I am sorry," says Ned.

Both men begin convulsing from the invisible destruction brought upon them by the General's Relic. They are dead a minute later. The General's Relic takes two more from the world and into oblivion.

When Captain Malcolm Sloan checks on the two privates the next morning, he finds lifeless corpses instead of his comrades. Captain Sloan does not approach any closer as he had read the report of the death of so many Confederate Soldiers after the failed experiment months before. He realizes what has happened, and he cannot believe the dangerous rock is in the open. He runs to his tent and grabs a bandanna he wraps across his nose and mouth. "Those two insubordinate idiots are going to get us all killed."

Captain Sloan uses a pole to roll the now cold relic into a specially designed lead-lined haversack and returns it to the gold box. The two privates are quietly given a Christian burial. Captain Malcolm Sloan and two privates dig the grave. Malcolm stands at a distance as the privates pull the bodies off of the burial wagon.

"Captain Sloan, this body feels warm under this oil cloth. No pulse. What could cause this?"

"Just bury the men for Pete's sake! These men died from awful causes. Don't languish or you too will perish!"

Chapter 5
April 1863

Captain Malcolm Sloan observes a Union signal station near Chancellorsville. He states what he is seeing through his binoculars to a private who quickly writes down the various flag colors and signals. Across the river, Joe Hooker's massive Union army is converging to deliver what he hopes will be a knockout blow to the Confederates. Back at headquarters the Rebels decipher the secret messages.

Jeb Stuart enters the staff officer's tent. He reads the Federal transcriptions. He looks up at Malcolm. "Looks like this message might be right up your alley? The Federals are holding a ball at a mansion across the river."

Malcolm rolls a cigarette. "Events like that are gold mines of information. Officers and women get to drinking and all sorts of secrets are divulged."

"Could be dangerous."

Malcolm takes a drag from his cigarette. "I've been on dozens of these information gathering trips, worse thing that can happen is a hangover from too much champagne. We have got to get some more information as to what the enemy is planning. I will ride over and join the Yankee's party."

Malcolm rides his horse, Argo, through the porous enemy lines and up close to where the party is being held at a large estate. He ties Argo to a tree in a grove of woods. He changes into a confiscated Federal officer's uniform. Malcolm slips in through some large boxwoods onto the patio of the mansion. Malcolm wrings his hands and looks around for some other officers to mingle with.

A servant walks up with a tray of drinks. "Sir, would you like a glass of champagne?"

Malcolm takes a glass, becoming more relaxed with something in his hands, and then walks in through the side door of the antebellum mansion.

A little later, a general asks, "That man over there, who is he?"

"He said his name is Malcolm Smith," replies a staff officer. "I haven't seen him before either. I ran a telegraph out to Washington and he checks out okay. He arrived from Lincoln's personal staff, a day ago."

Unbeknownst to the Federals, the Confederates have taken control of the telegraph line, intercepting the messages and putting in place their own deceiving information.

Late in the evening, Malcolm finds himself in the company of two beautiful Southern belles. One of the girls, a brunette named Emily with curly hair and blue eyes, is wearing a long, white ballroom gown with pink piping. The other girl, Sally, has red curly hair, green eyes, and wears an equally beautiful green ballroom dress. Malcolm tells the attentive girls his wartime adventure stories. The girls giggle and take more champagne.

Sally leans over to the disguised Rebel officer and whispers in Malcolm's ear, "I think you are a Rebel spy."

Emily waves her hand. "Don't mind her. Sally thinks everyone is a Rebel spy."

"Girls, I can assure you I am very loyal to the cause."

Sally asks, "Which cause is that?"

Emily interrupts, "I know what we can do. Let's continue this party over at my uncle's house."

"It is getting late. I must go."

Emily takes Malcolm's arm in hers. "Don't be silly, we have a carriage outside that we drove up here ourselves. Come and keep us company. We know you will be a perfect gentleman."

Malcolm concedes, "Well, just for a little while." The girls and Malcolm loaded up into the carriage.

A little down the road, Malcolm points off the road. "Right here, my horse is in that grove of trees. I will follow you to your uncle's house."

Arriving at the plantation house, it is evident that the girls have failed to mention a thing or two. Malcolm is surprised that the place looks abandoned.

"My uncle is gone off to war, fighting in the Confederate army. This place is still lightly staffed by his faithful servants," explains Emily.

The three walk into a parlor. A servant woman and man come to the entrance of the parlor. Emily steps out to talk to them. "It is good to see you, Miss Emily, but I don't think you two girls should be entertaining this strange man."

Emily puts her hand to her mouth. "Heavens, you two must think we are loose. We are always ladies. Do not say a word of this to my uncle."

Emily gives the servants a sharp look of warning and pulls the parlor doors shut.

Early the next morning, the servant woman puts up her daily laundry in a coded arrangement to let the Federal army, stationed on a faraway hilltop, know that a Rebel is at the plantation. Quickly a group of Federal cavalrymen ride down into the valley.

Malcolm now dressed in his full Confederate uniform, throws a kiss to the two beauties looking down at him from an upstairs balcony. Emily and Sally now dressed in morning gowns, throw kisses back to Malcolm. His large black stallion rears up his front legs kicking at the sky. Malcolm waves his plumed cavalry hat in a grand goodbye to the two girls.

A mile down the road, the Federal cavalry runs into Malcolm. A chase ensues. "You there, stop now!" The Federals begin to aggressively pursue Malcolm on their horses.

Malcolm is certain he will escape as always, but he begins to realize he is severely outnumbered. The Yankees spring a trap and Malcolm is soon surrounded with nowhere to turn.

Malcolm, in his full Confederate uniform, pleads, "Gentlemen, as you can see, I am an officer in the Confederate army. I am in uniform and deserve proper treatment."

"Let's hang him!" yells out a soldier from the crowd.

A Federal officer emerges from the crowd and points toward Malcolm. "I saw you last night at the party in a Federal uniform. How do you explain that, sir?"

"You must have me mistaken for someone else, sir. I was preoccupied last night with more attractive company, if you don't mind me saying." Malcolm looks up the road towards the mansion that he just rode from.

"No sir. I never forget a face. You were there, and today you will hang."

"This is outrageous! You all will be tried for war crimes if you proceed with this egregious offense," Malcolm yells out while the crowd of Yankees begins to close in on him.

His pleads fall on deaf ears. Malcolm is hanged as a spy by the Federal cavalry.

Later the next day, his comrades, who had intercepted the telegraph a day earlier, cut down his body. Many of the soldiers are in tears, as they carry Malcolm's remains back behind Confederate lines.

After the great victory by the Confederates at the Battle of Chancellorsville, Robert E. Lee is despondent about the loss of the great Stonewall Jackson, along with the loss of over twenty thousand of his best men. Also to add to the loss of men is one of Robert E. Lee's trusted staff officers who guarded the General's Relic. Robert E. Lee had been hesitant in the first place to have such a terrible weapon under his army.

Robert E. Lee comes to a conclusion that the General's Relic is cursed and that the relic is more of a danger to the Army of Virginia than to the enemy. Stonewall Jackson was the champion of the General's Relic. General Jackson felt that the weapon could be effective under the right circumstances, possibly bringing about a quick end to the war. Robert E. Lee summons the remaining General's Relic agents and gives them the commission of removing the General's Relic from his army and placing it under safe guard until further notice.

Henry and Walt, the two remaining Rebel agents initially involved in transporting the dangerous relic, agree to meet in a parlor of a two-story Victorian house to discuss where to hide the General's Relic. It's a hazy day in June and the house is peaceful, considering how close the house is located to the warzone.

Henry, standing in the parlor, adjusts his cavalier's hat in a mirror. "Well, where is the best place to store this devil plaything for safekeeping and secrecy? If that weapon ever falls into the Yankees hands, we will lose our cause for certain."

Walt, sitting at a table, turns his head and looks Henry in the eye. "My friend, I am going to let you in on something I know about that is top secret and highly classified," Walt leans forward rolls a cigarette and prepares to light it. "I know about this information due to my blockade running activities and ferrying supplies through the Yankee gauntlet."

Henry puts a hand on the table and leans forward listening. "Go on."

"I have been sworn to secrecy on the subject, but I think in light of our current mission you should know some facts and details that may help us achieve our goal. Jefferson Davis has commissioned a Confederate supply base and possible second capitol to be built in South America. You may have heard of rumors that a long-term goal of the Confederacy is to include South America and Mexico in our countries boundaries, resulting in a golden circle of Confederate States.

"Eventually, once the second Confederate capitol is complete, we will move the General's Relic and other Confederate assets to that location. The current plan is to fortify a temporary hiding place in a remote location for highly important items such as the Confederacy's gold reserves. God forbid the Yankees were to take Richmond, but we will lose the war for sure if either of these items falls into the enemy's hands. I know of a cave in Northwest Alabama. It is a perfect place to stash supplies. We will use this temporary location until we can move all assets to the South American base."

"That area is now crawling with the Yankee army and murdering thieves. We will be putting ourselves and our mission in great danger.

"I will admit it was easier to make the trip earlier in the war. Jefferson Davis expressed an interest in sending the Richmond gold reserves to Alabama if the war took a turn for the worse. That cave is a perfect hiding place. In September of 1862 after the battle of Antietam and Lincolns Emancipation Proclamation President Davis began to see that we might lose this war. I was commissioned at that time to move some of the gold reserves to the cave in Alabama."

The next day the two start working on a plan to make the long journey to move the General's Relic to the cave in Northwest Alabama, where it will be safe far behind enemy lines. The natural barrier of the mighty Tennessee River cutting through the Tennessee Valley provides a formable defense for the Rebel Army's supply routes.

The hidden cave was discovered years before by Walt, who was raised in the area before going off to the Eastern theatre of the war with an Alabama regiment.

The two Confederate Secret Servicemen discuss the perfect plan, one they pray over. The final decision is made to put the long-term fate of the Confederacy in the hands of a subordinate, who is a true patriot. The new agent would be a replacement for Captain Sloan, who had served honorably and made the ultimate sacrifice.

Walt leans over the table to extinguish his cigarette. "I would like to put in a request to replace Captain Sloan's position on our team. Virginia has lost a great patriot who will be sorely missed, but he would want us to carry on our mission."

Henry leans back in his chair. "General Nathan Bedford Forrest should be able to assign someone to a temporary special assignment."

The two Virginia agents submit their plans to their superiors and wait for a response to their requests and plans. They keep the General's Relic safe in the Victorian farmhouse near Richmond. The two perform chores and duties that will help the women of the farming community in their struggles going into the growing season.

A few weeks go by and a courier delivers a dispatch case with papers to Walt and Henry. The two agents proceed to the parlor of the farmhouse and begin working on decoding the correspondence with a closely guarded CSA encryption decoder.

Henry turns to Walt. "Jefferson Davis has approved our plan to hide the General's Relic in North Alabama. They've also found us a scout from Middle Tennessee who comes highly recommended. I figure we should ready the horses and wagon and head out in the morning. I've got to let the lady of the farm, Ms. Judy, know it might be a long time before we see her again."

Walt strokes his chin and raises one of his eyebrows. "It will be okay, Lincoln's administration is going to come to its senses. We have won every engagement and battle up to this point. Lincoln will have no choice but to withdraw his forces and understand we fully intend upon having a free and independent Confederacy!"

Chapter 6
February 1863

The new Confederate agent chosen to replace Malcolm is a young Rebel from the famed Coleman Scouts unit in Middle Tennessee named Andy McCarver. Famous for their horse riding skills this network of scouts was legendary across the Western Theatre of operations.

Andy is celebrating his seventeenth birthday. He only has one burning desire for his seventeenth birthday, which is to see his girlfriend, somcone hc has not visited in many months.

The visit is not only for pleasure though. Andy's girlfriend works behind enemy lines in one of the many brothels in downtown Nashville. Andy will receive valuable information on troop movements and operations of the Union soldiers in occupied Middle Tennessee. The battle of Stones River in Murfreesboro had recently been fought to a stalemate.

Andy approaches a two-story Antebellum home with large ornate columns on the front of it. The home is on the edge of Nashville on the outskirts of what is known as a no man's land that separates the safety the Union forces enjoy behind their fortifications, from the raids and scouting operations of Confederate cavalry. The weather is very cold, and it is starting to snow. Andy approaches the door of the stately manor and knocks a secret knock.

An old man dressed in a smoking robe comes to the door and opens it. "Andy, please, enter quickly! It has grown dangerous around here in last few weeks. The Union cavalry stop here nearly every day now asking questions and poking their noses in our homes and private affairs."

"Ah, don't worry about me. They will never catch me, and as you well know I have never failed at a mission to gather information." Andy is dressed in his finest grey military coat and cavalier's hat.

"Very well. You will have to join me for a drink. The weather is terrible out there, and a little whiskey, the best in Tennessee, will warm you up. Let's make a toast to friendship and the Southern Confederacy."

Andy raises his glass and clinks it against the Southern gentleman's glass. "To the Southern Confederacy, victory or death!"

The master of the house walks over to a bookshelf which hides a secret passage way. "I will open the secret passage for you. There are many issues I would like to talk about, but time is short, and Victoria is waiting for you in the King's Chamber. Her maps and information of enemy troop movements are precise as always."

The dark passageways under the streets of Nashville are old and date back to the days of the Indian wars. Many of the passageways were expanded and lined with brick. Some of the hidden chambers are quite extravagant and were designed as long-term hideouts. The tunnel Andy walks down is one of the old brick-lined passages. Flickering torches cast shadows on the tunnel walls.

Andy turns a corner and comes into the King's Chamber, which is decorated with old scenic pictures on the walls. Dozens of different sized candles light the room. A round banquet table with fine wood chairs is in the middle of the room. A beautiful brunette, wearing a green evening dress, smiles at Andy.

"Victoria!" Andy removes his hat, casts it to a chair, then rushes to embrace Victoria with a kiss.

"Andy, I have missed you terribly, why have you not visited me sooner?"

She giggles as she reaches her long slender fingers to Andy's face. Andy reaches for Victoria's hand and kisses it. They fall together on a couch laughing and kissing each other. The two lovers passionately frolic over each other for the remainder of their time together, as they both know they might never again have this opportunity.

The next morning, over breakfast, Andy asks, "How's about when this war is over we get married?"

Victoria blushes. "Andy, let's find a minister and get married today! We can run down to South America and put this miserable war behind us."

"I've made a promise to my comrades, my brothers in arms."

"Well, I will have to just keep procuring the very best intelligence to shorten this war, so we can get on with our lives together. Let's place this map on the table here and I will show you the weakest points of the Yankee occupation."

Chapter 7
June 1863

With the General's Relic, Walt and Henry begin their long journey to Northwest Alabama. The two are fortunate the trains are running. They travel comfortably in a plush railroad coach. The General's Relic is still in an ammo caisson, which is loaded onto the train in the same car with the two agents' mules and horses. The railroad journey itself is dangerous since bandits and bushwhackers, who show no loyalty to either side, frequently attack the trains.

Walt and Henry start out at Richmond, Virginia going further south to the great sea port of Wilmington, North Carolina, where so many Confederate supplies arrive from abroad. The next leg of the journey is to Orangeburg, South Carolina, skirting by Charleston. The train carries the two agents through Atlanta where they sightsee for a few hours while the train stops at the depot to load Confederate supplies from the Atlanta Arsenal.

The Confederate agents marvel at the size of the war materials operation, along with the number of people involved in the production of uniforms, bullets, and accouterments. They are told that nearly half the population is working around the clock producing everything imaginable for the military. The arsenal produces close to seventy thousand bullets daily. Once the train is loaded with supplies for the war efforts, the two continue their journey to Chattanooga and from there on across Alabama. The two Rebel agents wave at well-equipped infantry soldiers, part of the large Confederate army of Tennessee, camped along the railroad tracks in Tullahoma Tennessee.

Ever since the bloody Battle of Stones River was fought December 30 to 31 in 1862, the Rebels had held the Union army of the Cumberland at a standstill. Six months had passed. The Confederate army of Tennessee was still camped along the Duck River in Shelbyville and at Tullahoma in Middle Tennessee.

The two agents talked about the news of Nathan Bedford Forrest's chase, made famous by the tenacity and fierceness of the Confederate cavalry capturing Colonel Streight and his Mule Brigade. Forrest's heroic soldiers and fast thoroughbreds, relentlessly for days and without sleep, obstructed Colonel Streight and his doomed raid across North Alabama from cutting the railroad tracks in Rome, Georgia.

Walt and Henry arrive in Tuscumbia, Alabama late in the evening. They stay at a local inn there, getting a good night's sleep. The next day, the two secret service men get directions from the headquarters of General Roddy on where to meet the Coleman Scout from Middle Tennessee. While at the Tuscumbia headquarters camp, the two write letters to family members and marvel at the strong natural spring with water shooting up out of the small lake there.

Walt and Henry meet Andy on the banks of the Tennessee River. Andy holds up his hand, greeting the two with a wave. "Did you have any trouble finding my camp?"

Walt, getting down off his horse, surveys Andy's small camp with grey piercing eyes. "Nah! No trouble in finding the Tennessee River. You must be Andy. We've heard that you are a good shot."

"I guess that's a good reputation to have. I reckon I can hold my own with a rifle."

The camp is in a underneath a large old oak tree about fifty feet from the edge of the Tennessee River. Andy has a tent pitched and a good campfire going. "Would y'all like some hot coffee?"

Walt and Henry both contend that coffee would be much appreciated. They tie their horses and mules to nearby trees.

"This is a beautiful place here in the Tennessee Valley," says Henry.

"Yea, my ma has a place close by, where I was raised."

Walt looks out over the mighty Tennessee River. "Me too, I was raised in Lawrence county, but I have not been here since the war started."

Andy hands the two coffees, and the three take a seat on some rocks and a log close around the campfire.

Chapter 8

"How are you holding up under this War [illegible] Aggression? I will be glad when this war is o[illegible] the sooner the better."

"It's rough, we've lost a lot of good men. If not for General Roddy and General Forrest the entire area would be a desolate wasteland. Our forces here in North Alabama have provided a tremendous service in protecting the lives and property of the citizens. Areas outside of our immediate jurisdiction suffer terribly. You would not believe the stories we hear from the citizens who have suffered harm from Yankee cavalry and bushwhackers."

Walt lets out a sigh. "Andy, we are on an important mission to store a valuable item that may one day, if God is willing for it to be used, help us in our struggle for Southern independence, and stop once and for all the attacks on our homeland. The item is in that ammo caisson over there."

"What is the item?"

Henry, the older agent, answers, "The item is a weapon, a terrible weapon that can wipe out a twenty-thousand-man army with one shot from an artillery piece."

Andy squints his eyes and clasps his hands together. "Well, how can I be of service?"

Walt opens a haversack next to him and pulls out a solid brass belt buckle with a down-turned eagle on the front and the words The Southern Confederacy written out above the eagle. Walt brings the buckle closer to the campfire. "This buckle has an encrypted secret message engraved on the back of it. Both of us are wearing the same buckles, and ese are the only three buckles of this style in existence. The encrypted codes on the back of our buckles, when combined with this buckle, will produce a map that will lead to a secret hidden cave where the weapon and other treasures of the Confederacy will be stored. We need someone with high integrity, intelligence, and courage to join us in our mission to protect what we call the General's Relic and the Confederacy's treasures."

The Coleman scouts inquisitiveness leads him to ask, "Why don't you just tell me where the cave is?"

Walt replies, "In case of our capture, it is better you did not know the exact location of the cave. Our plan is for you to take this buckle and have knowledge of the treasure. With your skills we have no doubt you will be able to locate the treasure if anything happens to us. We have papers and personnel in place that will make sure that our possessions, namely our buckles with the clues, are to be delivered into your hands if we are killed in action."

The Coleman agent points at the belt plates. "I don't want to wear a gun belt buckle like the ones y'all are wearing. Those buckles look like they could belong to the president himself."

"Look, kid I—"

"I ain't no kid. I can outride, outshoot, and out-spy circles around the two of you!"

Walt offered an apology, "I meant no offense. Please join our cause. I promise you will not regret it."

Andy discarded his CSA belt plate for the ornate one. The new plate, stunning in its motif with the Southern Confederacy, brilliant eagle, wings turned down, and, to top it off, thirteen stars around its edge, one for each of the States in the young new Confederacy.

Chapter 9

At sunrise, Walt and Henry prepare to break camp and head to the hidden cave. There is a slight fog coming off the river, covering the ground, as the two Confederate Secret Service agents hitch up their horses. Andy is just getting out of his tent.

Henry asks, "How far away is the cave?"

"Won't take us more than an hour to reach it."

"Is there any chance someone else could stumble upon it?" Andy asks.

Walt looks over at Henry, as he tightens a strap on his horse saddle. "Not likely, the area is remote, plus there are legends of ghosts. Folks say it is an Indian burial ground. The entrance is hidden behind brush. We're going to seal the entrance with a rockslide. The rocks above the entrance are unstable. We can use a barrel of gunpowder to reopen it when needed."

Henry mounts his horse. His horse leads a mule pulling the ammunition caisson. "I am looking forward to seeing more of the valley. Maybe I will move my family down here after the war. Lots of wide open space here."

Walt mounts his horse, then turns in the saddle. "Hey, Andy, if you see any signs of trouble, fire off two warning shots. That will let us know to be on the lookout for trouble."

Andy, now the newest member of the Confederate Secret Service, could only wonder at the foolishness of sitting around a campfire by himself when he could be with his unit chasing down Yankees.

It wasn't until the next morning he saw a soul. Andy knew at once the three men riding towards him were deserters or bushwhackers or both. He muttered to himself, "Those murderers will kill me, along with my new friends, on a whim. I must do something."

Andy had stuffed his .44 Remington revolver in his waist. The three ride up and proceed to start up a conversation.

"Howdy! You wouldn't be a deserter now would ya?" The bushwhacker grins and shows his discolored teeth.

One of the other men in the party spits on the ground. "Boy, what unit you with?"

"I am a scout for Nathan Bedford Forrest."

The ruffians look up and around on the mention of the name of Forrest, afraid that Andy might be telling the truth.

"We would like some food if you have any extra; the Yankees have cleared out just about everything around here."

Andy replies, "I am on picket duty here. You three need to be moving on before I raise the alarm."

One of the dusty ruffians reaches down towards his pistol. "Now look here pup."

As soon as the word pup is off the end of his tongue, Andy is in action. Before anyone can blink, Andy has his .44 Remington out from behind his back. The three horsemen fall from their steeds, dead from three well-fired bullets to their chests.

"I have had it with being called kid and pup!" Andy shouts.

Not too far away Walt and Henry, done with the mission of hiding the General's Relic, are returning towards camp. They'd heard the sharp sound of gunfire in the distance. As they ride back into camp, Andy is finishing putting rocks on the last grave of the three men he killed.

Walt asks Andy, "What happened, kid?"

Andy replies, "Well these three men rode up and called me a 'pup' and 'kid.' I killed them, and now they are dead."

"You did a fine job of killing them."

Andy could not help but laugh.

Chapter 10

Henry returns north of the Mason Dixon line to help with espionage in Virginia. Forrest's cavalry are camped at Ringgold, Georgia on the eve of the battle. Walt and Andy fight alongside each other in the Battle of Chickamauga, riding and fighting in Nathan Bedford Forrest's dismounted cavalry forces. "Andy, have you got a minute?"

"Sure Walt, pull up a seat on that log there, I've got this rabbit grilling on the fire, and in a minute we will have some good eating. I always make the best rabbit traps."

Walt pulls his coat around him tighter. "We have confirmation the entire Yankee army is within a few miles of us. Tomorrow there will be a large battle."

Andy leans back against a log. "We always win when we are riding with Forrest."

"I know, Andy, it's just that, darn if I knew I should have sewed that button on tighter. I lost one of my Virginia buttons off my coat."

"So what's bothering you, Walt?"

"I don't think I will survive this war."

The next day opens early in the cold grey dawn. The Rebels move west towards Chickamauga Creek. The Confederate infantry in their crisp new uniforms spread out one mile before Reed Bridge. Most of the Federal army had crossed the bridge earlier to escape the Confederates coming towards them. About noon, Forrest's Cavalry moves in front of the Confederate Infantry to determine where the Yankees are located. Riding at a gait, Forrest's Cavalry gallop ahead and run directly into the waiting Yankee army. The Yankees are hidden on the edge of some woods. The Union army opens fire emptying several Rebel saddles. With the fog and cold of the morning now gone, the fight begins in earnest with the rattle of musketry.

Forrest yells, "Dismount, troopers!"

The Confederate cavalry and infantry mix together. The Confederate infantry and several hundred of Forrest's men push the Yankees back. The Confederates fight hard but cannot take Reed Bridge. Forrest rides south, looking for a ford over the creek, to flank the Union army. The Confederates at Reed Bridge stay pinned down from the heavy firepower of the Yankee army.

Returning an hour later, Forrest finds the Federals have crossed the bridge and are making a stand on the opposite side. The Yankees had pulled up the bridge planks and railing, throwing them in the river, on their way across. In spite of many shots ringing out from Federal sharpshooters, the Confederates repair the bridge with planks from the Reed house and barn. Some of the Confederate infantry manage to cross and begin to spread out on the west side of the bridge providing rifle fire against the Yankees.

Andy notices his horse is not acting normal. He looks back and down at his horse's right back hoof. Andy's horse is lifting his hoof up and down.

Walt shouts over to Andy, "Something's about to happen at the bridge, Andy! You better come over and watch this!"

"I'll be with y'all in minute." Andy takes his horse away from the action to inspect what is going on with his leg. Andy lifts up the horse's hoof and uses his cavalry pick to knock mud from the hoof. "Well, I'll be, look at that, there's a spent miniè ball stuck in your hoof, boy! Just stand still for a second and we'll have this out." Andy stands and pets his horse. "Good boy! That's got to feel a lot better."

A tremendous triumphant bellow comes up from the Confederate army of Tennessee. Andy ties his horse to a nearby tree and walks over to Walt. "What did I miss?"

Walt grins. "Forrest rode out and single handily whipped the whole Yankee army. They're on the run to Chattanooga. I told ya that you might miss something good! Let's mount up! Forrest will want to keep the scare on them!"

After a hard day of fighting, Forrest advanced on the enemy and camps close to the Alexander Bridge that night. Andy and Walt, tired and cold, slept in the same tent. Walt looked at a locket he'd pulled from under his shirt.

Andy asked, "What do you have there, Walt?"

Walt handed over the locket from around his neck. "This is a picture of my mother and father. I also have a younger brother who is too young to serve." Walt pauses as he looks at the fire, then out towards the woods. He lowers his head and pokes the fire with a stick. "My father is tough. He met my mom in an unusual circumstance. My father was a fur trader. One day he came by my mother's family home."

Walt stops poking at the fire and turns his head towards Andy. "Everyone at the home except my mother, Anna Belle, had been killed by rogue Indians. Father tracked her captives for two days before catching up with them. He slipped into the camp and killed two of them outright. The remaining Indian put my mom across the front of his horse and was preparing to ride off with her. Father picked up a tomahawk and made a perfect throw, hitting the Indian in the back as he was riding off."

"Sounds like the Indian got what he had coming to him."

"I visited them in Alabama recently. Yankees were afraid to go up to his cabin after hearing the local legends. It was hard work living on the mountain, but I am happy when I look at their picture. Andy, tomorrow is going to be an even bloodier day."

"Walt, we're gonna whip the Yankees tomorrow just like we did today."

*

Forrest realizes the next morning that the Federal army has outflanked him in the night. As Forrest moved down the Chickamauga creek, General Rosecrans had moved north to escape to Chattanooga. Forrest throws his troopers into action. Flanked and overwhelmed, with everyone ignoring his pleas for help, Forrest rides off and finds Colonel Claudius Wilson and General Walthall's brigade.

Forrest's troopers hang on under the cover of every log and tree they can find.

Andy ducks his head down behind the cover of some boulders. "How's our ammunition holding up?"

Walt hands Andy another cartridge. "We don't have much. Make every shot count."

"I never miss."

"You weren't kidding about being a good shot with that Sharps Carbine. You've hit every Yankee you've shot at."

Andy squeezes off another shot, dispatching a Yankee colonel. "You just keep that ammunition coming, Walt. We'll get out of this yet."

Running low on ammunition the two are elated once veteran Confederate infantry arrive. "Look over there, Andy, it's the Hardee Flag. Looks like reinforcements are finally here."

Andy lets out a Rebel yell and smiles.

The Confederate infantry close in right up to the Yankees, open fire, and drive off the enemy. In the thickest of the fight, Forrest is seen at his favorite position near Morton's guns, wearing a long tan duster, his pistols, and sword wrapped around him outside of his coat. Both flanks close in around Forrest. Canister shot and bullets fly all around him as he and his command fight like mad men to save the day. Overpowered by the advancing enemy, Forrest's cavalry falls back in one of many back and forth surges by both sides.

Walt sees a group of cannon with all of the horses shot dead. "Andy, quick, throw these ropes around your saddle horn. We have got to get these cannons out of here."

Walt waves his hand for help, and several more cavalrymen hook their horses up to the cannons, dragging them off through the woods to safety. Ector's Brigade comes up providing more reinforcements. At about 1:30 in the afternoon, Cleburne, of Cheatham's division, takes the field, sweeping everything before it.

*

The next day opens with Forrest advancing. The Confederate cavalry come upon Federal field hospitals.

Andy pauses his horse. "You were right, Walt, this is a terrible battle. I cannot believe how many men are wounded."

Walt dismounts and walks over to a wounded soldier to give him a drink from his canteen.

Upon returning to his horse, Walt overhears a scout reporting to Forrest, "A large amount of Yankees are approaching, sir."

Against orders Yankee General Gordon Granger is fast approaching with his reserve corps. Forrest brings up fourteen cannon, blasting the Yankees to bits, stopping Granger. The Federal army begins its retreat to Chattanooga. Forrest keeps the fight and chase on them the whole way.

The next day, Forrest is still chasing the Federal army. Along with General Armstrong, Forrest rides out onto Missionary Ridge, capturing Yankee lookouts in the trees. Climbing a tree himself, Forrest spots the Federal army evacuating across two pontoon bridges, boarding their trains and preparing to evacuate Chattanooga. Forrest lowers his binoculars and looks over at General Armstrong. "They're evacuating. I'll send a message to Bragg. If he can send us troops we can retake Chattanooga."

Forrest sends a dispatch to Bragg letting him know of the enemy's weakness in Chattanooga. Bragg does not reply and fails to send any troops.

Forrest brings up his cannon and shells the Yankees, but cannot dislodge them from their works. Soon the enemy is well entrenched and impenetrable.

To add to the disappointment of Braxton Bragg not following up after the great victory at Chickamauga, he sends a letter to Forrest on September 30 requesting him to turn his command over to Joe Wheeler. Forrest sends a dispatch to Bragg informing him he will be riding to personally respond to what he has just written.

Forrest meets with Bragg and lets him know he did not appreciate the attempted destruction of his Kentucky and West Tennessee operations. Dr. J. B. Cowan, chief surgeon of Forrest's Cavalry, is outside Bragg's tent when he hears Forrest say to Bragg that if he ever crosses the path of Nathan Bedford Forrest again he would do so at the peril of his life.

*

Andy is placed in General Joe Wheeler's cavalry. He goes on to serve loyally until the end of the war. Forrest resigns in protest of Bragg's order to turn his command over to Joe Wheeler, but Jefferson Davis refuses to accept his resignation. Instead Forrest is promoted to major general by President Davis and is given his own independent command in West Tennessee and North Mississippi.

Walt is sent to Charleston, South Carolina to reenter his profession as a proficient blockade-runner. His ability to leave and enter the Confederate mainland at will, bringing back supplies and selling cotton, becomes the lifeblood of the beleaguered Confederacy.

War moves on and so does the Confederacy's hopes for independence. Atlanta falls to the Yankees, and Jefferson Davis summons John Bell Hood to discuss alternatives to save the Southern cause. Jefferson Davis wants to replace Joe Johnston, the current commander of the Army of Tennessee, with John Bell Hood, a soldier known for his bravery and aggressiveness on the field.

Hood is untried with such a large command. Jefferson Davis knows it is a risk to place Hood in command, but he knows of a secret weapon that may turn the tide in the Confederates' favor. This knowledge gives him the confidence to make his decision, even though he has heard the rumors of a possible curse surrounding the General's Relic.

Jefferson Davis tells Hood of the existence of the General's Relic and of its strange powers that could make an army undefeatable in battle. Jefferson Davis informs Hood that the relic is in a secret hiding place in Northwest Alabama. Hood agrees that moving the Army of Tennessee to Northwest Alabama to acquire the General's Relic and then marching an undefeatable army into Middle Tennessee to destroy the Union supply line, running out of Nashville, could force Sherman out of Atlanta.

The move would be a strong strategy and might have a greater chance of success with the deadly General's Relic on the side of the Confederate army of Tennessee.

The Confederate Secret Service agents charged with protecting the relic have been disbursed throughout the Confederacy to ensure protecting the secrecy of the relic. Two of the agents have exact knowledge of the location of the General's Relic. One of the agents, Henry, serving under Jeb Stuart's old cavalry force is on an undercover espionage mission serving as a minister behind enemy lines in the D.C. area. The other, Walt, is currently serving on a special mission as a blockade-runner for the Confederacy. The third agent, Andy, is serving under the command of General Joe

Wheeler in the Western theatre of the war in the battles to contain Sherman's large army.

Jeff Davis sends couriers out with a message for the Confederate agents to retrieve the General's Relic from its hiding place and meet up with the Army of Tennessee in Northwest Alabama.

Chapter 11

It is eight o'clock at night. Henry's wife and infant son are sound asleep, while Henry is busy working on his weekly sermon. He wants to drive home a message to the soldiers to cease their ever-increasing practices of gambling and drinking.

Over the past few months whenever Henry was walking around the camps, surveying the lines of the fort for a potential weak point that the Confederate army could exploit, Henry had noticed a gambling fever coming over the men.

Looking in the eyes of the men he ministered to on Sundays, he could see a wild look in their eyes. Henry thinks to himself that the enlisted men he was preaching to would be wild eyed indeed if they knew he was a high-ranking officer in the Confederate Secret Service.

Henry's cat jumps atop his desk and levels her tabby face over the piece of paper Henry is writing on, demanding Henry acknowledge her presence.

"There now, Ms. Precious. You sure don't let this war stress you out now, do you?"

Henry had received an encrypted message to gather the General's Relic and report to General Hood in Northwest Alabama. He was deeply loyal to the Confederate cause, but he had a family to look after. He had hoped the war would be over by now.

He was in no hurry to ride off to the Deep South. His wife's father had made a lot of money in the railroad industry and had purchased them a house as a wedding present on the outskirts of the nation's capital. The house they lived in was a modest two-story brick house with a stable and carriage next to the house. Henry dreaded leaving the comforts of his home to head back to the frontlines.

A knock is heard at the front door, startling Henry and Precious. Henry's agents from the nearby farms frequently stopped by to exchange secret documents in the guise of dropping off eggs or milk, but rarely dropped by after dark.

Henry opens the door.

"Henry, we've come here to let you know your cover has possibly been blown. A detachment of the United States cavalry with fifty men at their disposal will be arriving at your doorstop within the hour. They have word that a Confederate spy is in the area. We are not certain, but they might be coming to arrest you. You must escape Washington. We cannot take the chance of losing you. If they have evidence of you being a Confederate sympathizer, they will imprison and hang you."

Henry knows he has no choice. He had been an undercover agent working for the Confederate Secret Service under the disguise as a minister for months.

"Thank you for the warning, gentlemen."

Henry issues an order that his network of spies stay low and not arouse any suspicion.

This would be Henry's burden alone to take on. Henry hurriedly addresses a letter to his wife, informing her that a family in a nearby town needs a minister to perform last rites and for her not to worry. Henry takes solace in that, if all went well, someday after the war was over, he would see his wife and child again.

Chapter 12

Henry rides out of the old musky barn and down a dark winding country road. Henry's thoughts are of country and patriotism. Henry is secure in the knowledge that the information he has sent to the Confederacy has helped in securing victories.

Henry approaches the Federal lines surrounding Washington. He knows if he is caught he will possibly be hanged on the spot. As Henry approaches the lines, he relaxes his grip on the horse's reins and slows to a trot.

A young Federal picket shouts out, "Halt, who goes there?" The young soldier with polished accouterments and a clean new uniform aggressively puts his bayonet tipped rifle out in front of him, bringing Henry to a stop.

Henry answers, "A friend of the Union army."

The Federal picket asks, "What is your business being on the road at this time of the night, sir, I mean Reverend?"

"I received an emergency telegraph of a severe sickness at the Jones' house. I've been summoned to prepare last rites. The password is lemons."

The young soldier tightens his grip on his rifle. "That was last week's password, Reverend."

"Young man, I must be on my way. It is … an emergency," Henry spurs his horse forward.

"I have received orders that any and all citizens are to be stopped and interrogated by my sergeant."

"Now see here, young fella, I have papers with permission to pass between the lines." Henry hands the soldier his pass granting permission to travel through the lines in the event of medical emergencies.

"Your fake Reb papers won't work with me, mister. Now get down off that horse right now."

Henry points up the hill as he leans forward in his saddle. "I have a good friend up at camp who can vouch for me. I strongly suggest you send someone up the hill to let my friend know Reverend Henry is down here."

"You hold real still there."

The Union picket sends a guard, and then pulls his blue wool uniform and overcoat tighter around himself.

The path is littered with rocks and is slippery from a recent rain. The young private, in his rush, slips and falls on the muddy ground, unbeknownst to him, his prized silver corps badge falls off of his coat and onto the ground. The private picks himself up, looking down he realizes his badge is gone. He looks around but cannot find the prized badge. Continuing on, he reaches the camp headquarters. Ravenalle is standing at the campfire.

"Gentleman, I am confident if any Rebel spies come this way there is no way for them to pass."

A captain in the group replies, "I have pickets spread apart at twenty paces between each man from Washington all the way to the river. A squirrel could not approach our lines without being noticed."

The young private runs up, muddy and wet from his fall, and stands at attention. "Permission requested to communicate with Sergeant Ravenalle, sir."

"Go ahead, private."

"Sir, a minister by the name of Henry says he must pass through the lines immediately."

"Henry and I grew up together. He is a good man." Ravenalle starts walking towards the tent flap. "Gentleman, I will return in just a moment, we will capture the Rebel spy and hang him. It is unfortunate but there is good evidence the Rebel spy has already passed valuable information on to the Confederate government that will greatly compromise the Union army's war strategies."

Ravenalle walks back to his tent and enters. He runs his long mustache between his fingers. He reaches his hand under his coat and pulls out a silver pocket watch. "Ten o'clock, it is getting late. I've known Henry all my life. There is no way my friend could be a Rebel spy."

It had been several months since Ravenalle and Henry had seen each other.

After fifteen eternal minutes, Henry's friend appears. Ravenalle slaps the young lookout across the back of his head.

"Are you crazy? This is the Reverend Henry."

"Sorry, sir! We've all been anxious to find the Rebel spy."

"Get back to your post before I have you court martialed! Henry, it would please me for you to join me and my command for a cup of coffee, and maybe you can say a prayer over our company's men."

"I would be delighted. But it can be only for a moment. I have a parishioner in need of last rites."

"Henry, it is dangerous for anyone to travel. The word is a Confederate spy will be trying to skirt Union lines and trigger fingers will be more jumpy than usual.

Ravenalle and Henry walk over to the fire which has died down to a few glowing red embers.

Henry turns and walks over to the woodpile. As Henry gathers kindling he reaches into his trench coat and pulls out a coal torpedo, normally used to blow up enemy steamboats.

Henry gets the fire going and drops the coal torpedo into the fire. He quickly lays a few pieces of firewood over the coal torpedo to hide it. The coal torpedo has been coated with bees wax and designed not to detonate for ten, even fifteen minutes after being applied to the heat of a fire.

Ravenalle calls out to the men in his company, "Men gather around, the good Reverend Henry is going to say a prayer for your safety and victory."

Henry offers a prayer to keep the men safe and to bring them victory in their war with the Rebels. The Reverend Henry thanks his friend for the warm coffee, and then asks that his friend do him a favor. "When you hear the bombs falling, promise me you will duck and fall to the ground."

"Henry, that is typically what we do, but it is mighty nice of you to think of my safety." Ravenalle watches Henry ride out of the camp into the night and says to the others, "What a good man."

Moments later Union cavalry, hot on the trail of Reverend Henry, come to a halt at Sergeant Ravenalle's post. The captain pulls the reins back on his horse trying to keep his mount still. "Ravenalle, have you seen anybody ride by here in the last few minutes."

"Only my friend Reverend Henry. We are keeping a close eye out for the Rebel spy."

The Union captain holds both his reins in one hand as he shakes his fist and yells at the sergeant, "You fool, the minister is the spy!"

At the very moment the captain yells at Ravenalle, a powerful explosion rocks the ground. The sergeant falls to the ground and is spared. Others are not as lucky. Blood is everywhere, and the large tent is engulfed in flames.

When Henry hears the explosion behind him, he reaches up and removes the minister's white collar and lets it fall to the ground below.

Chapter 13

Though Walt's blockade running adventures had led to a few close calls, the pay was good for moving goods to the Confederacy from Nassau. Walt came to enjoy walking along the beachfront barefoot. It was a favorite past time of his when he had the time. He came to especially enjoy the solitude of looking at the beauty of the ocean.

One afternoon, as a hint of rain lingered in the air, Walt's secluded routine stroll was abruptly broken by a woman's scream for help.

He turned to see two men, one on foot and the other on a large horse with a whip in his hand, chasing a woman. Walt pulled his Colt revolver from the satchel he has slung at his side, and ran, revolver in hand. Walt had been in the Ninth Alabama Infantry before being assigned to the Confederate Secret Service and Jeb Stuart's Cavalry. His powerful legs carried him to his quarry in the blink of an eye.

The man who'd been on foot was atop the woman, and it was obvious he meant to force himself upon her. The man's appearance was of a criminal. He looked up in shock just in time to see the explosion of Walt's Colt .44. The large caliber bullet entered his head over his right eye. He fell over to his side, dead. Most of his brains a few yards behind him.

In contrast to the dead man, his accomplice was well dressed and had been quick to take in that Walt was an immediate threat. The man threw down his whip and pulled out a breech-loading repeater rifle. The man raised the rifle and fired; the shot grazed Walt's shoulder. Walt kneels down, making himself a smaller target, steadying his aim.

Walt's shot hits the man above the heart near his collarbone. The man slumps in his saddle. Walt's next shot hits the man in his abdomen. The man falls backwards off his horse.

Walt tucks his revolvers under his belt. He asks the woman, "Are you hurt?"

The woman nods.

"How did you get mixed up with these bandits?"

"They shot at my carriage. I fell off, and then … they began to chase me."

"What are you doing out here alone?"

"I was going to the market."

"Where's your carriage?"

"Over here." Walt followed her towards her carriage.

"My name is Sara." She smiled. Walt smiled back.

"Walt."

The woman's horse seemed unharmed, but a wheel had fallen off her carriage, and straightaway Walt began to repair it.

"I'm sorry to do this ma'am, but now that your carriage is fixed, I'll need it to take those bodies and dump them in the ocean."

Sara looks over at the dead men. "I have no problem with that."

Walt loaded the bodies across the carriage rack. They drove the carriage down to the edge of the ocean. Walt disposed of the men's bodies, letting the tide carry their bodies out to sea.

Chapter 14

Walt found the Bahamian houses and buildings built from coral reefs elegant and beautiful and that banana and orange trees, along with the island's thick green foliage, provided decent enough shade. Even so, Walt held a white umbrella to keep the scorching sun off him.

He wore his usual dark business suit with a red vest. The coral dust of the street has settled on his suit giving it a tannish color.

Walt removed his tall, silk stovepipe hat as he entered the lower bar of the Royal Victorian Hotel.

The hotel built by the British government in 1862 was the favorite gathering place. Men played cards and fraternized with the local girls. The women of the island wore colorful dresses. Everywhere Walt looked, the men were dressed mostly in all white, wearing straw hats or colorful Arabian turbines. Walt adjusted his spectacles, patted the dust from his suit and walked up to the bar to get a pint of beer and a shot of whiskey.

"Looks like a storm brewing out there."

Walt picks up his drink. "Yea, I'll be leaving for the States tomorrow. I'll miss it here." Walt raised his whiskey then downed it.

A tall well-dressed man walked approached the bar and asked the bartender for a beer.

Walt motioned for the bartender to pour him another drink.

The bartender placed the drinks down in front of the men.

"I hear the penalty for murder is hanging." The stranger, who'd been looking forward, turned to Walt.

"Can I help you with something, sir?"

"I think you had something to do with the disappearance of a friend of mine. 'Bout a month ago. You know something about that, don't you, son?" The man stared hard at Walt.

"Sir, I am not your son, and your accusation is outrageous. I am a loyal citizen of the Confederate States of America here on business to transport goods to a port in the South."

"Is it? There was a witness to the incident."

Walt sipped his whiskey.

"The witness described a man of your exact description laying lead into two men near the ocean. He said a woman was there, too."

"Oh, that. I do recall a couple of men trying to have their way with a defenseless woman. I'm sorry to hear they were friends of yours. I just made sure it was a fair fight."

"Why you son of—"

The bartender's hands shifted under the bar, and a subtle click of a double-barreled shotgun was heard. "You best let Walt finish his drink in peace, mister."

The man paid for his beer. As he got up to leave, he sneered, "I'll see you hang yet, Reb!"

When Walt finished his drink, he walked upstairs and took a deep breath as he looked out over the island from the hotel's huge wrap-around balcony and watched the sun set one last time. After the huge orange fireball dropped into the ocean, Walt stealthily made an exit through a back door and ducked down several alleys in order to make his way unseen to a cottage not too far away from the blockade running ship he would be climbing aboard the next morning.

Walt had been through this port before, but this time was by far the most memorable. He had fallen in love with Sara, the beautiful local woman he'd rescued at the edge of the ocean.

Sara lived in a cottage with a small, lush garden full of fragrant flowers. Walt hurried up the path, stopping by a fountain to look back to make sure he wasn't being followed.

Before Walt could knock, Sara opened the door, a candleholder with a lit candle held in her long slender fingers. "I recognized your footsteps. Come in, come in."

Sara pulled her nightgown around her, as she stepped back to let Walt in, and then placed the candle on a table. Walt's hand came up and stroked Sara's face. The two embraced in a passionate kiss.

Walt stays with his lover, safe and secure from whoever it was who might be looking for him in town. His large, rough hands brush across her forehead and through her raven dark hair. The American Civil War seems far away, and Walt sighs as he leans over and kisses Sara, who wakes and pulls him closer to her.

"I don't want you to go," she whispers.

"I dread it, but I promise to return." He gives her a reassuring smile.

He knows he is needed on the frontlines. The past month had brought happiness. They had shared their dreams with each other underneath the palm trees.

Walt whispered, "This has been the best four weeks of my life."

Sara nudged him. "We can share a lifetime like this, stay with me. Don't go back!"

Walt was torn, but he had a mission. He had made a commitment to his fellow soldiers and the Confederate States of America Government.

Chapter 15

Walt awakens and watches Sara while she sleeps. He gets dressed, takes a drink of water, and looks around the cottage for his personal effects. When Sara wakes, she notices Walt is already dressed. He is wearing a seafaring sailor's frock coat and a seaman's hat.

Sara's dark brown eyes look down, not meeting Walt's. She begins to cry. "Is it morning already?"

"Oh, Sara. I promise to return. It's bad luck for a sailor to leave a crying woman."

"I am tired of hearing about this war of yours. I know you must be torn, but I love you, Walt."

Walt walks over and sits down on the edge of the bed. "Sara, I love you. Here, I want you to have this derringer while I am away so you can protect yourself."

"It would be better if I had you here as my protector. I owe you my life, Walt."

"I will be back in eight weeks, I promise."

Sara reaches her hands behind her neck and unfastens her necklace. "I have something for you as well." Sara takes her silver cross necklace and places it in Walt's hands. "I want you to have this while you are upon the ocean. This cross has always brought me luck. I love you, and I want you to come back safely to me."

Walt closes his hand around the cross. "I will. I promise."

Sara walks Walt to the door. She looks down as she closes the door. Walt pulls his seaman's hat down over his eyes, and walks into the garden. Out front, Walt looks back and sees Sara in the window crying. He waves goodbye and then turns his head toward the wharf and the waiting steamers.

Approaching one of the guards, Walt, with his hat pulled down to hide his tears, gives the password before the guard asks. There is no time to waste; the Army of Tennessee would be needing supplies for the oncoming winter, and the two fast ships before him were heavily loaded down with guns, ammunition, gunpowder, blankets, and food.

Captain Walt calls out, “All ready, mate.” Walt walks on the gangplank of one of the cruisers. He looks back towards town and the cottage. Walt has a feeling he will never see this shoreline again, or the woman whom had been his lover during his stay in Nassau.

Rolling out of Nassau, the sleek little cruisers are spotted by the large Union battleships. By the time the slow battleships can swing their cannons around, the cruisers blaze right on by into the darkness of the night. Upon reaching the Confederate coastal area of Charleston, South Carolina, all attention is on the black outline of the coast. Confederate sympathizers are positioned on the shoreline with lanterns to guide the cargo ships into the docks. Once the lanterns are spotted, it is no problem to arrive at the docks.

The cargo onboard is quickly loaded onto wagons and carried off to the thirty thousand man Army of Tennessee. Arriving in Charleston, Walt enters the Mills House Hotel. A special room is reserved for soldiers of Walt’s abilities. Walt writes letters, then hands them along with a map to a courier with special instructions.

Walt changes into his staff officer's uniform. The downturned eagle buttons glitter even in the low lamp light of the room. Walt belts on his College Hill CSA sword. The Southern Confederacy buckle with part of the code to the treasure is tightened against Walt's leather belt. Walt learns that Atlanta has fallen and that General John Bell Hood has waged fierce attacks against Sherman's forces.

It is also learned that General Joe Wheeler, with three thousand men, are following after Sherman's large sixty thousand man army, with orders to try and contain them as best they can while Hood starts a new campaign into Middle Tennessee. Walt figures General Joe Wheeler can use all the help he can get, as soon as possible.

Chapter 16

Walt looks out of his room on the second floor of the Mills House. Above him cotton ball clouds dot the blue sky. A woman with a basket of fruit walks by on the sidewalk beneath him. Across the street a group of worn Confederate soldiers dressed in butternut stand around with their rifles at support arms, the rifles upright in the nook of their left arms. The soldiers light tobacco in their pipes and engage in a serious looking conversation. No doubt they were discussing the folly of camping in Charleston while the Union Navy bombs them at will. An explosion occurs five blocks away causing the soldiers across the street to jump and the woman to run into the Mills House. Walt turns away from the window and walks to the bed. He lies down fully clothed and puts his hands behind his head.

Walt's thoughts go back to the horrors of the Battle of Chickamauga. The bloody action he and Andy had seen there had forever sealed his and Andy's relationship as brothers in arms. Walt thinks to himself that he will do whatever it takes to keep Andy alive. The small cavalry unit commanded by Joe Wheeler was no match for the entire army that Sherman was bringing to bear on Georgia. Andy would be killed in action in Wheeler's command. Walt did not want Andy to perish like Captain Malcolm Sloan did.

Andy sits in the entrance to his small tent. A slight misty rain is falling in the Georgia night, as the candlelight illuminates the inside of his tent. Andy writes in his journal.

North Georgia

Dear Journal,

We had a rough fight today, and we lost three of our most gallant soldiers during a cavalry skirmish with Yankee cavalry. During these past two or three weeks, time has become a black blur, and we have seen continuous fighting. I see no hope for the Confederacy surviving, but we will see this to the last breath in our bodies. The forces we are opposing are legion. On scout duty, we look out over their encampments, and as far as the eye can see is Sherman's army. The rape and pillaging of our woman and citizens is a daily occurrence and so far there is little we can do about it. Only when the Yankees stray too far away from the main body of their army, can we inflict any harm to them. It has rained nonstop for a month. I am in good spirits, although there is nothing I would not do for a good home cooked meal. I have to wonder what those two cavalrymen, Walt and Henry, are up to right now. The two are a mysterious pair. Wherever they are I am sure they are forwarding our cause. My thoughts go back to my girlfriend in Nashville. I hope after the War, I might see her again although, I have come to doubt that will ever happen.

Off in the distant mountains of Georgia, massive bolts of lightning startle Andy. He closes his journal and lays his head down on his saddle bed. As he drifts off, the rain starts to come down even harder.

Chapter 17

Walt walks down the semi-deserted streets. For a moment, the constant bombardment by the Yankee blockade ships has a mild lull. Walt has been at sea for days and even with the bombardment, he is glad to be on dry land and enjoying the Southern hospitality of Charleston, South Carolina. The bars are open and are in full defiance of the blockade. It is business as usual with plays being performed in the downtown theatre, as the sound of explosions are heard over the actors' and actresses' lines.

Walt has a few beers at a local tavern and then walks to a friend's house. His friend is secretly a member of the Knights of the Golden Circle. Walt raps out a secret knock on the large oak door. His friend, an astute lawyer and planter experienced in dealing with people, opens the door. Sir Francis is dressed in a smoking jacket. Swirls from his pipe fill the room with the pleasant fragrance of tobacco.

"Walt, what a pleasant surprise, come in, come in."

"I see our enemies are still attacking the city."

"Yes, but our spirit of resistance remains strong."

Sir Francis leads Walt to his trophy room. The room has all of the beautiful elegance of a Victorian home, befitting a Southern planter.

Walt asks, "How are the crops doing this year?"

"I haven't been out to the plantation yet this season because of the steady bombardment, but don't worry we will have a nice crop of cotton for you to run through the blockade in a few months."

After a few more cordial exchanges, a cigar and a drink, Sir Francis asks, "Tell me, how are the plans going for the new Southern Confederacy Capitol building in Brazil?"

"The location is remote, and thus far we have been able to keep our plans secret. Eventually we will have even larger, grander plans to create towns and centers of trade to further our plans of manifest destiny throughout South America."

Sir Francis draws a puff off his pipe and exhales. "Do you think we will succeed in creating the Golden Circle Empire, Walt?"

"Yes, yes. I do think we will succeed in having a colony in South America. Even if we lose this war we are laying the groundwork for a long-term political movement that, if necessary, can be revived even after a hundred years of dormancy."

Sir Francis and Walt laugh and talk about politics and adventures on into the evening.

Later, as Walt is getting ready to leave, Sir Francis says to Walt, "Come with me out to the stables, I know it's late, but I want to show you something."

Walt and Sir Francis step out onto the back veranda and head to the stables.

"I have to show you the world's most beautiful stallion." Sir Francis opens the stable doors.

Several horses are there, but one stands out above all the rest, a beautiful black stallion. Walt runs his hand over the horse's long mane. The horse throws his head up and down, neighing, nervous at the sound of exploding shells falling close by.

"Sir Francis, this is the most exquisite stallion I have ever seen." Walt offers the horse a sugar cube as a treat, a rare commodity, but one he had procured through blockade running. The horse calms and nudges his head towards Walt, enjoying the treat Walt has brought to him.

"You always know how to make a new friend."

"You certainly have a beauty on your hands with this magnificent beast!"

"Walt, I want you to have him. You have been a loyal friend. He is my gift to you. I know you have a strenuous journey ahead to Georgia. You will need a strong horse."

"I don't know what to say. Thank you, sir. I am honored, and I will take good care of him."

The next night Walt bids his friend farewell. He climbs upon the excited half-wild steed. The stallion rears onto his back legs with his front legs pawing at the night sky. In an instant, Walt is riding with the wind to get to his old unit and offer his services.

About this same time, his friend and co-agent, Henry, stationed at a picket post in Petersburg, Virginia is also embarking on an equally dangerous journey after receiving orders from a Confederate courier.

Chapter 18

The moonlight glistens off Captain Henry's uniform buttons, sword, and belt plate. He rides astride his horse along a road in West Tennessee. To his right are trees with a hill rising up. The ground is covered with leaves. To his left is a deep ravine with a creek meandering over large boulders. The roadbed is pebbled with small rocks. He pulls the reins on his horse, and rider and horse come to a stop. Henry pulls a worn map out of his haversack. The map shows current Union positions and picket posts. Up ahead is a town that is occupied by Union forces per the map. A path is marked on the map that will take Henry through a tough valley trail that will cross a Confederate friendly farm and a small creek. He puts the map away and turns his horse off into the trees and down into the ravine. He finds a well-worn trail hidden from the road that follows the creek. The map Henry is using is kept up to date by Confederate couriers and scouts that take their maps deadly serious. A mismarked map meant death by bushwhackers or being hung for spying.

After bypassing the Union-controlled town Henry sees a yellow dot rising between two mountain peaks, the sky is reddish purple with gold up amongst the grey clouds. The hills in the distance are a deep blue. He smiles. This is his favorite time of the day. A time of reflection and a time to get off the road and into woods where he can pitch his tent for rest during the daytime when he is most likely to be seen even from a long ways away. At dusk Henry breaks camp and continues on his journey to Northwest Alabama where he will meet up with Walt and General John Bell Hoods

Confederate Army. God willing they would retrieve the General's Relic from its hiding place and move towards Nashville, Tennessee.

Henry is nearing his destination in Alabama; he has been riding hard and is tired and dusty. His large white mare is thundering down the narrow Alabama roads. The cavalryman's cape bellows in the wind behind him.

It is twilight with dawn approaching, and the visibility in the forest is low. The cavalryman does not see the bushwhacking cowards that are about to cut him down until it is too late. A hail of bullets enters the body of the cavalryman, and he falls to the hard, cold roadbed beneath him.

The bushwhackers are upon his dying body in a second. They rustle through his clothes trying to find anything of value. They hear a noise. Horses are coming down the road. They get on their horses and ride off quickly, for the penalty for bushwhacking is hanging. The gallant cavalryman's horse strides over to his stricken master. The mare gently nudges the dying soldier. Together they had fought in many battles and dispatched many a foe.

Two Rebel cavalry scouts ride upon the stricken soldier and dismount to help him.

"Sir, can you hear me? Sir?"

"His wounds look bad."

They can see by the stricken soldier's wounds he has but a few hours of life in his body.

"I doubt he will make it through the night."

They move the soldier closer to a nearby creek. The two cavalry scouts decide they will strike camp and return to their unit in the morning.

The cavalryman is dying and close to delirium. Henry removes his buckle.

"He's moving! Sir, what is it?"

Henry coughs up blood.

"Get him some water from the canteen."

Henry coughs again and in a scraggily voice says, "Take the buckle."

"What did he say?"

"He said take the buckle." One of the scouts takes the buckle from the dying man.

"Map …" Henry is able to say before coughing.

"Give him more water!"

"He says this is a map." The soldier points to the back of the buckle.

"Get … get it to Jeff … Davis."

"Yes, sir, we will get this to Jefferson Davis."

"Gold …" Henry slowly raises his hand and points towards his saddlebag.

Henry begins to start coughing and cannot stop. Bullets have pierced one of his lungs.

The scout gives him another swig of water. "Rest for now."

After looking after Henry, the two scouts cook their evening meal around a campfire and keep lookout in case the bushwhackers return.

During the night, Henry, the gallant Confederate cavalryman, takes his last breath, and at first light, the scouts bury the cavalryman near the water's edge.

"What should we do about the buckle and gold?"

"We've been gone so long; I know we will be reprimanded. There is no telling what our captain will do with the map on the back of the buckle."

The scouts decide to bury the treasure map buckle and the small bag of gold. The unit's camp would not be a safe place for any valuables. The scouts distrusted their captain for he was a mean disciplinarian and would more than likely take anything of any value for his own personal gain.

The two scouts arrive back at their unit on Whitney Hill a short time later with the dead cavalry man's horse in tow and proceed to their captain's quarters. The captain goes into a rage.

"Deserters, that's what you fools are! Now, you're out of food, so you had to come back to camp!"

The scouts explain to the captain what had happened to delay them. The captain does not listen to any of their pleas and goes so far as to accuse the scouts of being the ones who are the bushwhackers. The two scouts are put into the stockade, and the captain makes plans to have the two men executed before a firing squad.

Word gets out that two scouts are to be executed before a firing squad for the minor infraction of getting back from leave late. Sam Lambert's sweetheart upon hearing of this outrageous horror rides at once for the town of Jonesboro to get a pardon for the two scouts from the commander of the psychotic captain. The beautiful bride to be rides hard to get back to her sweetheart to prevent the worst.

Torrential rains hold her up from crossing one of the fords. Once she finds another way across the creek, she rides with all speed possible. Unfortunately, she is too late. She arrives only in time to see her future husband shot down by the firing squad. The captain, believing that the two are bushwhackers and may reveal bushwhacked loot, hold back loved ones from coming near them until they have breathed their last breath. The secret of where the buckle is buried, with the treasure map etched on the back of it, goes with the two scouts into oblivion.

Chapter 19

Walt catches up with Joe Wheeler's cavalry in the mountains of Georgia. He has been riding nonstop to get back to his unit. Walt arrives in the Rebel camp and is surprised to find a desolate and tattered cavalry force.

Walt spots Andy poking at a fire with a tasty looking rabbit stew cooking. Andy looks up and smiles. "Well, well. We thought we had seen the last of you, Walt."

Andy looks gaunt. It seemed pretty clear rabbit stew was a rare commodity in the camp. Andy offers Walt some stew, and not having anything to eat for the last twenty-four hours, Walt gladly accepts.

"How are the men holding up here. Are they in good spirits?"

"Pretty good, all things considered. That damn Sherman would pillage and burn the whole state if we were not keeping him somewhat contained."

Walt learns that Wheeler's men are planning a raid in the morning on a group of Sherman's cavalry that had strayed away from the main body of the Union army.

In the dark, a dispatch courier rides into camp and is escorted to General Joe Wheeler's tent. General Wheeler comes out of his tent a few minutes later.

The General replies, "Walt, I hate to tell you this, but General Hood has need of your services in Northern Alabama and orders have been written to that effect."

Walt knows that in the morning, his mates will be riding out to battle with Sherman's cavalry, and it sored him deeply he could not ride into battle with his comrades.

Chapter 20

In the morning, Walt walked over to Andy. "You take care, kid, don't get yourself killed."

Andy replies, "You better be the one looking out. You've got to ride out into dangerous country with nothing but murderers and thieves running amok."

"If anything happens to me, remember to follow the clues I have left. We have a duty and obligation to the Confederacy and to the cause for state's rights. I know you will follow the clues and I have no doubt you will succeed in finding the General's Relic."

Walt finds a few of his mates and bids them farewell. He mounts his horse, waving his hat in a grand goodbye as his powerful black steed rises up and bucks his front hooves into the air. He rides away from the rising dawn and early foggy grey twilight, into the darkness.

Andy knew that this would be a tough fight. The Confederate cavalry was outnumbered ten to one. They would hit the flank of the Union cavalry and thereby hope to keep them from maundering the surrounding townspeople quite as badly.

The Confederate cavalry raise the Rebel yell and charge out of a section of woods, across a field towards the unsuspecting Union cavalry. Pickets of the Union cavalry rise up out of their slumbering positions they had kept all night. A few companies of the large Union cavalry brigade, in the middle of the camp, had slept on their arms during the night and are ready for the Rebel charge. A terrific volley is fired into the oncoming Rebels and several horses go down.

The Union soldier's repeating rifles repulse Wheelers' cavalry.

Andy's horse is shot from under him. Both rider and horse tumble, hitting the ground hard. Andy's horse falls on him pinning his leg to the ground. Yankee bullets are popping all around him, and he is sure this will be the end for him. Andy looks over his shoulder towards the sound of a running horse to see a large black steed and rider come galloping towards him. It is Walt. Walt reaches out his hand at the same instant Andy's horse rolls off of his leg. Andy grabs Walt's hand and pulls himself up onto Walt's horse. The two ride off with a hail of Yankee bullets whizzing around them.

The two are now separated from the main body of Joe Wheeler's cavalry and it seems as though the entire Yankee cavalry are chasing after them. Walt turns in his saddle and fires his Colt .44s, but that only seems to make the Yankees close the distance between them faster. Walt continues firing, throwing his empty pistols down. The big black stallion carries the two through a pine thicket going up alongside a river. Walt pulls the stallion up for a second. He realizes that the Union cavalry will soon have them surrounded and will close in for the kill.

It is lighter now. Walt and Andy can see the enemy. Walt thinks to himself that something looks familiar about this particular company of Union cavalry.

Walt pulls his binoculars out and cannot believe his eyes, riding up to meet them is the captain who had murdered his brother-in-arms Captain Sloan many months ago. Walt had served with the man at West Point and had never liked him.

"We will not be taken prisoner by these ruffians, Andy!"

"Yes, sir! Let's get 'em!"

Up farther they ride into the pine thickets and over rocks. The path leads along a cliff overlooking a river running beside it. Walt pulls up and stops again. The Yankees are closing fast, and bullets are popping off the surrounding trees.

"Pull out those last two Colt revolvers for me, Andy."

Andy reaches into the saddlebag behind him and pulls out .44 Colt revolvers, handing them to Walt. "You're a hell of a shot with them pistols, Walt. You've killed half of the Yankees following us."

With loaded Colts in hand, Walt hunkers down over the stallion and whirls the big horse around. He puts the horse's reins between his teeth. Walt and Andy emerge out of the pines and charge directly towards the cliff's edge. Walt is still turning in the saddle and firing the whole time. Walt can see Captain Sloan's killer clearly now. The man is only about a hundred feet back. The enemy will not catch the Rebel's today. The black stallion, sweat pouring out of him and all of hell's fury directing him, leaps over the edge of the cliff. Walt standing in the stirrups leaps up and whirls out of the saddle, firing as horse and men go over the cliff. The remaining shots in the pistols are now used.

As he is in midair, Walt takes one last careful shot at Malcolm's killer. The shot hits the Union soldier square in the chest. There is no doubt in Walt's mind the man who killed his friend was as good as dead. The man falls from his horse in a clump on the ground.

As Walt is falling to the river below he keeps firing the twin Colts up towards the cliffs edge, probably not doing any more harm but certainly making him feel better about the situation. Walt's back hits the water with a terrible blow. Walt cannot feel anything. His back is broken from hitting the water's surface.

Andy swims to the edge of the riverbank and retrieves the stallion. Andy does not see his friend in the river. Walt had already slipped beneath the water's surface, and his body now drifted downstream.

As the last rays of life drift out of Walt's consciousness, his mind returns to a better day of peace and happiness when he was growing up. His father and mother are there. His younger brother greets him on the steps of their log cabin. Sara is there on the porch, her dark hair flowing over her shoulders. Walt was home for good, and the war was over. The waters of North Georgia gently carried his body to his last resting place on the edge of a riverbank in Georgia, the secret of the General's Relic to rest there with him forever.

Chapter 21
September 2015

An old timer told Carter, an attorney from the area who now lives in Birmingham, about a treasure story of lost gold buried by Confederate soldiers, somewhere along Masterson Creek.

Carter had enlisted his detecting buddy, Blake, who grew more and more frustrated at having found nothing, save a few deeply buried aluminum cans along the old creek in Northwest Alabama.

Blake and Carter had spent many weekends together looking for Civil War artifacts over the past several years. They realized they would make a good team when they had met at a group relic hunt in Tennessee. Blake brought his people skills he had learned in business and the military to the team. Carter was the researcher that could find productive sites to detect.

It was a hot September day. The woods were thick with summer growth. Blake and Carter are wearing snake chaps for protection, as they hack their way with machetes through bamboo and underbrush.

Old Masterson Creek is dry for the most part. The water level is low due to lack of rain. The woods are quiet. Blake and Carter see and hear a few birds and animals, but for the most part it is silent.

Blake had been a Navy Seal. He'd seen extensive combat and also worked as a private contractor in various parts of the world. He had close encounters with danger and death during his service to his country and time abroad. Though Blake mentally cursed Carter for dragging him on this trip, Blake was more than up to this little excursion into the woods. A few snakes would not bother him.

Blake saw a black snake slither into a patch of water in a semi-dry creek bed. "Man, there is nothing out here but copperheads and water moccasins!"

Carter, not accustomed to hiking this far, grimaced in pain. "Blake, I've got a major blister coming up on my heel. Maybe we should turn back?"

Blake was not one to give up so easily, especially after driving all the way from Nashville. "Let's push on. I think there's something to the story. I researched the story and it is based upon actual events. Involved a mean captain. He killed his own men when they wouldn't tell him where the gold was buried."

Blake pulls out his canteen strapped to his survival belt and takes a good long swig. Blake is dressed in camouflage pants and a green, army-issue short sleeve shirt. His military outfit serves him well in the harsh undergrowth and briars of Masterson Creek. Always prepared, Blake keeps a Ruger .380 auto loader in his front right pants pocket in case of any trouble; wild hogs were known to roam the area. Be it varmint or criminals, he was not one to take any chances.

The two had permission from the landowner, and there, of course, should not be any troublemakers out in the woods, but Blake's mindset never allowed him to go anywhere without a gun. Carter wore a more civilian-style outfit, with khaki cargo shorts, a blue short-sleeved shirt, fanny pack with water and gear, as well as a small, loaded revolver.

Metal detecting wasn't for the weak—and they took relic hunting very seriously.

Startled by a loud, smooth beep, Carter looks at the numbers on his detector's display screen. He cannot believe he has finally got a solid hit and the depth finder indicates that the object is close to the surface, only a few inches deep. He sends up a quick silent prayer of thanks for that much. Carter finds the center for the object by going around the outer perimeter of the object with his detector.

He whispers to himself, "This might be a bullet!" He puts his shovel to the ground, digs, and then pops up a clump of dirt.

Both Carter and Blake had started out strong earlier in the day, but digging out iffy trash signals of iron and foil along with countless aluminum cans, from the creeks flood plain was beginning to wear on them.

Carter picks up the clump of rich Tennessee Valley soil and passes it underneath his detector. He pulls apart the rich, dark root-encrusted soil. His eyes widen as he sees what he is holding. Between his thumb and first finger Carter holds a raised ringer miniè ball.

Blake rushes over, "What did you find?"

"Check it out. It's a miniè ball, the kind used by the Confederacy."

Blake holds up the miniè ball that Carter just pulled from the soil. "It looks like that old timer knew what he was talking about. That is definitely a bullet that the Confederates used. Let's spread out. I've a feeling we are standing in the middle of a rebel camp."

Carter and Blake find the perimeter of the camp and detect, slowly, listening for any hint of relics.

Blake finds an infantry eagle button and walks over to show Carter his find. A few more relics are found and then Blake gets a strong reading on his detector, he digs up an 1857 twenty-dollar gold coin.

"Carter, come here! You are not going to believe this. My first gold coin!"

Carter takes the shiny coin out of Blake's hand. "We have found the site we were looking for! Let's keep searching."

Within a few minutes, Carter also finds his first gold coin, and within an hour, between the two of them, they pull eight more gold coins from the ground.

Carter turns to Blake. "It looks as though the creek might have washed away some of the coins over the years."

Carter gets a hit with his metal detector near a medium-sized oak tree. After digging a few inches, roots start to impede his search. Always prepared he pulls out his hand hatchet from his tool belt and proceeds to go to work on a century's worth of roots.

Carter finally reaches the find and pulls out what he knows at once to be a buckle. Carter yells to his friend, "Civil War belt buckle! I've found a buckle!"

Carter brushes the dirt off of the oval buckle, and an eagle with down-turned wings appears in the center of the plate. Wiping away more of the moist dirt from the top, Carter makes out the words "The Southern Confederacy" across the top. Thirteen stars appear around the edge of the buckle, as he pours water and more dirt is removed.

Carter hands his friend Blake the buckle. "Be careful, don't want to damage this beauty. It looks like it is in pretty good shape."

Blake takes the plate from Carter, being careful not to drop it. "Congratulations on a stunning find. It's unusual to find a buckle of this quality. This seems like a buckle that would come out of Virginia. I wonder what the soldier who dropped this was doing way down here in Northwest Alabama."

Blake gently hands the plate back to Carter.

Carter turns the buckle over and notices engravings on the back of the buckle. "Blake, take a look at this. There are numbers and letters etched into the back of the buckle." He gently brushes the plate with a hand towel and holds the plate at eye level. "I'll have to clean this buckle up a little more to see what the numbers and letters represent."

"Be careful about cleaning it up too much. You don't want to take that beautiful patina off and destroy the value of the buckle."

Carter walks over to Blake after retrieving his metal detector. "On this note, I think we should call it a day. We both have a long drive home."

"You're right, and it doesn't get much better than this. You'll want to get that beauty home. Don't forget to send me a picture."

After hiking back to where they started, Carter and Blake load up their gear into separate trucks and head out.

*

When Blake got back to Nashville he opened his email. Carter had already washed most of the dirt off of the buckle and had sent him pictures of it. Blake began researching the buckle on the Internet and learned that only two others like it are known to exist. A cavalry soldier who fought in the "War Between the States" once owned the buckle in Richmond per an article on the Internet. One of the buckles is an un-dug example and is on display at a museum in Richmond, Virginia. The other buckle was found years ago in the mountains of North Georgia. Blake emails Carter the information.

Carter arrives at his office on Monday morning. His thoughts are a mixture of his busy day and the fantastic find from the weekend. Carter can't stop thinking about his incredible find. Carter opens an email from Blake. At about 10:30 a.m. Carter makes a call to the Virginia museum housing the buckle.

The woman who answers the phone tells Carter in a very pleasant voice that she will need to transfer him to the curator of the museum.

The museum curator comes on the phone. "Hello, how can I assist you?"

"My name is Carter Oakland, I am an attorney in Birmingham, Alabama, and I am calling about a buckle your museum has on display."

"We have several buckles on display. Which one do you have a question about?"

"The buckle with the down-turned eagle wings with the words 'The Southern Confederacy' across the top of it and thirteen stars surrounding the eagle. I would like to have a copy of the front and back of the buckle emailed or faxed to me. I recently found a buckle like the one you have on display."

The museum curator pauses. Carter wonders if he has lost him for a minute. The curator clears his throat and replies. "The buckle you are inquiring about is on loan to the museum and permission from the owner of the buckle must be given for anyone to take pictures of it."

Carter asks, "Can you please look at the buckle and tell me if there is any writing or letters on the back of the buckle?"

The museum curator pauses again, and then politely replies, "Let me get your name and number, and I will have the owner contact you."

"Sure, sounds great." Carter gives the curator his cell phone number.

"I will pass your information onto the buckle's owner."

"Awesome, I really appreciate it. I hope you have a terrific day."

"The same to you," the curator says, as he hangs up the phone.

Carter's curiosity was fully piqued.

Chapter 22

A few days go by before Carter receives a mysterious call from the owner of the buckle. The voice on the other end of the phone is coarse, like that of a heavy smoker. Carter notices the man is short of breath. Carter guesses he is probably short of time as well.

"Mr. Oakland, I understand you're interested in a family heirloom of mine."

"Yes!" Carter leans over his desk. "Very interested! Thank you so much for returning my call, sir."

"First things first, please call me Robert."

"And call me Carter. I found a buckle that seems to be an exact match to yours."

Robert's tone turned serious. "I know you're excited, but there is some history you need to know about the buckles, a history that goes back to the war. I would prefer not to talk about the information over the phone. If you can travel here to Richmond, I will tell you the story behind the buckles and let you examine mine."

"I'll check with my boss and call you back with some dates."

"You might want to make it sooner than later. As you can probably tell by the way I sound, I'm battling some health issues. I have advanced lung cancer."

"I'm sorry to hear that, Robert. I'll keep you in my prayers."

"Yeah, I don't know how much time prayers will give me, but thanks. And, like I said, get your plans straight and try to get here as soon as you can."

After work Carter called Blake's cell phone on his drive home. "Blake, Carter here, have you got a second?"

"Sure, I can talk for a minute. What's up?"

"I was able to get in touch with the owner of the buckle. He said there is something he wants to talk to me about concerning the buckle, and the only way he will give me any information is if I drive up to Virginia and meet him face to face. How does a short trip to Virginia sound to you?"

"I'm certainly game. We could also tour some of the battlefields while we are there." Blake starts thinking about who can cover his territory and assist his customers for the week.

"Let's do it. We need to meet with the buckle's owner, pronto. He's battling lung cancer, and the man sounds like he is on his last leg."

"Do you want to fly or drive up to Richmond?"

"Man, by the time you try to fly, with security and layovers, we could already be there! It'll take about eight hours, but I can probably get us there in seven. And besides if we fly we'd be risking damage to our detectors. If we get an early start, it won't be too bad."

"All right it's a plan!" replies Blake.

"I figure we'll drive up there on Wednesday, meet with Robert on Thursday morning and that will give us the rest of the weekend to see the battlefields." Carter starts mapping out the visit in his head.

"Sounds good to me, book it."

"I'll let Robert know we're coming."

Carter and Blake finalize their drive to Virginia. They are excited. Neither had ever toured the battlefields. Carter makes the decision to rent an SUV for the trip. His jeep is a classic but not the most comfortable vehicle on a long distance road trip. Carter arrives at the rental place the day before the trip to secure an SUV. The representative sets him up with a beautiful black Suburban with tinted windows.

"Wow, we will look like government officials riding around in this thing!"

The rep laughs. "Where are you going?"

Carter replies, "We're taking it to Virginia."

"Well then, it might not be a bad idea to look like a government official. Might keep you safe!"

Carter leaves out early the next day and arrives at Blake's house at 8:00 a.m. to pick him up.

Blake walks out of his house as Carter pulls up. "Wow, man, this is a sweet ride! This isn't yours, is it?"

Carter beams. "It is for a few days, my friend. Hop in!"

Blake loads his gear up in the back and the two guys hit the road, Virginia-bound.

Carter starts shuffling through some papers he stuffed in the center console.

"You might want to watch the road, can I help you find something?"

"I want to show you what I found on the Internet about Robert, the owner of the buckle. Ah, here it is," Carter hands Blake a printout. "So check this out, Robert McCarver is actually Sir Robert McCarver. Back in the day, when he was in the Marine Corps, he rescued a member of the British royal family who was kidnapped by some bad guys in the Middle East. He got knighted for returning the prince safely. Isn't that cool?"

"We'll be meeting a celebrity, huh?"

"I just hope he provides us the information we need."

Blake leans his seat back and tilts his hat down. "Maybe my service record will help us build rapport."

Blake rests, and Carter concentrates on the drive. He turns on some alternative rock and accelerates on down the interstate.

They arrive close to Richmond that night and check into their hotel. The two are up early the next day to meet the owner of the other buckle.

Chapter 23

Carter and Blake ride up the long driveway to Robert's mansion. "My gosh, look at this place, Carter!"

The driveway is lined with old oaks on one side, with an old stone wall just beyond the tree line. A pretty creek winds its way across the property on the other side.

"Sir Robert's family certainly must have done well after the Civil War."

Carter notices a historical plaque on the stone entranceway listing the date the mansion was built shortly after the American Civil War in 1867.

Blake and Carter walk up the stone steps to the wide porch of the old mansion. The mansion has large twin chimneys on either side of it. The house itself is wood with large columns stretching out across the front of the home. Sir Robert comes to the door. He is dressed in brown khakis, a dark blue shirt, and black boots.

"I was starting to think you might have gotten lost or decided to take a detour. You must be Carter."

Carter reaches his hand out and shakes Robert's hand. "Yes, sir, it's a pleasure to meet you. We did get into a little more traffic than I bargained for. Things move a little slower down in the Deep South."

A golden retriever waddles over in front of Robert. Blake reaches down to pet it.

Robert puts his hands on his hips and looks down. "This is Jake. I have had him since he was a puppy. He's elderly but is still getting around pretty good. Well, come on in, we have a lot to talk about."

Blake shakes Robert's hand on entering the front door. "Blake Dossman. It is an honor to meet you. That is the friendliest dog I have ever seen."

Robert leads the gentlemen into his home. "You must be a dog person. Jake can sense it. Well, welcome to my home. Are you guys thirsty?"

"Yes, I could go for something," says Carter.

"How about some sweet tea?"

"Yes, sir, that sounds good."

Robert prepares sweet tea for his two guests and guides them into a library study beyond a grand entranceway. As soon as he enters back into the house, Robert wraps an air tube across his nostrils and around the back of his ears. The air tube is attached to a tank that he rolls around.

Years of smoking left his voice thick and raspy. His breathing is labored.

"Did you boys have any problem finding this place?"

Carter and Blake politely shake their heads.

"No," says Carter. "We didn't have any trouble at all. This is a beautiful place you have here, Robert. I mean, Sir Robert."

Robert laughs. "I see you made an Internet search of me, huh? It's not every day you get knighted." He continues, "My granddaughter looks after the flowers here, and my son and his wife take care of the horses. Up until lately, I have managed to do a little, but as you can see I am getting on up in age now. These days, I do pretty good to look after ole Jake and myself."

Blake asks, "How long have you lived here?"

"I've lived on this farm and in this house my entire life, raised a family of my own here. It's a piece of heaven and in my opinion there is no better place to live."

The gentlemen all take a sip of their sweet tea, and then seem to experience an awkward silence. Carter can tell Robert is scoping them out. Carter looks at Blake and raises his eyebrows. "Blake, were you ever out this way with the Navy?"

Robert looks over at Blake. "Ah, a Navy man. When were you in the service?"

"I had two tours in Iraq and two in Afghanistan. It was intense being there but exhilarating! Sometimes I miss it, but I sure love the conveniences we have in America. People here seem to take our freedom for granted sometimes."

Robert nods his head. "Yes, the camaraderie established in battle is unbreakable. I miss my old command. So many of those fellows have gone on to be with the good Lord. We lost some on the battlefield, but at this point, many are dying from illness and age."

Robert relaxes a little. He leans back in his chair. "Yeah, I have a long line of ancestors who served in the military. My dad was in World War II, my granddad was in the Spanish-American War, and my great-granddad was in the Civil War."

The guys lean in. Robert pauses for a moment as to collect his thoughts. "I know you didn't come all this way to hear me talk about my family tree."

Blake leans back, crosses his arms, and then rubs his chin. "Sir, it is an honor to sit here with you and hear about your ancestor's accomplishments."

Robert smiles. "I know you are probably itching to hear the story behind the buckles. Let me see what you've got."

Carter brings the carrying case out of his pocket. He gently lays the buckle on Robert's desk and takes the pins out that hold the glass top down onto the case. "Here you go. This is, by far, the best thing I've ever found metal detecting."

Robert picks up the buckle and examines it. "This is a beautiful find. I will tell you the story."

Chapter 24

"My great grandfather, Andy McCarver, in that picture, fought in the Civil War and was a scout during the War of Northern Aggression. Legend has it Andy belonged to an elite division of the Confederate Secret Service and that the inscriptions on the back of three buckles would produce a map leading to a great treasure. Of course, now you know that my grandfather had one of the buckles, and for years I wondered if there were others like my great grandfather's belt plate. We also now know that the two other belt plates were indeed lost during the war."

Blake and Carter lean in, with their full focus on what Robert has to tell them.

"Legend has it that the two belt buckles that were lost during the war were worn by men with larger-than-life personalities. One of the soldiers, Captain Walt Henson, died going over a cliff in the mountains of Northern Georgia, still firing both his pistols at the Yankees on his way to oblivion. That story is documented in the regimental histories of both the North and South. As for the other soldier, Captain Henry Washington, we never knew what happened to him. It was a mystery to Andy. It was like Captain Washington was swallowed up into another dimension. Andy thought he must have been killed by bushwhackers and buried in an unmarked grave somewhere in the Deep South."

Robert clears his throat and inhales deeply from his oxygen machine. "I guess I've been doing all of the talking. I might need to take a break and let my lungs catch up. Now please tell me, exactly where did you find your buckle? I'm curious to know the whereabouts."

Carter proceeds to tell the story of his best relic-hunting day ever.

"An older gentleman told me two Confederate soldiers had buried gold on Masterson Creek. We dug a lot of deep aluminum cans before we found the site and started digging gold coins. There seemed to be a small cache. It was hot. At one point, I thought I was going to pass out, and then I uncovered this beautiful buckle."

Robert develops a curious look while holding his chin. "I bet you young men were standing right beside Henry's grave. It sounds like he was waylaid by criminals and murdered. It is almost for certain you found Henry's haversack that had the gold coins in it. Well now, I will tell you Andy McCarver's story, as best it can be told without his missing journal."

Carter and Blake exchange excited looks. They can see it in each other's eyes.

Blake looks at Sir Robert and leans forward. "Missing journal?"

"Yes, we know Andy kept a journal. He mentions it in several of his letters. We have searched but haven't found it. Several years ago my friend Jedediah Smith at the museum started examining Andy McCarver's old Civil War papers and his regiment's movements. He called me and said he thought he could locate the site of my great grandfather's camp, right before Walt was killed and his buckle lost. Jed was determined to find the site. He has an old war wound in his leg that limits his physical endurance at times. We drove down to the site and, amazingly, found the camp. Using the best metal detectors available back then, we dug hard for about four and a half hours. Jed was rewarded with a C. S. spur, which was the best thing we found in the camp. We dug a few eagle and flower buttons along with some flat buttons. We did not find a lot of bullets. The Confederates never could afford to lose much."

Sir Robert shifts in his chair and winces. He reaches out for his glass of sweet tea wincing again.

Blake reaches out and hands him his glass.

Sir Robert takes a drink then gazes off in the distance with a thousand-yard stare before he continues. "We found the spot where we thought Andy and Walt charged over the cliff and into the water. We decided to hunt along the riverbank to see if we could find a spot where Walt's body could have washed up. It was fall, when the leaves offer their most vibrant and brightest change in color. We were checking out an area, when we noticed an old man walking along the river. We started up a conversation with him, and it turned out he was looking for Civil War bullets and Indian artifacts. We asked him if he'd ever heard of anyone who had ever found any belt plates along the river. The old relic hunter said that years before he had been walking on one of the shoals and half buried in the sandy edge of the water he had spied a Civil War belt buckle. He described it, and I was nearly certain the plate was the one we were looking for. We could not believe our luck! Jed asked if he would be interested in selling it, but the old timer said he did not want to part with the belt buckle. Luckily, he did let us take pictures of it."

Chapter 25

Sir Robert reaches into a desk drawer. "I want to show you this." Sir Robert pulls out a faded manila envelope. The pictures he pulled from the envelope are color images of the North Georgia buckle. Sir Robert handed the pictures to Carter and Blake, who are both very excited.

Carter holds the pictures so Blake can see. "Wow this buckle has a beautiful green patina! I see an engraving on the back of the buckle that spells out something."

Sir Robert's old gray eyes light up and twinkle. "Yes, it does spell out something. On the back of the buckle found in North Georgia there is an engraving. 'Let us cross over the river and rest under the shade of the trees.' Here, I know that you history buffs know exactly where that saying came from."

"Yes, those were Stonewall Jackson's last words before he passed away," says Carter.

"I don't know what it means. I have wondered if maybe the phrase somehow breaks a secret code. I also think it is possible that Stonewall Jackson's last words may have been describing a real location. Maybe Jackson knew something and the buckles are supposed to lead us to whatever that something is. As you can see there are other markings and characters on the buckle. I have worked on this mystery, but time is growing short for me. Hopefully, you two can make some sense of it."

Sir Robert starts to cough. He keeps coughing, and then reaches for a handkerchief and coughs again. Carter notices blood coming up in the old man's cough.

Sir Robert takes another deep grasp of air from his oxygen machine. "I've got to let you know something. I am dying, and I don't have any family that will take this treasure story seriously. I was hoping I could get my son interested, but sadly he has never shown any interest in taking up the legacy of the McCarver treasure. You two seem like nice guys. I am going to turn over to you all of the research and Civil War documents that I have been able to gather on Andy McCarver's lost treasure story."

Sir Robert opens a briefcase and reaches out to hand Carter a piece of paper. "Here is a picture of Andy McCarver's buckle. It is more in line with your buckle but with different encryptions."

Blake and Carter examine the front and back pictures of the buckle, looking for clues.

"I don't know where these mysterious buckles will take you."

After coughing up some more phlegm, Sir Robert regains his voice.

"A few years ago I had a friend look at the buckle's engraving to see if he could make any sense as to a possible secret code. This friend of mine was in charge of counter intelligence with the Central Intelligence Agency. His expertise was deciphering secret codes that the Russians were sending back and forth to America during the Cold War. He said that without a specific decryption key he felt that the code could never be broken."

Sir Robert reaches for his oxygen, but he continues on.

"I have studied the buckle's engravings on and off over the years, but I have not been able to crack its secrets. If you succeed in decoding the buckle's secret you will have succeeded where some of the best code breakers in the world have failed." Sir Robert leans his head back and sighs. He looks Carter and then Blake in the eye. "I worked in counter insurgency for most of my career. My job was to uncover secrets. I have seen my share of action. I've had thoughts of writing my memoirs, but many of my Cold War missions are still classified. I lost several friends in combat, and I have seen my share of war. I was right in the middle of some of the darkest moments of the twentieth century. The Russians are not our friends and we should always be on guard against them."

Sir Robert looks off to his left and gets a faraway look in his eyes as though he is remembering a particular scene from his past. He takes a deep struggled breath.

"Gentlemen, I want to show you around my home. I have gathered artifacts and weapons from various parts of the world. First let's step out on the balcony. There is a beautiful view of the valley that runs behind my property. I also want to have a puff on my pipe."

Standing on the Balcony Blake asks, "Sir Robert would you care if we scan your yard with our metal detectors to see if we can find any Civil War relics."

"Sure go ahead. I don't think you will find anything as this place was built after the war."

Chapter 26

With the sun falling fast this time of the year, darkness would arrive in a matter of minutes. Carter and Blake pop the hatch on the back of their SUV and slip off their nice shoes to exchange them for old hunting boots. The two pull out their detectors, turn them on, slip on their headphones, and began swinging their detectors over the rich Virginia soil.

Blake hits a signal and digs out a small plug of dirt. "I've got an Indian Head penny that predates the Civil War … 1860!"

Carter walks over to examine the coin. He hands the coin back to Blake after admiring it. "We've got to hunt hard before the sun goes down."

Blake secures the coin in a plastic container. "Have you found anything good?"

Carter reaches in his bag, pulls out some of his trash finds, and holds out his hand for Blake to see. "I can tell from a nail I found, plus these other objects and the old glass and pottery in the ground, that there was a homestead here that predates the current house. This house site is older than the Civil War."

Carter walks back to his shovel and detector. He follows Blake by finding two Indian Head pennies with dates of 1859 and 1860. Blake finds a miniè ball and a few coin buttons.

After about thirty minutes of hunting, Carter gets a strong signal, digs, and pulls up a beautiful Virginia Military Institute button. Carter gives a celebratory yell, "Wahoo! Pay dirt!" He runs over to Blake to show him his great find.

The two relic hunters manage to get two and a half good hours of hunting in before darkness overtakes the day. Besides the V.M.I. button and coins, the two find a Mississippi infantry button, a few eagle buttons, and an "A" artillery button. The two also manage to find a handful of bullets. They also find a two-piece "I" button, as well as an 1852 Seated Liberty dime, the first either of them had ever found. One of Carter's last finds, before it became too dark to see, is an ornate, Civil War era, skeleton key with mysterious letters running up one side of it and cryptic numbers running down the other side.

When Carter and Blake decided it is time to quit, they walk up to the large old mahogany door and knock. Sir Robert comes onto the front porch and lights his pipe. As Carter and Blake show Sir Robert the various items that have come out of his yard, his eyes grow wide with wonder. Sir Robert picks up the Mississippi Infantry button, admiring the remaining gold gilt on the button. "You boys found all of this in just two hours?"

Carter smiles. "Yes sir, we hit it pretty hard. We have some good detectors, too. It takes some time to get use to our machines, but once you understand the sounds, you know pretty easily when you hear a good signal and when you hear something that might not be as good."

Blake laughs. "Yeah, but Carter fails to mention that sometimes bad items ring as good tones. Don't let him fool you, Sir Robert, we dig a lot of junk to find relics!"

Carter and Blake give Sir Robert a few of the bullets and buttons they had dug.

Carter shakes Robert's hand. "You know if you let us bring a mini dozier in here, there would be tons of relics that come out of the ground!"

Blake raises an eyebrow at Carter and rubs his chin. He is afraid that Carter may have stepped out of bounds with the dozier question.

Sir Robert laughs. "I don't know about all that. Probably when I'm dead and gone, they'll bulldoze my old place to build another shopping center. I don't understand how these stores can keep going up. Do people really do that much shopping?"

Blake relaxes and looks out over the beautiful estate. "Folks need to get outdoors more."

Carter finishes loading up his gear. "We value the information you shared with us. It's been a true pleasure getting to hang out with you today."

Robert smiles. "I wish my son felt the same way. Hey, do you guys want to come in and have a beer with me to celebrate your finds? I might even be able to find some aged brandy tucked away. I might as well drink it, right?"

Carter looks over at Blake and shrugs his shoulders. "Sounds great!"

Blake says, "I could sure go for a drink."

Sir Robert ironically coughing less now that he has smoked his pipe leads Carter and Blake off of the bricked front porch and to a side entranceway. After entering an elegant hallway, Sir Robert presses a button to summon an elevator that takes them to the basement.

Carter is impressed. "Wow, now this is a cool way to get around your home!"

"Thank you, you two will like where I'm taking you."

Getting off the elevator, the guests are stunned by a truly awesome man cave. The room has oak-lined walls with moose head, bison, deer, and other animals covering the walls. In the center is a billiards table.

Sir Robert proceeds over to a granite countertop bar. "Y'all can probably tell this is my favorite room."

A bookshelf running along one entire wall is full of Civil War books as well as a number on regimental histories of Confederate units. There are still other books on the great European wars, as well as a section on Far East military history. Blake runs his finger along some of the titles.

Sir Robert pours three brandy sifters. "Pull any of those books off the shelves and look at them. Better yet, if you see one or two of them you like, feel free to take them home with you." He hands the drinks to Blake and Carter, along with beers for chasers. "Cheers, guys! Thank you for driving up to Virginia. I really appreciate your interest in this treasure story I have been chasing all these years."

The three sip their brandy.

Carter sets his down. "This hits the spot after a hard day of metal detecting."

Sir Robert looks at Carter and stands up a little straighter, grinning. "Well, I'd like for you guys to keep secret what I want to show you next. Check this out."

Sir Robert pulls out an oversized book on the history of George Washington, reaches into the shelf and pushes a button. One of the oak panels pops open and swings outward revealing a hidden chamber cleverly disguised by what must have been a master carpenter.

Blake asks, “Did you build this yourself?

“I did. My grandfather had a woodshop. I picked up carpentry skills from him.”

Mounted on the walls are full auto 5.56 rifles, AR 15s, Uzi submachine guns, semi-auto handguns, revolvers, and a .50 caliber Barret rifle. Every variety of web gear and military-weaponry imaginable is in the chamber.

Sir Robert picks up an M1 Garand rifle that Blake is eyeing and hands it to him. “I have kept this room a secret for many years. Only my wife and a few other trusted associates know of its existence. I never revealed it to my children.”

Carter leans over admiring the .50 caliber Barret rifle. “I know where we will be coming if the Russkies ever invade.”

Sir Robert laughs. “If the Russkies do invade, ‘they will find a rifle behind every blade of grass’ here in the States.”

Chapter 27

The next day Carter and Blake drive their rented SUV to look at artifacts and see Andy McCarver's buckle. They arrive at the museum at around 10:00 a.m. The building appears to be an old structure, possibly period. As they approach they can see that the newer stone siding is covering a much older exterior.

Carter and Blake enter the structure and begin to look around. The museum's curator makes his way over to them. "Good morning, fellows! Welcome to our museum. My name is Jedediah Smith, named after the famous Jedediah Hotchkiss. Unfortunately no relation, I go by Jed for short."

"Very nice to meet you, sir. My name is Carter, and this is Blake. We have traveled over from Middle Tennessee to do some research. Sir Robert McCarver told us you have a very interesting museum."

"Robert told me about you boys. Well, come on over and sign my guest book. Would you like any coffee or to take a tour of the museum?" Jed smiles politely.

"We stocked up on coffee this morning, but we're interested in a tour."

"Don't get many folks visiting these days for tours."

Jed walks over behind the shop's counter and pushes a guestbook to the edge of the counter. Blake and Carter walk over to sign it.

"Sir Robert McCarver and I have been friends all of our lives. Not a finer man can be found in Virginia. A true patriot. He has a long line of military service in his family. Did he tell you guys about his ancestors?"

"Yes sir, he did. Quite an impressive bloodline." Carter and Blake follow Jed into the main part of the museum. Carter and Blake see many swords and uniforms, and learned some history they did not know.

Coming around a corner, Jed holds his hand out towards a specific glass case. "This is what you came to see, one of this county's most famous citizens, the Confederate Secret Service Agent Andy McCarver's belt plate and accouterments. Be careful, boys. No leaning on the glass, please."

Blake looks over at Carter and rolls his eyes.

The display includes Andy McCarver's grey Confederate uniform with down-turned eagle buttons and the insignia for a captain's rank he held at the end of the war. Also in the case are his slouch hat, full regalia belt with cartridge box, sword, pistols, and the mysterious Southern Confederacy belt plate.

"As you might already know, this plate design is one of only three that has been found. This belt plate as well as the one found in North Georgia has symbols all over the back of it. The few who have studied the symbols have been unable to crack the code. It may well lead to a fabulous treasure, as the Confederacy's recorded gold reserves have never been completely accounted for. Does the belt plate you found have symbols on it?"

Yes it does. But we don't know what the symbols mean. Carter bends down to the case to get a better look. "If only these relics could talk, imagine the stories that they could tell."

"Well, relics don't talk. You gotta do the research to find the story."

Blake looks at Carter and rolls his eyes a second time.

"We have Andy McCarver's uniform, accouterments, and wartime papers. What we are missing is the diary we know he kept from the letters he wrote. Andy's diary may hold some important clues as to what the encryptions on the back of the buckles mean."

At the end of the tour, Carter and Blake shake Jed's hand. Jed watches out a window as the two walk to the parking lot. Carter and Blake wave goodbye, get into their SUV, and head to the once bloody Virginia battlefields.

After they leave the museum, Jed places the ten-dollar bill from Carter into his register. He murmurs, "I gave them more than ten dollars' worth of information."

Jed picks up his phone and places a suspicious call to a person at an overseas phone number. "I've found the boys that you are looking for. The two who have uncovered the third buckle came in to visit the museum, I have their names and addresses in my guest book and I will email the information over at once."

"Excellent. Payment will be on the way within the next three days. Once again, it is a pleasure doing business with you."

"How much did you say… one thousand dollars for the names?" But all Jed hears is a dial tone.

Chapter 28

Carter and Blake roll down the windows on the SUV to enjoy the crisp autumn air. The fall colors added to the scenery, as they began to explore the battlefields before heading back to Nashville.

Carter knew Blake had studied the Virginia theater of battle extensively; he had an idea Blake would know of a great place to start a sightseeing tour. "We've still got plenty of daylight. Where should we start?"

"Let's see," Blake studies a battle map of the area. He runs his hand over his stubbly military haircut and adjusts his sunglasses. "If it is okay with you, I would like to ride over to the Chancellorsville Battlefield. I have always wanted to see where Robert E. Lee and Stonewall Jackson had their last meeting. I also would like to see where Stonewall Jackson fell. That moment, more than any other during the war, sealed the fate of the Confederacy."

The guys take in all they can get of the beautiful landscape of Virginia. The rolling hills, green pastures, churches sitting perfectly on the hills, with the sunlight beaming on them display a view straight from heaven.

Carter says, "Blake, I would like to move to a place like this. The countryside is beautiful. Birmingham is nice, but I really love being here in Virginia."

Blake looks up from the tour map and over at Carter. "Virginia is beautiful, but I have a hard time understanding what people are saying sometimes."

Carter laughs. "What do you mean?"

"Seriously, Carter? Do you like digging in the 'dut' or dirt?"

Carter smiles. "I like the accent, I could get used to it."

Blake shrugs. "Whatever, man, I'm ready to get back to Tennessee twang!"

On the Chancellorsville Battlefield a short distance away, the ghosts of fallen soldiers await Carter and Blake's tour. On this historically significant battlefield, General Lee had his greatest victory by splitting his army into two parts. It is also where Stonewall Jackson made the ultimate sacrifice.

Blake and Carter decide to head back to the hotel and have an early dinner after their battlefield tours. They have a long drive home the next day. The two leave the hotel in Richmond at 5:00 a.m. and arrive back in Nashville at about 3:00 p.m.

The guys pull up to Blake's house. Blake sees his Harlequin Great Dane, Roscoe, pawing at the gate in the backyard.

"Looks like you've been missed. My employees take good care of him when I am away, but it's not the same as when I'm here with him. You go ahead and make yourself at home. The guest bedroom should be pretty clean."

Carter pokes his head in the room. "Looks good, man, I appreciate it."

Blake puts his bags in his room and pops his head into Carter's room. "How does a night out on the town in Nash Vegas sound? I love touring the countryside, but I'm ready for some longneck bottles, neon lights, and live music."

Carter laughs. "Let's do it, man! I've got tomorrow off, and I am certainly up for a night out."

"Great it's settled then."

Blake goes out back to play with Roscoe for a while before coming back in and taking a quick power nap.

Carter carries his luggage to the guest room. He takes the buckle out of his travel bag and studies it.

"I wonder where you will lead us?" He puts the buckle on the nightstand. "I'm talking to a buckle … I guess I do need a nap."

Carter lies down to rest. Three hours later the two are ready for the honkytonks on lower Broadway.

"Carter, you're not going to take your buckle downtown with us, are you? We can lock it up in my wall safe."

Carter had already thought about it.

"No way! I am going to keep this buckle right by my side until I can get it to the safety deposit box in Birmingham."

Blake shrugs. "Suit yourself."

"It's Nashville. Surely, we can stay out of trouble."

After relaxing down on lower Broadway, Blake and Carter decide to journey to a little sports bar on Second Avenue. As the two make the turn from Broadway to Second Avenue, they hear someone calling from behind them.

"You two out on date night?"

Blake notices two thugs in black suits following them.

"Keep moving, Carter. It's just a couple of drunks."

Blake and Carter keep walking, when one of the guys yells, "Hey, I'm talking to you."

The guy grabs Blake's shoulder, and in one swift motion Blake grabs the guy's wrist, dragging him painfully down to the ground. With another swift motion, Blake's left leg flies up with a karate kick to the other goon's chin. The second guy falls to the ground with a busted lip. Both of the well-dressed men are on the ground, their faces grimacing, in pain.

Blake stands over the two ruffians. "You two are obviously not from around here. I'm a lot nicer than most, but if you don't back off, I'll be glad to show you how we handle big mouths here in the South. Now get the hell out of here!"

The two troublemakers beat a quick and hasty retreat.

"So much for Southern hospitality."

"No, that was weird. I have never had any confrontations down here before. People are partying hard and they start drinking early in the day. I know we are getting more and more tourists downtown."

Carter checks his pocket to make sure the buckle is secure. "Those guys had accents. Possibly Belgium?"

"I don't know, but I could tell they had a different accent," says Blake.

"They were a little too anxious to pick a fight with us. Something ain't right," says Carter, as he looks over his shoulder. "You think they followed us?"

Blake cracks his knuckles. "Ever since we've picked up that buckle …"

"Do you think we should check out the house?"

"Nah, my alarm system will send me a call if anything happens at the house."

Blake and Carter pass several more bars before reaching one of Blake's favorite watering holes, a sports bar in a basement with different beers on tap.

"Wow, man, this is a hidden jewel down here!"

"Yeah, it's a cool place. I'll grab us a pitcher."

"Awesome man, I'll go see if I can get a pool table."

Carter walks over to the pool table and puts quarters on the table to challenge the folks currently on the table. Blake takes the pitcher and a couple of glasses over to a table, where Carter joins him.

"These are a few of my favorite things. Cold beer, good music, pool, and women."

"If I lived here, I would be a regular here."

"Don't you shoot pool in a league down in Birmingham?"

"I do. I've been shooting since I was a kid." Carter sees the eight ball go rolling into the corner pocket, along with the cue ball into the other. "Looks like I'm up, this should be fun!"

Chapter 29

After ordering a second pitcher of beer, Blake and Carter concur they made a wise decision in coming downtown to pop into Blake's favorite local bar on Second Avenue. Carter manages to strike up a friendly game of pool, drawing a good bit of attention to himself with his pool-shooting abilities.

Carter pours beer into his glass. "Playing with the league pays off, man. You get some great training with the pros, and it makes it a lot easier playing against folks who've had a few brews."

Carter walks back to the pool table and recalls one pro in particular who would come up to the table, start shooting pool with a cigarette in his mouth, barely looking at the table, then run it out every time.

He doesn't know what skill level his opponent might be, so Carter proceeds to run the table. He doesn't get good shape on a shot and is forced to play a safety.

As he is waiting his turn, Carter looks across the bar and notices Blake has managed to attract two lovely ladies to their table, one a striking brunette and the other a petite redhead. Blake waves at Carter and motions for him to come over whenever he gets a chance. The brunette is sitting close to Blake, and it is evident that the two have met before tonight.

"Blake's always been a ladies man," Carter says to no one in particular, as he steps up and hits the cue ball with his pool stick, zipping the eight ball in for another victory.

Carter decides not to give the pool table up just yet. He is having a good time beating the tar out of his challengers.

After a few more games he tells the crowd around him he needs to quit for the night. "That's it, guys, no more for me tonight, I'm going to join my friends over there."

The guys he's been shooting against roll their eyes, call him a pool shark, and shake their heads before starting a new game. Carter walks over to his friend across the bar.

Blake introduces Carter to the girls, "Ladies, this is a dear friend of mine, Carter, aka pool shark."

"Man, don't say that. Those guys over there were about ready to throw some punches over a couple of games of pool. Ladies, I'm no pool shark, just well trained!"

The brunette looks to be about twenty-seven or twenty-eight while the redhead was likely in her early to mid-thirties.

The redhead extends her petite hand to shake Carter's hand. "My name is Pam, and I must say, wow you're really good at shooting pool!"

Carter puffs out his chest and then laughs. "Well, what can I say? I practice a good bit."

Carter likes the way Pam smiles. She also seems pretty intrigued with him; he was always a sucker for a redhead with green eyes.

"Where are you from, Pam?"

"I am originally from Ireland but I live in London England now. My Irish heritage brings me luck."

Carter picks up on some possible chemistry between him and Pam.

"You know, I'm quite the historian. I could help you trace your family tree if you haven't already."

Pam laughs. "I've never heard that used before as a pickup line."

The brunette extends her hand. "I'm Victoria, but my friends call me Vicki."

"That's a pretty name."

Vicki smiles. "It's a family name, seems very formal to me and I'm pretty laid back, so I like people to call me Vicki. Anyway, y'all, it's getting late, how about y'all follow us over to my place in Brentwood. We'll continue our party over there?"

Neither Blake nor Carter has an issue with Vickie's invitation and load up in the SUV rental, while the ladies get into Vicki's plush new convertible.

"Man, Blake, Vicki must do well!"

"Yeah, that's an understatement. She does extremely well. She is a consultant for the government, black ops kind of stuff, man."

"You date her?"

"We're friends. I served in the military with her husband."

On the way to Vicki's house, Blake explains to Carter that Vicki's husband was killed while working as a military contractor supplying guns to insurgencies and guerrilla fighters in Syria.

Blake didn't know the specifics of what had happened to Vicki's husband, but he knew it was something unexpected and out of the ordinary, even for a weapons supplier. He continues, "Probably someone put a hit on him for one reason or another."

Blake started to reminisce his time in the service with Vicki's husband. He recalled him being a loyal friend and a hell of a good soldier. Blake recalls the first time he met Vicki at a fundraiser for veterans. He pictures her in that sleek black dress and her bright red lipstick. Blake had also seen her out on occasion since her husband had been killed.

Blake glances over at Carter. "I didn't really think she was interested in me. She surely never invited me to her place before." Blake goes on to say, "Maybe you are bringing me some good luck, bro!"

Carter looks over and smiles. "Might be the luck of the Irish redhead!"

Vicki's house is fixed on a high hill overlooking the beauty of the forested areas surrounding Brentwood, Tennessee. The house is a ranch style with a huge window in front. With a full moon out, Carter and Blake can appreciate the slope of the hill they have to walk up.

Carter asks, "What do they do if it snows?"

"They leave the car at the bottom of the hill and hike up."

The girls motion for the two men to hurry into the house.

Vicki breaks open a few bottles of beer and pours the beer into glasses. She opens a cabinet. "Anyone up for tequila shots?"

They toast to friendship and good times. The four hang out for a while in the expansive living room. A nice fire is roaring, and stories are exchanged.

Carter shares his story of finding the Southern Confederacy belt buckle. He shows them the plate.

Vicki motions to Blake. "I've got something I would like to show you. Follow me."

Blake and Vicki shuffle down the long center hall to other parts of the house leaving Carter and his new friend, Pam, to themselves.

Pam asks, "Can I see that relic again?"

Carter pulls the Civil War belt plate from his pocket and carefully hands it to Pam.

Pam holds the buckle with both hands. "The workmanship that went into this is impressive. You haven't had any luck in decoding these symbols, huh?"

"No. I wish I could. The story goes that once the code is deciphered, a fantastic treasure will be found." Carter shrugs, he looks up from the buckle at Pam and continues, "Those brave soldiers gave everything they had in that horrible war."

"I think your hobby is cool. I mean just think of all the history this buckle has seen. It sounds like a great adventure you two are going on."

Pam hands the buckle back to Carter. He returns it to his cargo pants then leans back on the couch, gazing into the flickering embers in the fireplace. "It is not every day you meet someone who is able to see and admire another time and place when people were more interested in their culture and traditions. Folks in the 1800s practically worshipped their history and the Founding Fathers."

Pam nods her head, as she scoots a little closer. "I like your passion for history. So many people nowadays have no idea of our past."

Carter puts his arm around Pam. He leans over and kisses her. "You are really sweet, you know that?"

Pam smiles. "Are you sure it's not the beer?"

"No, it's not the beer. Would you mind if I kiss you again?"

"Such a gentleman, but no, I wouldn't mind that at all."

Carter kisses Pam on her lips and then on her neck.

"I like that."

"Yeah, me too. There is a lot more where that came from."

Carter and Pam embrace, gradually sliding down onto the carpeted floor in front of the fireplace.

Meanwhile Vicki has led Blake to a far back corner of the house stopping at a hardened steel door that looks out of place at a ranch house in Brentwood, Tennessee.

Vickie looks Blake in the eyes. "I know you will appreciate this setup. Uncle Sam has invested a lot of money in outfitting its contractors."

Beside the door is an elaborate electronic keypad and hand scanner locking system. Vicki keys in the password, scans her hand, and enters into a room that looks like, from Blake's combat experience, a Special Operations Command Center.

"My late husband probably told you he performed special, sometimes top secret, missions for the government. One of the requirements and perks was that we would need a command center to run and coordinate black operation's teams. From here any special ops mission, in any part of the world, can be viewed and coordinated in real time via drones linked to satellites. If you ever get in a bind and need help, call me at the number on this card I am giving you and I will help out in any way I can."

"This is an incredible setup!"

Blake admires the intricate technology and layout of the room. Vicki reaches down and touches Blake's hand.

"You are a good man, Blake. I could tell that when I first met you at the fundraiser."

"The fundraiser? Do you remember seeing me there? I definitely remember seeing you!"

"Of course, I remember you."

"I couldn't get you out of my mind with that black dress and your red lipstick."

Vicki likes that comment and reaches for Blake. The two embrace each other in a heated kiss, and then Vicki leads Blake farther down the hallway to her bedroom.

"If you liked me in that black dress, wait until you see me in this." Vicki begins to unbutton her blouse to reveal a black lace corset.

"Um, I like that very much!"

*

The next morning Vicki makes coffee for everyone and turns on a TV in the kitchen, switching it over to a news channel. She glues into a story about a successful raid by U.S. Special Ops in the Middle East. "Everyone seems pretty quiet this morning. Have any of you heard the story about the raid last night?"

Blake looking at his phone sees he has a text message from the alarm company and from a friend of his that works at the police department.

Blake looks up. "Sounds like my house was broken into last night!"

"Are you serious?"

"I need to go check on everything. Ladies, we had a lovely evening. We will catch up with y'all soon," says Blake.

Blake and Carter grab their belongings and head to Blake's house. Upon arriving, they see police cars surrounding it, he is worried about what might be missing.

The police approach Blake. "Well, your electronics are all here, doesn't look like they got away with much. Only a few drawers were pulled out."

Blake rubs his chin. "Hmm … like someone was looking for something specific."

The officer hands Blake a copy of the report. "Exactly, they seemed to be looking for something in particular."

The officers walk off to finish their inspection.

Carter looks over to Blake. "Man, they were looking for the buckle!"

"Shhh, no need in bringing that up to the police right now. I don't know who is behind this, but we better lay low until we sort this out."

"You're right, Blake. I better head back to Birmingham and check out my place. I'll catch up with you soon."

Chapter 30

Driving home, Carter thinks about the trip to Virginia. The history they had seen refuels his passion for the American Civil War. Carter's thoughts turn to the mystery of the buckles. He thinks to himself that he should try and contact the relic hunter in Georgia about the buckle that was dug up along a riverbank there. Sir Robert had provided Carter the phone number and address of the owner of the Southern Confederacy belt plate dug in Georgia.

The next day Carter makes a phone call during his lunch hour and gets in touch with the relic hunter who found the buckle in Georgia. The relic hunter is an elderly gentleman who had found the buckle years earlier.

Carter introduces himself. "Um, yes, I know you don't know me, but believe it or not, I have found a Southern Confederacy belt plate almost identical to yours."

"Really? I didn't think another one would be found. I sold mine a few years ago. I regret it now."

"Would it be okay to ask who bought it?"

"I sold it at a Civil War show to a man who supposedly had a relic booth. I didn't want to sell it, but the price he offered was incredible. I sold it for thirty-five thousand dollars cash."

"That's a nice price. May I ask if there was anything unusual about the man who purchased the buckle?"

"I thought it was odd anyone would pull out that kind of cash. The man had more cash in a small suitcase … a lot more. The man said he was from Belgium. Strange thing is I tried to contact him to see if I could buy back the plate, but the number he'd given me was disconnected and I could find no trace of his relic shop being in business anymore. I've seen no trace of the plate anywhere on the Internet. It's like the man was a ghost and fell off the face of the earth."

Carter's stomach sinks a little on hearing the details of the buckle's mysterious disappearance. "Would any of the other relic dealers in the area know how to get in touch with the buyer?"

"Believe me when I tell you I contacted everyone who had a booth that weekend. No one knew much about him. They had dealings with him for a few years themselves and then they never saw him again. I think the relic shop was real, but he must have closed it up. Perhaps he retired."

"Were you or anyone else able to make anything out of the letters and numbers on the back of the buckle?"

The relic hunter pauses. "I made a serious attempt to see if the markings might make a treasure map, but nothing ever came of it. Some map experts decided the markings might relate to troop movements during the war or that it might be a treasure map but that it was unlikely. The experts mostly agreed the markings were likely the carvings of a bored soldier longing for home."

Carter asks, "What do you think?"

The old timer pauses again. "I believe it's a treasure map."

Carter thanks the man for his help and promises to let him know if he and his partner uncover the meaning behind the buckles' markings.

With the three buckles pieced together, neither Blake nor Carter can decipher the puzzle of the cryptic etchings.

Carter begins to realize that professional assistance would be needed if the inscriptions on the buckles is to ever be deciphered. The only person Carter knows who is an expert in code-breaking is an old girlfriend he had dated in college who now works as an analyst with the FBI, specializing in deciphering encrypted messages between criminal organizations throughout the world.

In college, Rachel had made a hobby of solving puzzles and had won some prizes in nationally organized treasure hunts. Rachel and Carter had gone on several of the treasure trips together. Rachel was passionate about treasure hunting, even a little obsessed. The two had been close in college, but that changed when Rachel was offered a position as an analytical engineer in New York City. Carter was hoping Rachel would help him with this puzzle, but he wasn't sure about contacting her.

He decides he doesn't have many other options and on a crisp fall day he calls her to see if she might have time to assist with the puzzle. Carter dials Rachel's cell phone number, thinking she might have changed her number, but then she answered.

"Hello, this is Rachel."

"Rachel, hey, it's Carter. Have you got a minute?"

After a slight hesitation, Rachel replies, "It's been a while, but yeah, what's up?"

"I was wondering if you'd take a look at encrypted messages on an old Civil War belt buckle I found."

Rachel bites her lip. "What does the message look like?"

"There are three belt plates with numbers, letters, and symbols engraved on the back of the plates. I haven't been able to make anything out of it. You always had a knack for such things."

"Let me give you my email address, so you can scan it over to me. Please include any details you can think of in your email."

Rachel's heart was pounding. Carter had really hurt her by not making more of an effort to rekindle their relationship after she had relocated closer to home from New York. Rachel had missed Atlanta and her family especially. She and Carter had grown further and further apart, even though their cities weren't that far apart.

Carter was sorry for the awkwardness that his call to Rachel had created, but he knew that Rachel would not hesitate to become involved in a treasure quest. Rachel was the best code breaker in the country. If the code could be broken, she could do it. Carter's thoughts drift back in time to when he and Rachel would look for treasure clues in parks. The memories they had shared together were priceless. Carter knew that his behavior was a lot of the reason their relationship had faltered. He had a problem making commitments. A long term relationship had so far been an elusive thing for him.

Chapter 31

Rachel calls Carter a week later. "There's definitely a coded message. What's missing are the decoder keys. It's unlikely this puzzle can be deciphered without finding the right key to decode it."

Carter opens his desk drawer thinking about the key he'd found at the Andy McCarver House. "Rachel, you are not going to believe this, but I found a key with Roman numerals and letters on it at an old home in Virginia where one of the soldiers connected to the buckles lived after the war. I never gave it much thought. The key is loaded with Roman numerals and letters along the entire length of it."

Rachel replies after a grasp of aggravation at Carter's lack of perception. "Please scan the key and email it to me. I'll have you an answer tonight. You most likely have had the encryption key the entire time I have been working on this puzzle!"

There is a momentary pause and a second of awkwardness between the two as their calls used to end in "I love you."

After the call, Rachel mummers to herself, "Carter does not think. How could he have missed such an obvious clue?"

Rachel gets home and checks her email, nothing as usual, no email yet from Carter.

Rachel changes out of her office clothes and slips into her workout attire. Rachel's keen discipline keeps her on a set routine of exercise and training. Rachel walks into the workout room, turns on the lights, and climbs onto the treadmill with her television remote control in her hand. Rachel turns on her favorite television show, a show about romance and adventures in the early 1900s, and begins her daily five-mile run.

Rachel reflects on her past. She'd lived in the Big Apple for two years after college and had been an analyst for one of the firms in the North Tower of the World Trade Center, until that nightmarish day she had nearly lost her life. She hated the terrorist organization that had almost taken her life away from her on that September day.

Rachel survived that horrendous day and swore an oath that she would do her best to contribute to winning the war that had come to America.

When she decided to move to Atlanta, Georgia, Rachel applied for an analyst position with the Federal Bureau of Investigation and to her surprise received an offer.

Rachel gets a text from her roommate Christie that she is picking up Chinese food on her way home from the photography studio where she works. Rachel replies that Chinese sounds good and not to worry about wine as she had picked up a few bottles.

Rachel reminiscences back to her and Christie's days in college. Back then all they could afford was half a case of beer. Rachel was happy that Christie had decided to move to Atlanta from Washington, DC. After Rachel finishes her run, along with her television show, she opens her laptop to check her email again. Carter has followed through and sent a picture of the key. Rachel begins to read the email and reminisces of the times she and Carter shared together.

Carter was someone Rachel could have seen herself settling down with… unfortunately it hadn't been in the cards.

Rachel opens the attachment and inspects the image of an old stylish key from the Victorian era. Rachel studies the encryptions running along the length of the key on both sides.

Rachel thinks to herself that the key is probably not the only one like it that was made. The key was made from a mold and was cast brass. From the relic reference books she had thumbed through when she and Carter used to date, she could not remember anything quite like it. After carefully studying and examining the key and trying to use it to decipher the codes on the back of the buckles, she was still at a dead end.

Rachel was ready to give Carter the bad news. Rachel rings Carter. Carter picks up after one ring. "Rachel, I've been waiting on your call! What do you think?"

"The key does not appear to be made to decode the symbols and letters on the back of the buckles. I am going to study the buckles closer to see if I can come up with anything."

"I really appreciate you looking into it. There has got to be something we are missing."

"Perhaps so, I will call you if I find anything."

She hangs the phone up and continues to examine the pictures of the buckle on her laptop. She uses the zoom feature to enlarge the picture. She applies the invert feature as she browses across the back of the plate's cryptic symbols and letters.

She thinks to herself that there must be something else here. Then in the lower right hand part of Carter's buckle, she spots what appears to be, a tiny part of a symbol. Rachel rubs her eyes. She brings the zoom to this spot and brings up a full screen of the area.

By darkening the image and bringing more contrast, what looks like a symbol, begins to appear. It is an image that everyone had missed before, up until this point. Rachel emails Carter, asking him to take a closer look at the lower right hand corner of the buckle. She explains that where there is a small dirt smudge, there appears to be a symbol partially hidden by the dirt.

Nine minutes later Rachel receives the email from Carter. He explains that the belt plate is locked up in a safety deposit box and is inaccessible until the next day. Rachel excitedly opens the attachment and a high resolution picture of the back of the buckle confirms what she suspected.

The symbols that she can make out for certain are a crescent moon and possibly a heart. If there was a third symbol, it is completely covered with the dirt smudge. Rachel pulls up an old cryptologist book she used a lot back in her treasure hunting days with Carter. The reference book indicates that the symbols could be Masonic in nature or could represent regimental corps in the Confederate or Union armies.

The next day Carter opens and reads an email sent from Rachel late the night before explaining what she had been able to find. He drives to the bank on his lunch break and retrieves the plate from the safety deposit box. Once in his vehicle, he uses a rag, small soft brush, and water to clean the suspect area on the buckle. Sure enough with a magnifying glass, three symbols appear.

"The symbols are a crescent moon, a heart, and a triangle." Carter looks up and thinks about the symbols for a few seconds. "I have seen the triangle symbol on one of Captain Andy McCarver's papers!"

Carter takes a picture of the symbol area of the plate with his phone. After returning the plate to the bank's safety deposit box, he emails Rachel.

Later that evening, on a hunch, he examines the online records of Captain McCarver. He finds the exact same supply requisition form signed by General Nathan Bedford Forrest that he now has in his possession. Carter assumes Sir Robert must have sent Captain McCarver's service records to the Civil War soldier's site. Carter emails Rachel the supply requisition form asking her if the triangle might be a clue.

Rachel, after opening the email, examines the document and, sure enough, right in the middle of the document along with some kind of reference numbers, part of a code perhaps, was a triangle symbol. It couldn't be a coincidence.

Rachel was at her wits end trying to solve the mysterious puzzle that had been methodically left behind by a group of Confederate Secret Service scouts. The requisition supply form was for shirts, hats, pants, and corn for cavalry horses. Rachel had her head in her hands from looking at the information for so long. She goes into the kitchen to pour some coffee. All of a sudden, an idea pops into her head. She calls Carter.

"Carter, are you doing anything right now?"

"No. What's up?"

"Are you close to the supply order document with the triangle?"

"I have it right here. Have you come up with any solutions to a coded message in the form?"

"Not yet, but I have an idea. If it's okay with you, I want you to carefully wave the paper over a light bulb. It is just a hunch, but I am wondering if the Confederate scouts or Captain McCarver may have written an invisible coded message on the paper that will only be seen, if it is applied to heat."

"You don't think it'll hurt the document?" Carter pauses as he delicately moves the document closer to the bulb. "Rachel, you're a genius. There's something written on the back of the requisition form!"

The hidden message, now appearing before Carter's eyes, describes the hiding place of the wartime diary and memoirs of Captain McCarver. The diary book is hidden in a secret hiding spot in Sir Robert's mansion.

Carter calls Sir Robert. "Sir Robert, you won't believe this. One of the documents you gave us has a hidden message that tells us exactly where to look for Andy McCarver's lost diary."

After the brief call from Carter, Sir Robert hangs up the phone and walks straight to his garage to retrieve a crowbar. With crowbar in hand, he walks to the room mentioned in the hidden message and begins to remove the baseboards from what had been for many years the library room of the McCarver mansion. Carter had let Sir Robert know that the diary was hidden behind the library baseboards in a recessed area behind the walls. The invisible letter on the back of the supply requisition form said he would see a symbol of a heart behind the library baseboards that would reveal the hiding place of Captain McCarver's journals.

Sure enough, Robert spots the symbol, a heart, and breaks a hole in the wall at that spot. He puts his hand and a flashlight in the hole, and there behind the wall is the long lost, sought-after diary, along with letters, memoirs, business journals, and a small box of gold and silver coins.

Carter has Sir Robert make a copy of the diary and memoirs and then express mail the copies to him. Once Carter receives the package, he excitedly opens it. Carter pours over the information scanning through the pages to see if he can find a quick clue. In the back cover of the diary, along with other notes, Carter sees a crescent moon symbol with the number 157 beside it. Carter flips to page 157 and begins to read about how Captain McCarver tells of the defeat of the Army of Tennessee in Nashville. While the Army of Tennessee was fighting its way into Middle Tennessee, Captain McCarver and several scouts were on a mission to ride into Ohio in search of new recruits, in advance of the Confederate army's planned push to the Ohio River.

As Andy came back through Tennessee on Hood's retreat, he realized from the reports coming in that it would be only a matter of time before the surrender of the Confederate army and the end of the war.

In an entry dated January 20, 1865, Captain McCarver stopped at a friend's house in Nashville. In the library of the friend's mansion was a hidden entrance, behind a bookshelf, that led to secret underground passageways beneath the city of Nashville.

Captain McCarver described that these tunnels were extensive and elaborate, leading into the very heart of the city itself, even to the Nashville Capitol Building. The Confederate Secret Service had a broad network of spies, and the tunnels were used to transport information out of the city.

During the retreat from Nashville, Andy, knowing the danger of letting the dying Confederacy's most important secrets fall into the hands of the Yankees, hid an important sword in these tunnels. Henry and Walt gave the sword to Andy with a message that the sword, with its encryptions and hidden coded message, along with the three buckles would lead to a great treasure and a weapon. The weapon, known as the General's Relic, could destroy an entire city or army if deployed.

Per an entry in Captain Andrew McCarver's memoirs, the General's Relic would never be of use to Hood's Army of Tennessee since the only two people who knew where it was were dead or presumed dead, and now two of the belt plates were missing.

Andy hid the sword in a secret room beneath the mansion. After the war the entrance to the room was sealed up with bricks and mortar. Carter reads aloud, "Only ruins are left there now after a fire destroyed the old house. I am sure the sword is buried beneath tons of rubble. I leave the details of my adventures as a Confederate spy to a future generation that may find use of this information. Not enough years have yet passed to safely release the secret information in my journals."

Carter sighs and says to himself, "I need to get to Nashville."

Carter loads his jeep. He calls Blake and leaves him a message on his phone. "Blake, you are not going to believe what I have discovered. I'm heading to your house first thing in the morning. See you soon."

Carter arrives at Blake's house around mid-morning. He opens the jeep door on the passenger side, grabs a toolbox, and pops the hood. He had heard a clunking noise on the journey to Nashville and decides to check it out. He tightens down a loose bolt, fixing the problem.

As Carter closes the hood, he notices Blake's Great Dane is sitting in the passenger side of his jeep looking at him inquisitively. Carter politely pokes at the behemoth of a dog. "Come on, Roscoe. Out!"

Blake walks out of his house. "Ah, come on Carter, give Roscoe a break. Besides, if you want to convince him not to go, be my guest." Roscoe tilts his head and perks up his big floppy ears.

Carter hands Roscoe a treat. "Okay, Roscoe! Just stay out of trouble."

Carter, Blake, and Roscoe drive to the ruins of the lost and forgotten mansion. Blake pets Roscoe, who has his massive head over the seat from the back, slobbering a little to the distress of Carter.

Blake adjusts his hat after Roscoe nudges it sideways. "I know this area pretty well. I have been given permission to metal detect here. All I found was a bunch of beer cans and pop tops, seemed to be a big party spot in the past."

"Do you think the landowner will mind us exploring the cellar?"

"Nah, like I said, the landowner already gave me permission to metal detect anytime I like. Let's go on in!"

Carter pulls off Franklin Pike and parks the jeep on a dirt driveway. The treasure hunters unload their gear and begin to hike towards the ruins, leaving Roscoe to keep watch.

"I've seen the cellar before, follow me." Blake leads Carter to the ruins of the old mansion and points down to a large hole in the ground. "See, the cellar is still intact!"

After examining the area, a symbol of a crescent moon is spotted on one of the walls amongst graffiti.

"Wow, Blake, check it out! There is the crescent moon symbol we are looking for! Let's see if we can break through this wall."

After breaking open an entry with a pick, the two find the secret underground room. The furniture, candles, and wall pictures are still there, untouched after one hundred and fifty years.

"I have been over this property numerous times and had no idea this hidden room was here." Blake shines his flashlight around, amazed at what he's seeing.

Carter walks forward into the dust. "Check behind the pictures! We need to find another symbol." Behind one of the pictures, a heart symbol is spotted. The two know what to do. They break open a hole, and there behind the old mortar is the sword wrapped in a Confederate grey overcoat.

"Jackpot!"

"This is a fifty-thousand-dollar coat! And it's in impeccable condition! We better get this treasure to a safer place."

The guys are hiking back to the jeep, when they hear Roscoe growling. "Roscoe sounds irritated!" They run over logs and scramble through the brush.

When the two come out of the undergrowth, a man is waiting for them with a knife pointed towards them.

"Stop where you are and don't move. Trust me I am handy with this knife. I will take whatever you found."

Carter is carrying their equipment and is few steps in front of Blake who has the sword and coat cradled in both arms. Blake hesitates on going for his .380 pistol for fear of Carter being stabbed by the man's knife.

Roscoe has had enough at this point, and uses his teeth to tear through the plastic of the back window of Carter's jeep. Roscoe darts to the man and makes a flying leap onto the villain. The large man staggers but keeps his balance. Roscoe manages to disarm the man after grabbing ahold of his arm with his teeth and shaking his powerful neck.

"Get this beast off of me!"

The man trips and falls to the ground. Roscoe jumps on his chest. The huge Great Dane pins the man to the ground with his enormous paws, snarling and biting with the slightest bit of movement from the bad guy.

"I love that dog!" Blake calls the police and requests assistance.

The police arrest the man, who admitted he was homeless and had intentions of lifting the wallets of the two young men. Blake and Carter had doubts about the man's story. He didn't seem homeless, and he hadn't asked for their wallets, only the treasure in their hands. After talking it over, Carter and Blake are convinced coconspirators dropped the man off to rob them of the treasure clues.

Chapter 32

Carter sends Rachel a picture of the sword found in the cellar. He asks her if she thinks she can decipher the symbols. Rachel's keen analytical mind quickly sees that with a little work the symbols on the sword will solve the secret of the three buckles.

In further studying the symbols, she discovers what might be coordinates. She becomes convinced she has deciphered the latitude and longitude coordinates to … somewhere. Rachel pulls up a global topographical website on her laptop, plugs the coordinates into the topographical program, and, to her surprise, the coordinates are not in the United States. The coordinates mark a point in the Amazon Jungle in Brazil, South America.

Rachel emails Carter back. "Carter, I have solved the code. Give me a call tomorrow evening, and I'll tell you everything I have discovered. The answer will definitely surprise you!"

Carter arrives home and opens up his laptop, excited at possibly receiving an email from Rachel. Carter reads the email and picks up the phone to call Rachel.

"Sounds like you have something exciting to share, Rachel!"

"Carter, it's a remarkable find."

Unknown to Carter, an agent hired by a large international overseas corporation has been able to bypass his alarm system by crawling under his house, drilling a hole underneath the floor, and placing a listening device in his house. All plans and conversations regarding the lost treasure are now being listened to and recorded.

"In examining the sword, I spotted a triangle, crescent moon, and heart symbols; each of the symbols are followed by cryptic letters and numbers. The symbols on the sword were in a different order than the ones on your buckle. Without the two together, I would not have been able to solve the puzzle. Putting everything together, I have deciphered coordinates. You are not going to believe this: the coordinates point to the Amazon Jungle."

"Why would anyone go through so much trouble to leave clues about a place in the Amazon Jungle?"

"My guess is buried treasure."

"You really think so?"

"I do, and when I pulled up satellite maps to look at the area, it is still very much undeveloped. Whatever was hidden there one hundred fifty years ago is probably still going to be there. Carter, I have one request. I want to go along with you."

Carter smiles. "Rachel, I wouldn't think of leaving you out of a treasure hunt."

"Is Blake still single?"

Rachel closes her eyes. She remembers the kiss she had planted on Blake's lips while on that organized group metal detecting trip with Carter years before. She and Blake were sitting on a rock beside a spring and creek. Carter was fighting spider webs and a briar patch that Blake and Rachel did not want to go into. The kiss lasted only thirty seconds but she had leaned into Blake and kissed him. Not that Blake put up a fight. Blake being such a gentleman apologized.

Carter of course would never find out about that. She realizes her question came out awkwardly.

"Umm, if so I have a roommate that might be a good match. I mean, she specializes in outdoor photography. And a big plus will be that we will have someone to professionally document our adventure. Well, I guess what I'm saying is can she come with us, too?"

"Yeah, Rachel. I guess so. The more the merrier! Just kidding. Let's keep it to you and your friend. We will need to plan on taking this journey soon."

Rachel asks her friend Christie, who has had a few documentaries of her own on television, if she is game for a treasure quest into the Amazon Jungle. Rachel lets Christie know that her old boyfriend, Carter, has a good looking friend who will be coming along for the trip.

"Christie, I need for you to come on this trip. I have been through a lot with Carter; I need a good girl friend to be there to back me up."

"Sounds good, Rachel. Count me in."

In the meantime the team notice mysterious vans parked outside their homes, along with dogs barking at odd hours of the night. They suspect they are being watched and followed.

*

"Blake, I have got some outstanding news!" Carter says after Blake answers his phone.

"Don't tell me anything over the phone. You won't believe it, but I was in my test garden trying out some new settings on my metal detector, and I found a bug."

“You’re kidding! I tell you someone is trying to reach the treasure before us. I will send you a secure email later tonight with some details of what I have found out.”

Blake continues, “I ran an extensive search and I found bugs all over the house, even one under the house. Someone means us trouble. Let’s keep the phone calls brief till we are sure we both have a secure line of communication.”

“You bet, man, keep a close lookout. I’ll do the same. I will send a secure email shortly.”

Chapter 33

Blake, Rachel, Carter, and Christie begin to plan a trip to the Amazon Jungle in search of treasure using the coordinates that Rachel has plotted from the maze of symbols on three old Confederate belt buckles and a sword. All of the relic's secrets had been lost to the ages, but they were now found anew thanks to Andy McCarver's diary being discovered.

Three weeks later, after the group finalize their work schedules, four excited treasure hunters are ready for the trip of a lifetime to the Amazon River basin in South America. The team gathers together at the Atlanta airport. Christie drags her three large pieces of luggage behind her into the airport.

"Hi, Christie. I'm Carter. It's nice to finally meet you in person."

"Nice to meet you, too, Carter. Can you please help me with my luggage?"

"Sure, but you know there is no way you can lug all of this around in the Amazon in a backpack." Carter looks at her luggage and scratches his head in dismay.

"Well, we won't just be in the jungle, right? Aren't we going to sightsee and do some of the tourist stuff while we're there?"

"I don't know, Christie. I think the boys have a pretty strict agenda for us to follow while we're there." Rachel, coming straight from work, approaches her with one small carryon.

"Rachel, is that all you are bringing with you? Oh my. I can't even fathom how you packed everything you'll need into one piece of luggage!"

Blake approaches the group and smiles. "It takes a good planner to do that."

"Rachel is definitely a planner! Maybe to a fault." Carter winks at Rachel.

Christie reaches out her hand towards Blake. "And you must be Blake, nice to put a face with a name. Would you mind grabbing one of my bags, too?"

"Christie, you must be planning a trip to Paris rather than the Amazon. This is an adventure, not a grand tour," Rachel says and smiles.

"I don't care. I'm taking what I need. Y'all can try to survive with your one piece of luggage, but don't be running to me every time you need something!"

The group laughs and begin their journey. They walk to their plane's loading ramp to start their fourteen-hour flight. They catch a flight into Miami, then on to Manaus, Brazil.

*

After landing, the group picks up their luggage and heads out of the airport to find their taxi or shuttle driver. They notice a gentleman holding a sign with their names.

"This must be us! I guess we are already on a first name basis." Carter points towards a small man in baggy pants with a collar shirt and a Rebel kepi hat.

"Is he wearing a kepi?" Blake asks.

"Sure enough! How cool is that?" says Carter. The team approach the young man.

"Are you the American team here to find treasure in the Amazon?"

Carter laughs. "We sure hope so! What's your name?"

"I'm Rodrigo, and I have been assigned to be your tour guide."

"Well, Rodrigo, where did you get that nice kepi?"

"Huh? Keeppii?"

"The hat?" Blake points to Rodrigo's head.

"Oh yes, the hat. I heard your team was interested in Civil War history. I know a fellow that is also interested in the American Civil War here in the Amazon. He told me you would recognize me if I wore this hat."

"Yeah, I would say you kind of stand out!" Christie giggles.

"Let me just say, we are excited you are here and I am eager to be your guide during your visit." Rodrigo gestures towards the car.

"Hey Christie, maybe you can set up a booth and sell some of your stuff on the street here." Rachel laughs.

Rodrigo frowns when he sees Christie's luggage. "You have a lot of bags for your journey. Did you make it to the correct destination?"

Christie shrugs and smiles. "I'm not sure yet!"

Rodrigo points to an older model burnt orange Brasilia convertible. "Wow, Rodrigo, this must be a collector's item!" says Blake.

"Yeah, it gets me around. I like it pretty good. Are you interested in it?"

Blake smiles. "Nah, man, but it looks like a fun ride."

The team pile into the old Brasilia and head to the hotel.

"I have been to the location you want to journey to while here." Rodrigo's smile fades away. "The area has not been heavily explored. The jungle is dangerous. Not that long ago, my grandfather tried to explore that area of the jungle and was completely thrown off track. Thankfully, he was rescued, but he never was the same."

"Did he have health issues?" Christie asks.

"No, not that. He was only a little dehydrated after they rescued him. But he kept mumbling about ghosts he saw and some lost city in the jungle. It was like he had gone mad while out there or something."

Carter looks out the window and then toward Rodrigo. "I've seen some crazy things in my lifetime. In the Deep South, in Alabama, we have a lot of ghost stories. You add a little dehydration in and things happen that you can't explain. I can see someone getting confused."

"Anyway, we are almost there." Rodrigo turns on some Brazilian tunes.

Blake leans over and whispers to Carter, "Strange things or not, I did bring a few items to protect us from bad guys, ghosts, or whatever."

"How did you do that?"

"I got friends in the right places. I went through the proper channels."

Carter begins to ask another question, but the car pulls up to a large extravagant hotel.

"We're here!" Rodrigo says, smiling.

*

Blake, Rachel, Carter, and Christie have dinner at a restaurant overlooking the Rio Negro River.

"I don't understand why we have not kept in closer contact over the years?" Carter gazes at Rachel, flirtingly.

Rachel shrugs. "Life gets busy and priorities change, I guess."

"What does that mean?"

"I don't know. Why do you have to get so deep right now?" Rachel looks across the table towards Blake.

"Life gets busy? Seriously?"

"Don't take offense. You are a good friend, Carter. Truly."

Blake catches a glance from Rachel that makes him wonder what she is talking about with Carter. Blake senses he and Rachel might have some chemistry going on between the two of them.

"What are y'all over there talking about?" asks Blake.

"Oh, just catching up on old times," says Rachel, as she flips her wrist and lowers her head.

"Sounds sentimental."

"Not really." Rachel blushes and then smiles at Blake.

He catches Carter rolling his eyes at Rachel. Blake turns and looks out on the exotic view of the river. "I'm going to step out on the balcony to get some fresh air y'all."

Rachel, looking for an escape, scoots out of the booth. "Great idea, I might join you!"

Carter mumbles to himself, "Great idea." He downs his drink in one gulp.

Christie, with her chin resting on her hand and her elbow on the table says, "I know you and Rachel go way back. Do you still have a thing for her?"

"Definitely not. Why do you ask?"

Christie clasps her hands together on the table and smiles. "I don't know, I think you're cute, and I don't want to cross any lines with my best friend."

Carter puffs his chest out a little and picks up the bottle of wine from the table. He freshens up his and Christie's glasses.

"Aren't you into photography?"

"You could say that. I work as a freelance photographer. I get to travel some for my work. It has its perks, but it can also be pretty grueling at times."

The two talk for a while, getting to know each other. Christie lets him know of the travels she has been on throughout the world.

"What is your favorite part of the world to take photographs of?"

"I would have to say Africa."

"Really, Africa? Isn't there a lot of danger there?"

"Well, yeah, but the beauty of the savannas in Africa is so incredible, that once you are there you will never want to leave." Christie pauses and gets a sad look on her face. "It's unfortunate that where there is so much beauty, there is also a lot of pain and death."

"Did you experience any danger while there?"

"You can't go to Africa and not see or experience some type of danger. It's a part of life there."

"That is pretty brave of you to take on an adventure like that!"

"You think?" Christie smiles again. "I've been multiple times, I love the adventure there." Christie swirls her wine.

"You know, there are a lot of beautiful places to see in the States."

"Africa is the most beautiful place I have been to, by far. Imagine the sun setting and a group of giraffes on the grasslands of Africa crossing in front of you. It is breathtakingly scenic."

Carter looks down, rubs his chin, then looks into Christie's brown eyes, and smiles. I know where you would like to go. You have got to see Yellowstone National Park. The prairie lands used to be full of buffalos, deer, and antelope. Parts of the prairie still resemble Africa."

"I've been meaning to make a trip out that way."

Carter pours more wine into their glasses.

Meanwhile, on the balcony, Rachel and Blake are enjoying a breathtaking sunset. Rachel leaning over the rail on her elbows, her hands clasped together, looks over at Blake. "You know there is no place I would rather be than on this adventure right now."

The sky glows orange through the clouds. The dark waters of the Rio Negro River gives the two a spectacular treat as the sun's fading rays shine through the crystal clear waters, colored a hue of yellowish red to a rich coffee color farther away in the distance.

Blake makes a toast, "To a great adventure and new friends." The two clink their glasses together and gaze into each other's eyes as the energy between them builds.

Blake, never one to let an opportunity go by, leans over and kisses Rachel. Rachel reciprocates, then pulls back. "Wow, this must be some strong wine! We had better stay focused—"

"I am focused … focused on you."

The two move a little closer to each other, entwining their hands, enjoying the romantic Manaus skyline.

Carter calls out, "Looks like the sun has gone down. What are you two doing out there?"

Blake and Rachel come in from the balcony.

Carter points towards his watch. "I guess we need to head back to the hotel. We have a big day tomorrow."

The group piles into a taxi to start the journey back to the hotel.

"Blake, have you noticed the black sedan that has been tailing us since we left the restaurant?" asks Carter.

Rachel stops writing in her journal and looks over her shoulder. "You're right. I noticed the same sedan at the hotel. I've had a strange feeling we're being watched."

"Well then, we must be onto something!" Christie says.

Blake turns his head from the rear window towards Rachel, then Carter. "There is definitely something mysterious about these old buckles. I don't know what kind of story we're uncovering. But it seems like someone doesn't want us to uncover it, or they want to be the ones to solve the mystery first."

Carter glances back behind them and no longer sees the black car. "Looks like they're gone. Maybe it's just a coincidence."

*

The next day, the treasure hunters begin their tour up the great Amazon River. The team approaches the dock and begins to look around at the boats.

Rachel reads on her checklist from Rodrigo that they're supposed to catch a boat ride with Captain Marcelo. Rachel looks up from her clipboard and puts her hand up above her eyes to shield the morning sun. "We are looking for Captain Marcelo's boat. I'm not sure how we will know which one is his, but maybe we'll have some luck."

Carter calls out to the team, "Hey y'all, I think this is it down here!" Carter points to an old cardboard sign with the words Marcelo painted on it.

Christie frowns. "Seriously? This boat looks like it might not make it off the dock!"

"Oh Christie, they all look like this. It's part of the experience!" says Carter.

"I am here for an adventure not a disaster, Carter."

"Lighten up and think positive. This boat appears to be in fine shape. I've seen a lot worse!" Blake pats Christie on her shoulder, then hops on the boat.

"Ahh! The historians, you made it!" Rodrigo welcomes the team with his big smile, wearing his kepi.

"Yeah, we made it. Was that in question, Rodrigo?" Carter shakes Rodrigo's hand.

"Oh no, I'm just glad you didn't get nervous and turn back."

Christie looks at Rachel and asks, “Should we be nervous?”

“There are a couple of cabins left on the boat. Should I escort the ladies and then you guys can join me on the deck in the hammocks?” asks Rodrigo.

“Are there not enough cabins for all of us?” Carter asks.

“No, not really, sir. This is kind of how we do things. The ladies take the cabins, and the men take the hammocks.”

Blake surveys their accommodations. “Looks like you’re going to be roughing it with me, Carter!”

“Well, I guess it’s just for a couple of days.” Carter scratches his head and looks over at the twenty people hanging out near the hammock area.

Rodrigo escorts the ladies to their cabin, while Blake and Carter scout out for hammock space. The guys opt for the hammocks swinging close to the front, between the two sides of the riverboat.

“This will work, huh, Carter?” Blake drops his bag on the hanging bed.

“I guess it’ll have to. Man, I hope the ladies have a better situation than we do.”

Rodrigo opens up the door to the cabin so Rachel and Christie can enter.

“Oops, Rodrigo, this one won’t work, looks like it’s already taken.” Rachel starts to back out of the cabin.

“This one is fine and can hold both of you.” Rodrigo smiles and holds his arm out, gesturing for the ladies to enter. Rachel and Christie enter the room and begin to throw their bags above their bunks in the storage bins.

The women have their gear, plus the gear from the guys, so they can keep it somewhat protected in the cabin. Blake's M4 rifle is disguised in a specialized backpack.

"I'll leave you ladies to settle in," Rodrigo says, as he closes the door.

Christie and Rachel look at the other two women. Christie waves to one of them. "Hello, my name is Christie."

The woman looks at her friend and shrugs her shoulders.

Christie presses her hand to her chest and repeats, "My name is Christie."

"*Me chamo* Maria." The lady smiles and then points to her friend. "*Me chamo* Sophie." Both ladies smile and begin talking quickly in Portugeuse.

Rachel looking at her translation book leans forward. "*Me chamo*, Rachel, *falas ingles*?"

Both ladies say, "No!" Then start laughing.

"This is going to be an interesting trip," Rachel says to Christie.

*

Back on the deck, Blake begins to go through his carry-on bag. He smiles and is glad he remembered to bring along a speaker to pump out music from his MP3, thinking ahead in case there was no music onboard.

"Did you really bring your speaker?" Carter picks up the little boom box.

"Yeah man, I thought we might enjoy some tunes while cruising down the river."

Blake turns on the music and out comes classic country at its finest, jamming out over the Amazon. The other men on the deck begin to walk over. Some start to clap and others begin to dance.

Rodrigo meets back up with the guys. “I like the music, guys. You are growing in popularity.”

Carter looks around. “Do you think they’ve ever heard country music before?”

Blake laughs. “Well if they haven’t, they should’ve. They sure seem to be enjoying it!”

The girls rejoin the guys back on deck, and begin soaking in the vast beauty and scenery they begin to encounter going up the river.

“I thought I heard some music coming from somewhere!” Christie says, as Rachel gives her a dance twirl. “Country music on the Amazon, now that’s what I’m talking about!”

“You guys are making me want a cold one.” Rachel smiles and points towards a little bar.

“I’m on it!” Carter starts over to the bar. “They don’t have much, but they have some beer, and it seems cold.”

“Carter, remember to put a lime in my beer, if they have any,” yells Rachel.

“I’ll take four of those, please,” Carter says. “Oh and please make sure that one has a lime.”

Blake wraps his muscular arms around Rachel. “This is kind of romantic, huh?” Blake grips Rachel in his arms. Rachel smiles, as they engage in a kiss.

As Carter approaches the group with the cans of beer, he sees Rachel cuddled up to Blake. At first he feels a sense of jealousy, but Rachel had made it pretty clear about where things stood between him and her. Ultimately though, Carter is pleased that Rachel seems happy.

The group gets a treat of seeing the famous sight of the Rio Negro River and the waters of the Amazon in confluence, as the dark yellowish red waters of the Rio Negro meet the brown silty waters of the Amazon near Manaus, Brazil. The captain begins to make his rounds and stops over on the deck to chat with the team.

Rachel asks, "Captain Marcelo, are there ever any accidents that occur on the tour?"

Captain Marcelo reassures the four, "You are perfectly safe with me. I have been operating this boat for ten years. I have been traveling these waters for over twenty years. It has been a family tradition."

The team all laugh. Christie asks, "Have you heard any country music before Captain Marcelo?"

"No, I have not."

Christie smiles. "Well, I think it will grow on ya!"

"I like the music, everyone is having a great time." The Captain strolls off and begins to check on the other passengers.

That evening the treasure hunting team steps out to view the Southern Cross constellation. Rachel leans up against Blake's muscular frame, as Carter steals a first kiss from Christie beneath the starry night sky.

Chapter 34

After a journey of three long days, the team begins to get anxious to get off the boat.

"I am ready to get back on land," Christie says.

"Definitely, the scenery is nice, but we've pretty much been looking at the same thing over the last few days," says Carter.

"Team, patience is a virtue," Blake quips back. "We won't be exiting the boat to a five-star resort or anything like it. Y'all better get used to roughing it for a while."

"Here comes Captain Marcelo," Rachel points out.

"Well, historians, I'm afraid this is as far as I can take you."

"That's a relief," Carter says under his breath.

"You will need to travel by a smaller boat to the village that you want to visit."

"Great, another boat," Carter says a little too loudly.

Rachel elbows him.

"From there, Rodrigo will continue to guide you to your destination by way of pack mules and horses used by tourists to explore the more remote areas," Captain Marcelo explains, as he reaches out his arm and waves it across the vast open area.

Rachel, with her arms crossed asks, "How remote are we talking about?"

Captain Marcello turns to Rachel. "The area you want to go to is extremely remote. There are many stories of the dangers in that area but one that you might find interesting is that shortly after your American Civil War, soldiers dressed in grey uniforms traveled to the same area your team is going to. They disappeared never to come back out of the jungle. There were rumors that they found another way out of the jungle. It is easy to get turned around in the brush."

Carter and Blake look at each other on this comment and Carter starts to speak but is cut short.

Rodrigo raises his hand to get everyone's attention. "It takes approximately three hours in the smaller boat to reach the remote isolated village. We are almost at the dock where we can retrieve the smaller boat."

Blake with his arms crossed says, "Well, I guess we better get our gear together!"

The team reaches the dock; they thank Captain Marcelo for a safe journey and then exit the large tour boat.

"Where is the boat? All I see around here are canoes," Christie notices.

"Yes, yes, this is our boat!" Rodrigo points to a slender green boat that looks like it will barely fit the team in it.

"Uh, this is a canoe, Rodrigo." Carter raises his eyebrows and begins to rub his head.

"Rodrigo said this is our boat. Load up, team!" yells Blake.

The group begins their journey through the murky waters to the small village.

Christie gets her camera out and begins snapping pictures. "Carter smile for me." Christie snaps Carter's picture. "I love being out in nature and capturing the beauty of the great outdoors!"

"Oh yeah, capture that!" Carter points over to a snake slithering by in the water.

"Yikes, let's keep moving," says Rachel.

Several more snakes slither by. Rodrigo notices the group's reactions. "I wouldn't worry about those snakes, they are harmless. But keep your eyes out for anacondas and piranhas."

"What! Anacondas and piranhas!" Carter begins to look around nervously.

Rodrigo laughs. "Sorry Carter, those only show up in the movies. What you really need to keep an eye out for are other people. There are some in this jungle who seek to rob and bring harm to others. Those are the real monsters of the jungle you need to watch out for."

Rodrigo points out various birds, brilliantly colored parrots, small cute monkeys that look out with wise inquisitive eyes, and alligators. The four tourists' heads and eyes are constantly moving while observing the spectacular scenery. A special treat is seeing a group of pink Amazon dolphins. The group also spots a golden leopard jaguar sunning in a tree close to the water. Christie takes lots of pictures, while Rachel uses a book to help identify the wildlife.

The four finally reach their destination, a small isolated village in a remote part of the jungle. Rodrigo guides the motorized canoe to a secluded landing and moors it with a rope to the entwining roots of a large jungle tree, reaching down to the water.

"We finally made it!" Carter jumps out of the canoe, almost overturning it.

"Careful, Carter!" Rachel yells.

Blake helps Rachel and Christie out of the boat.

Rodrigo takes the four to the main thatched roof cabin in the village that houses the tour guides. The different tours available consist of trails and canoe rides where tourists can view the wildlife and plants up close.

"Impressive, they offer more than I expected," says Christie.

Blake sets his backpack down. "Might be worth looking into one day. But we are on a mission!"

Carter sees Rodrigo coming back towards them with a strange look on his face.

"We should make a change of plans. I was looking at your map with the elder. The route you want to take is more than the standard three-day hike and is no longer accessible from this trailhead. In the last month, down the trail you guys want to use, several attacks have occurred from robbers taking advantage of the remoteness of some of the longer trails. The villagers are now afraid to go into that area."

"Well, what are we going to do now? We've come so far!" Blake asks.

"I have a plan, if it is okay with you." Rodrigo smiles.

"Well, yeah, let's hear it!" Rachel reaches her hands out to Rodrigo gesturing for him to continue.

"The village has a helicopter pad that receives supplies once a week from Manaus. For a reasonable fee, the helicopter pilot can take you to a location in the higher elevations. There are some remote trails up there that tourists are flown to from Manaus by helicopters. It will be a little farther to your destination, but our company can make arrangements with the tour guides up there to have horses ready that you can ride to get to your coordinates by one of those trails. My apologies, but this will be a much safer route. The best news is that there is a pilot here today unloading supplies. Normally a guide has to be booked in advance, but if money is not an issue they are always willing to accommodate a tour on short notice."

"How much money are we talking about, Rodrigo?" Carter frowns.

"How much do you have?" Rodrigo gives Carter a serious look.

Before Carter can reply, Rodrigo starts laughing. "I'm guessing one hundred American dollars should do it."

"Well, that's a relief." Carter takes a deep breath.

After walking down a well-worn path, the group begins to approach a wide clearing where the helicopter is sitting on a landing pad.

Christie looks over at Rodrigo. "Why don't we just have the helicopter take us directly to where we want to go?"

"Because there is not a clearing wide enough for the helicopter to land where you want to go."

From the village, the helicopter will carry the group to a smaller more primitive village where the treasure team has agreed they should start the final leg of their journey.

The team loads up, and the helicopter takes off. After a while in flight, Rachel, studying her handheld GPS unit, says, "Looks like we are getting close to our destination."

"All I see are trees, is there a place coming up for us to land?" Carter stares out of the window and begins to scratch his head.

"Carter, Rodrigo already mentioned that the terrain is rough and we'll need to hike to the coordinates," Blake says, as he punches Carter on the arm.

"Man, I'm starting to miss treasure hunting in the cotton fields of Alabama."

The tops of the trees above their destination can be seen in the distance. Rachel leans forward to the pilot and Rodrigo in the front. "Can we make a fly over of our coordinates, right over there?" Rachel points to the tall trees on the horizon.

The pilot turns his head back to Rachel sitting behind him. "Negative, it is pointless to try a fly over of that part of the rain forest. The jungle growth is so thick at the treetops that sunlight cannot reach the ground."

The team keeps staring at the tree line like they might be able to force a glimpse of a treasure that is hiding beneath the thick trees. Below them is a wide valley with a river going through it, winding around patches of high rugged areas. At points, the jungle basin shoots straight up into high cliffs and beautiful ravines.

The four have a smooth ride in the helicopter. The chopper begins to descend and lands in the small village, resting on higher elevation, a little to the north but close to the group's coordinates.

"This should get you close to where you want to be." The pilot grins and prepares for a landing. The team thanks the pilot, pay him for the ride, and unload their gear.

Rodrigo pulls out a map and asks the team to huddle around him for minute. "Yes, the tours at this location specialize in more rugged hikes that vary from two to three day excursions to view the jungle further away from civilization. The landscape at this higher elevation consists of larger trees and a denser forest. The plants and wildlife are different here, due to the dense attributes of the jungle keeping out the sunlight. The tour trail also has examples of shelters and traps the natives use for survival in remote areas. These are very interesting and useful if you get lost in the jungle."

Christie and Carter give each other a concerned look. "Treasure hunters lost in the Amazon. I can see the headlines now," Carter says under his breath

Rodrigo nods over towards the huts. "We will need to head over to the check-in area."

The group proceeds to one of the larger thatched cabins, with some sturdy looking horses and pack mules in a fenced coral next to it.

"Welcome, Americans! Glad you finally made it!" A man with strong sinewy arms approaches them. The man is wearing tattered cargo pants, a tank top, and an army green safari hat.

"Yes, finally!" Carter shakes the man's hand.

"I am Sabio."

"Sabio, that is an interesting name." Christie smiles and shakes his hand.

"Yes, yes, it was my grandfather's name. The name means that I am very knowledgeable." Sabio continues to hold Christie's hand.

Christie's eyebrows raise and she begins to giggle. "Alright, anyway, Sabio, let me introduce you to the others." Carter brings Blake and Rachel over to meet him.

"Glad to take you into the jungle, American friends. Let me show you my map." Sabio goes behind the counter and pulls out an old dingy map.

"We actually have one." Carter pulls out his crisp map.

"That will do you no good here. Tell them Rodrigo."

"Sabio knows this area well. You can trust him."

Sabio puffs out his chest. "Yes you can!" He smiles and winks at Christie. "The area that you want to explore is only a few miles into the jungle off of one of the main trails, but the problem is that the jungle can be almost impenetrable from that trail," Sabio explains.

"Well, where will that trail lead us?" Rachel points to another trail on Sabio's map.

Sabio smiles. "Yes, you know maps, huh? That trail is up above one of the canyon tributaries. It will make it even easier to reach your destination. The only drawback is that there are some narrow ledges on the trail that are a little scary if any of you are afraid of heights."

"What kind of heights are we talking about, Sabio?" Carter begins to anxiously look around at the team.

"I don't know, like three hundred feet or so," Sabio says casually and smiles again at Christie.

"Three hundred feet, seriously!" Carter looks around at the group for a reaction.

"Carter, you've been on hikes in places that tall, like Fall Creek Falls," says Rachel.

"Yeah, but those are regulated parks with anchors and fences. And if you recall, I didn't venture down some of those trails that had the steep edged drop-offs."

"Oh man, you'll be fine. Did I see a bar out front?" Blake throws his bag across his back.

Sabio points back to the map. "Okay then, it is settled, I recommend this trail here. You can load your gear, food, and water on our horses and we'll move down this trail to get you close to your coordinates. We will then use machetes to cut out a new trail to get you where you want to go, but it might still be slow going. The jungle can be very tough through the densest parts, but this will still be the easiest route by far."

Carter mumbles, "Easiest by far, he says. I doubt that."

Sabio motions to the front of the cabin. "Please check out the bar while Rodrigo and I grab a few more supplies from the back. The bartender makes the best *caipirinhas* you will find in the Amazon."

The thatched roof cabin has a patio bar for tourists. All four get beers and tropical drinks at the bar then pull up chairs to a table.

Carter sips his colorful drink through a straw.

Out of the corner of his eye, Blake spots something nailed on a wall of one of the nearby buildings. Blake gets up and walks on a path to get a closer look. Blake's eyes start to widen upon seeing the familiar relic. He runs his fingers over the old rusted remains of an item that seems to be out of place. It is a Civil War era bayonet. Blake waves at Carter for him to come over.

"This is unbelievable! The tags on these artifacts say that they were dug here in the area."

Horseshoes and a few other old items, including the rusted remains of what looks like a Colt army revolver, surround the bayonet.

A sign indicating a scenic walking trail intrigues Rachel and Christie. They let Carter and Blake know they will be back shortly. The short walking trail leads from the tavern, over a creek, and back around to the banks of the main tributary. The exotic plants and animals they see leave them wanting to see more of the beautiful jungle.

Rodrigo comes out of the cabin and Blake calls for him to come over. "Rodrigo, do you know anything about these old relics on the side of the building?"

"I know they are old. They had something to do with your Civil War?"

"Yes, that is correct." Blake strokes his chin.

"I know a man that might be able to help you. His name is Gustavo and he runs a store where I purchased this kepi. His store is just a few buildings down. Would you like to meet him?"

"I would like very much to meet him!" Blake pats Carter on the shoulder. "Come on man, let's check out some relics."

Chapter 35

Rodrigo escorts Blake and Carter to a small cabin a short walk down from the tour cabin.

Rodrigo knocks on the door before entering. “Gustavo, hello! Anyone here?”

A bearded man wearing a New York Yankees baseball cap and white oxford, opens the front door of the shop. Rodrigo explains in Portuguese to the man that the Americans are preparing for a journey into the jungle and that they are interested in his relics. The man motions for the three to enter into his thatched cabin.

Carter looks up at a muzzleloader on the wall. “The air conditioning feels good in here.”

Blake looks over at Carter and shakes his head. “Better enjoy it while you can, it is going to be hot out in that jungle.”

Carter and Blake’s eyes scan over to a point on the wall where a nice top of the line metal detector is leaning against the wall.

Gustavo reaches for a bag and brings out a handful of miniè and round balls to show the group. “I have been digging in this area for a long time. See all of the bullets that I have found. I’m selling them for a dollar each.”

“Thank you sir, we’ll take a few. Hopefully, we can get through customs with them.” Blake picks out a few bullets from the bin in the front.

Carter walks up to Blake. “From what we’ve learned so far, I am beginning to think this area was to be a new colony for the Confederate States. Before the Civil War, the

Knights of the Golden Circle were working on expanding the slave states and form a circle of power that would never be challenged. The K.G.C. had agents in South America, the Caribbeans, and Mexico. The invasion of Mexico by France in 1861 was put into motion by these powers that be. The entire Golden Circle was to be ruled by French decree. France made Ferdinand Maximilian their ruler of Mexico. After the Civil War the United States focused on defeating French troops in Mexico. The invasion ended when Ferdinand Maximilian was executed by Mexican forces in 1867. The American Civil War was global in its scope."

Blake rubs his chin, "That is why I like metal detecting with you, Carter. You are a walking encyclopedia of knowledge."

Carter and Blake's curiosity is piqued. Gustavo can see how excited both are about the artifacts. After receiving payment for the bullets, he says something in Portuguese to Rodrigo. Rodrigo nods his head yes.

"Do you gentlemen want to see more?" Gustavo asks.

"Sure!" says Carter.

Gustavo smiles and nods his head. "Be right back."

He returns with a large case. Carter and Blake can't believe their eyes.

Carter points to the relics in the case. "Wow, those are coin buttons, a droop winged eagle button from a Confederate staff officer's uniform, infantry cast "I" buttons, and a few South Carolina Palmetto buttons."

Blake's eye catches a favorite relic in the case. "Ah, man! Check out the Alabama Volunteer Corps button!"

Old muzzleloaders and shotguns in excellent condition are standing up in the corners, some canteens are also about the room.

Carter and Blake note that Gustavo's cabin is a time capsule of relics from the surrounding jungle. There are the remains of an artillery jacket laid out in a display case and some excavated accouterment plates are hanging on the walls of the cabin. Gustavo's artifact collection also contains examples of ancient Stone Age pottery and arrowheads. Also on exhibit are a few modern weapons that are rusted and in excavated condition.

Gustavo walks around his cabin and explains the collection to the adventurers. "What I love most about the Amazon River Basin is that mysteries abound here. The jungle is frozen in a moment of time. Anybody who wants to disappear or hide something comes to South America. Living here, I have found remnants of every civilization and government that has ever existed on earth. In parts of the jungle, we find a timeline of everything from AK-47s and German luger pistols, to ancient Egyptian stoneware. The outside world would not believe most of the secrets the jungle holds, so the jungle keeps its secrets by de facto."

Carter and Blake ask Gustavo if he will reveal where he had uncovered the relics.

"For now, I want to keep the site a secret. I hope my children will take an interest in the hobby. I don't know if that will happen. You cannot teach passion."

"No, sir, kids always seem to go a different direction," Carter says, while looking at relics in a tall standup display case.

"We don't blame you for wanting to keep it a secret," Carter says, as his eyes continue to roam across all of the artifacts.

Gustavo asks, "Do you guys have time for a story?"

"Yes, sir, we do," says Blake.

"Many years ago when I was in the Peruvian army, a group of girls from a village were kidnapped and marched out into a remote part of the jungle. One of the girls was the daughter of an important dignitary. We were called upon to flush the kidnappers out of their hideout. We marched for several days and had to resort to using machetes to enter an impassable area. Eventually we located the girls and freed them."

Gustavo leans forward and puts both of his large hands on the counter near a relic case. "One of the remote trails we hacked through in the jungle came to a clear plateau that was relatively free of jungle growth. I saw the remains of an abandoned village there. The village had stone fences and hand-dug wells. I could make out the depressions of long decayed structures. I went back to the spot in search of treasure and started finding what you see now."

"I guess what you call the relic bug bit me. It is an addicting hobby. There might be more American Civil War forts and villages out there like the one I happened upon. This area has drawn people of European descent for nearly five hundred years. Manaus, as you know, started out as a European fort in the 1600s, later becoming a boomtown due to the rubber industry. There are remnants of Spanish, French, German, and Russian armies in the jungle … you name it they were here."

"That is quite a story, sir, thank you for sharing," says Blake.

"You're welcome. I'll be right back. I need to put this case back up." Gustavo walks to the back.

Rodrigo says to Blake and Carter, "Gustavo must have found the Civil War relics in a higher elevation where the jungle is less explored. He never tires, that is why I like having him work as a tour guide with my company. He brings one hundred percent to everything he does. He also buys and sells on eBay. Many of the items you see here are for sale."

Blake and Carter see Sabio escorting the girls back towards the cabin.

"I'll be right back. I'm going to let the girls know that we are over here." Carter darts out to get their attention, waving them over.

Sabio waves bye to the girls. "Rest up. We will have a busy day tomorrow."

Rachel and Christie walk with Carter back to Gustavo's store to check out the artifacts.

Rachel walks around the cabin viewing the collection. "Wow, this is quite an impressive collection."

Gustavo clears his throat and raises his eyebrows at the group.

"I apologize. Christie and Rachel, this is Gustavo," Blake motions for the girls to come over towards Gustavo.

"Welcome to my store, do you have the same passion for history as your two male companions?"

Rachel looks up from a display case. "Yes, sir."

"And you?" Gustavo motions towards Christie.

"I enjoy capturing history through photography. Would you mind if I take a few photographs of your artifacts?"

"I don't mind. I will even pose for you." Gustavo goes to the back and reappears with a CSA belt plate.

"Wow, Gustavo, you didn't show us that!" says Carter.

"The young lady wants a photograph and I thought this would be appropriate. Don't you think?"

"Well, yeah!" Carter runs over towards the buckle to check it out. "Where in the world did you find that?"

"Right here, where I found the other artifacts."

"Yeah, you weren't just whistling Dixie!" Carter laughs.

"How do you whistle Dixie?" Gustavo asks.

"Proudly!" Rachel smiles and taps Gustavo on his arm. The group all burst out in laughter.

Carter and Blake purchase a few of the miniè balls and one of the more expensive buttons he has for sale, a South Carolina Palmetto Tree button. They thank Gustavo for his time and exit the store to head back over to the tour cabin.

Blake asks Carter, "Do you think that Gustavo actually dug those artifacts out in this jungle?"

"I don't know, Blake. Who would have ever thought that a treasure map would be on the back of a buckle?"

Rachel runs her fingers over the bayonet of a muzzleloader. "Stranger things have happened."

Carter admires the gold gilt on the SC button he purchased, and then looks up at Rachel and Blake. "Gustavo's collection gives me hope that we might stumble upon some great relics here. We have a map and we know there's treasure."

"I just hope that all of the relics haven't already been excavated by Gustavo."

"No way, I have yet to find a truly hunted-out site," says Carter.

Rachel looks at Carter, then Blake. "Boys, I am going to lead you to the best metal detecting adventure you could have ever imagined."

Carter looks over at Blake as they walk back to the main cabin. "Rachel has never failed in a Treasure hunt. We are going to find the Treasure."

*

The group enjoys another incredible dinner that night. They share ideas of what and who might be driving their search for treasure. They all agree it's clear the men entrusted with the secret coordinates had contact with the highest levels of the Confederate government, meaning they possibly had access to military strategies, as well as the hidden gold reserves.

The next day starts early. Rodrigo and Sabio meet the tourists on the front porch after breakfast and guide them over to a stable where a team of sturdy horses and pack mules has been outfitted to carry them into the jungle.

"These are some beautiful horses," Christie says, as she begins to pet a stunning white horse with a black mane.

"Yes, Ms. Christie, this is the one I selected for you. She is my most beautiful trail horse and well mannered, too," Sabio says, as he hands the reigns over to Christie.

"Carter, you better watch out, man. Sabio has got the moves." Blake hits Carter's shoulder.

"I see that. What about us, Sabio? Which horses are for us?"

"Ah yes, this one is for Rachel." Sabio hands the reigns of a beautiful chestnut mare over to Rachel.

"And this one is for Blake. This is one of my oldest and most well-trained trail horses." Blake rubs the horse's forehead.

"And Carter, this horse is for you," Sabio motions towards a beautiful young mustang with a lot of spirit in her eyes. The horse begins to raise her head up and down once Carter takes the reigns from Sabio. "Thanks, Sabio, is she well trained too?"

"She is getting there. This will be her first trip on the trails. But she is a very good horse."

"First time on the trail? Are you for real, Sabio?"

"Yes, she is a good horse."

"Oh, Carter, quit whining!" Rachel laughs, then smiles at Carter.

"Let's review the map again before we hit the trail." Sabio pulls out his well-worn, heavily marked map and lays it on a table nearby. "I have explored a lot of the area. However, there are sections I haven't ventured into."

Rachel points to a small section on the map. "This is the area we really want to get to."

"Yes, yes, as I said yesterday that is an area I haven't fully explored. The jungle is … possibly impassable."

"We can handle some brush. We have some good gear," says Blake.

Rodrigo scratches his head. “What Sabio means is that it might be impassable for more reasons than just the brush.”

“What do you mean?”

“Remember what I told you when you first arrived?”

Blake pats Rodrigo on the back. “We have some good gear for superstitions and vermin. Don’t worry. We are prepared for any trouble that comes our way.”

Sabio pushes his hat up on his head. “I can get us close to that spot, but then we will need to use our machetes to hack the rest of the way. At that point, we will need to carry all of our supplies on our backs. My horse handlers will ride with us up to this point, then bring our horses and mules back to the cabin.”

“How will we get the horses back when we need them?” asks Christie.

“Don’t worry about that, Ms. Christie. I have that figured out. This is how we do things.” Sabio shows Christie his satellite phone in his backpack. “What is your number, Christie? I can plug it into my phone.”

“Aha.” Christie gestures.

“I can also send an email from my laptop by satellite connection,” Blake tells the group.

“Excellent, okay.” Sabio hands machetes to the men.

“I’ll take one, too, Sabio,” Rachel motions her hand toward him and grabs a machete. Rachel asks Christie, “Do you want one?”

“Ms. Christie can follow behind me, and I will carve out a trail for her,” Sabio says while smiling at Christie.

“Thank you, Sabio, that is sweet. Maybe I should take one too, just in case.”

The excitement builds as the group begins the process of checking packs and preparing their equipment for the journey. The adventurers mount their horses and ride at a brisk pace through the most beautiful exotic terrain any of them had ever seen.

Carter holds the reigns of his horse tightly. "I did not know that the Amazon had valleys and cliffs along the streams like this. I always pictured the Amazon as being one big thick jungle."

Sabio replies, "We haven't reached the rough stuff yet, the jungle trails are clear one day and nearly impassable the next. The weather can also change without notice as you have already seen. During the rainy season the waters can rise very fast."

The group continues along the narrow passages through several spots where there are sheer cliff drop-offs. Over a few hours, the trail gradually brings the party to a much lower elevation.

Sabio finally locates a clear spot for the adventurers. "We can camp here for the night, tomorrow we will get off of the trail. My horse handlers will take the horses and mules along with any excess bags back to the village, then the real work begins."

Chapter 36

The next day, the team brings out machetes, and they begin hacking their way into the dense jungle vegetation.

Carter swings his way through the massive jungle foliage, sweat pouring off him, and mosquitos relentlessly attacking, even with DEET repellant reapplied every few hours. "Y'all, there must be a trail of some sort that will lead to the area indicated on our map!"

"I sure hope so, this is getting to be more than I signed up for," Christie says, as she spits out a bug.

"Ms. Christie, you should walk right behind me, and I will clear your path!" Sabio looks at Christie with his chest out and his machete in the air.

"Hey man, be careful with that thing," says Carter.

The going is slow even though they have a point on their GPS to follow.

Rodrigo notices it is getting late and calls out to the group, "We need to break for camp soon since we haven't reached our destination yet, and we don't know how far we have left to travel."

Rodrigo did not want to be setting up camp in a dark jungle. The group has packed elevated two-man tents with mosquito netting and rain tarps. They string the tents between several trees about five feet high off the ground.

"With all of the research done by you Americans, I'm sure you know pit vipers are a reptile best to be avoided at all costs," says Sabio.

"Yes, I did see some information about the vipers online." Rachel cringes.

"I have some anti-venom, but it's a dangerous snake. Just be aware," Rodrigo says, as he begins to unpack his gear.

Blake clears out a spot for his and Carter's tent with a machete. Carter clears out an area for the girls' tent. Sabio and Rodrigo string up their military style hammocks with mosquito netting and rain tarps close to the other tents. A clothesline is run and all of the group hangs their clothes and socks on the line to dry.

Rodrigo says to the group, "Make sure you take special care to air out your socks or change them daily. I also have foot powder that each of you must use. I want you to inspect and clean your feet nightly with the alcohol cleaning swabs I have provided. Clip your toenails as short as you can. If your feet catch jungle rot, it can cause tissue loss after just twelve hours, and your adventure will end with a helicopter rescue basket carrying you out of the jungle."

"Lovely, thank you for the advice, Rodrigo," Christie says, with a smirk. Christie walks around and begins to snap pictures of the camp. "Looks like we are definitely roughing it. We should be able to make it into some of the larger national publications or something close to them with these photos."

Rachel climbs a rope ladder into her tent. "These tents are a trip."

"I thought you would like these! They keep the pit vipers out, right, Rodrigo?" Blake smiles.

"Yes, those are nice tents. You did your research."

"I always do when it comes to protecting myself and my friends," Blake says, while Rachel smiles at him.

The group feels the temperature drop, and then the sky starts to drop rain in a torrential downpour. They all feel secure and cozy in the floating tents. The men stay in their tent and the woman in theirs. Blake and Carter read their Civil War books from the kindles they have packed in waterproof sealed bags. The girls play cards until they are tired. At night, as the group start to slip into sleep, it seems as though every insect in the jungle is trying their luck to see if they can find a way through the mosquito meshing and make a meal on the adventurers.

Everyone is happy and grateful to see the mesh work and they are glad to have invested in proper tents.

The next day, the group's adventure continues. There are many sights and sounds that none of them have ever heard or seen.

Blake spots a scarlet macaw. "Even if this is a bust of a trip into the jungle, I'm still having a wonderful time. We may never see anything like this again."

"If we do see anything like this again in our lifetime, I hope I am as able bodied to handle it as I am now," says Rachel. "This is a fairly intense workout."

As the four are walking through the jungle, Carter spies in the distance a cylindrical-shaped rusted object rising high above the dense vegetation of the jungle floor.

Carter stops mid-step. "Man! Check it out, guys, what is that up ahead of us?"

As the four get nearer to the object Blake sees it's the bow of a large ship. He blinks his eyes. Although he cannot believe it, rising up out of the jungle floor is what appears to be an old side-wheel blockade-runner. "Check it out y'all. We have found an iron clad blockade-runner!"

Christie says, "I bet it has to be Civil War-related if you and Carter know what it is. What exactly is a blockade-runner?"

Carter touches the rusting front of the leaning hull. "During the war, the British would send supplies, clothing, and weapons to Nassau, Bahamas. From there the supplies would be loaded on fast sleek steam ships called blockade-runners. About 80 percent of the runs were successful. The Confederacy didn't run out of supplies, it ran out of men. This one must have been carrying something important to have been iron clad."

As the four walk around the old ruined ship, Christie asks, "How can a ship end up here on dry land?"

Rodrigo explains, "The waterway that brought the ship here changed its course. Many of the Amazon inlets will change direction over time."

Rachel studies her GPS unit. "Our coordinates show we are close to the treasure. We are about half a mile away from our destination."

Carter and Blake crawl though some of the wreckage of the old ship, which is half-rotted with great gaping openings in its hull. The two can find no obvious traces of the remains of the ship's cargo or what it might have been carrying.

Carter and Blake return from inside the hull and spot a young lad crouching in the jungle observing them.

The boy becomes startled after being exposed from behind a hollow log. He quickly turns and runs down a well-worn path.

Carter yells out, “Wait, come back!”

They start down the trail, thinking the cut path might get them closer to the treasure. The boy continues to run, occasionally looking over his shoulder as the group follows him.

The guide sees the boy off in the distance and calls after him, but he keeps way ahead of them. Rodrigo tells the party that a small native village must be close by and the boy must live there. The group keeps moving forward. As they come upon a ridge, they are able to look out over a little valley with a village at the bottom. They see the boy enter one of the buildings in the village.

Sabio summons the group to a halt. He turns to them with a worrisome look. “We should go back and continue with our plans to cut a path to our coordinates. The young lad was curious as to why we are traveling in this secluded part of the jungle and what that might mean to his tribe. Many of the Indian villages still have limited visitation from the outside world and they prefer it that way. Some of the tribes have been abused by big corporations that wish to exploit the resources in this part of the world.”

“You’re right Sabio, We really scared that boy,” Carter says, while looking down into the valley.

The boy upon arriving in the village informs one of the elders that there are strangers in the jungle that appear as if they might be lost.

The young lad relays to the elder that another group of men, twenty plus in number and heavily armed are shadowing the smaller party, and they look like they are up to no good.

Chapter 37

On into the jungle, the six begin again to hack their way through thick brush.

Rodrigo explains the sudden change in scenery. "The larger jungle trees we are approaching choke off vegetation at ground level creating clearings like the one we see now. How far are we from the GPS coordinates?"

Rachel pulls her GPS unit out of its pouch on her utility belt and studies it. "Not far!"

The jungle begins to open up and becomes clearer. Blake knocks down a patch of vegetation. He stops and gazes. A magnificent structure has appeared directly in front of the adventurers. "Wow, look at this! We've found what we are looking for and it is incredible!"

The domed capitol building that appears in front of the adventurers is built of marble, in the same Greek revival style as the Washington, DC Capitol and Supreme Court buildings.

Rachel takes off her backpack. "How is it possible this can be here and no one knows about it?"

Rodrigo replies to Rachel after taking a swig of water. "This jungle can swallow up an entire city and it would stay hidden for a thousand years."

Carter walks up and throws his machete in the ground point first. "This is proof of Confederate colonies in South America. This is a fantastic discovery y'all!"

Christie walks ahead with her camera snapping pictures. "Whoever built this must have been planning to establish a government at this location. It might be the cornerstone of a lost settlement. Okay, I want everyone to gather in front of the capitol building for a group picture before it gets dark."

The steep granite steps going up towards the marble structure and the marble columns are overgrown with vines. Along the top of the monument engraved in the marble are the words: "The Southern Confederacy."

The group walks up the steep, oversized steps towards the impressive structure's porch. At the top, the group stands in front of massive doors. The great circular seal of the Confederacy, *Deo Vindice*, or "God will vindicate" with George Washington on horseback centered in the seal is on both sides of the two massive doors. Onc of the doors is shut and the other is swung partially open.

Carter thinks about the engraving on the back of the buckle found in the mountain streams of Georgia. "Blake, you remember that engraving on the back of the buckle? 'Let us cross over the river and rest under the shade of the trees?'"

Blake nods his head. "Yeah?"

"Those words kind of match this location."

At the top of the stairs on the porch, old rotted boxes, which would have contained armaments, ammunition, and other supplies, lay around. The remains of a rusted old wagon now rotted and disappearing into the jungle are spotted to the side of the structure.

Blake moves the lid to an ammunition box over to one side. "Hey, check it out. This box still contains the remains of miniè balls and some black powder. Whoever built this place must have had some heavy funding. Getting materials this deep into the jungle would have been difficult and expensive. A lot of people must have stayed here"

"Okay everyone let's keep a sharp eye out for clues. There's got to be a treasure hiding here somewhere," says Rachel.

Rachel pushes on the partially open door. It grudgingly opens wider, and she squeezes sideways through the thick steel doors.

Rachel gets a chill up her spine. She looks back as Carter slides through the doors. "It looks like no one has been here since the end of the American Civil War."

Inside the Southern Confederacy Capitol Building is a time capsule of American Civil War relics. Carter walks over to a smooth bore muzzleloader, picks it up and points it towards a wall. "Looks like Santa came early this year. We have got to file a treasure claim and try to get these relics out of here and into a collection or museum."

Carbine rifles and shotguns are standing up in the corners, some canteens are scattered around the place. The remains of several old Civil War jackets and accouterment plates are laying about the room.

Blake walks over and picks up an eagle sword belt plate. "I can't believe it, I always wondered when and where I would find my first sword belt plate. I could never have imagined it would be in the middle of the Amazon."

Carter walks over and picks up two fork tongues and a CS clip corner buckle with the leather still attached. "These are wonderful relics, my first fork tongue buckle."

Several boxes are found that are packed with accouterment plates, with leather still attached to them. A few old bottles and jars from the nineteenth century are also spotted in one of the front rooms. Over all it appeared that no one had been here since the mid-1800s.

Past the front foyer, a large room opens up to the center of the structure. Rodrigo is the first through the archway. "Hey guys, you have got to see this next room. It is astonishing."

A beautiful glass domed ceiling covers the center room. Vines and jungle growth had broken through part of the glass ceiling along the back of the room.

Carter walks into the room next and places his hand onto one of thirteen panels surrounding the room. "I know what these are. These are the state seals of the Confederate States of America."

Along the circular wall in the main room are engraved panels of the state seals from all of the thirteen States of the Confederacy. There is a panel for each of the recognized States at the end of the Civil War plus Kentucky and Missouri, the two States that did not officially succeed from the Union.

The engraved panels wrapping around the room included, a pelican feeding her young for Louisiana; a star for Texas; three columned arches with the word "Constitution" for Georgia; an eagle with downturned wings spread out for Mississippi; a map on a tree for Alabama; two grizzly bears for Missouri; the Goddess of Liberty for Arkansas; a boat and plow for Tennessee; a palmetto tree and crescent moon for South Carolina; the Greek goddess Athena for North Carolina; clasped hands for Kentucky;

eagle in flight for Florida; and a soldier holding a spear with foot on tyranny for Virginia.

The team gazes in awe at the panels.

Chapter 38

As the group continues farther into the Southern Confederacy Capitol Building, their eyes are riveted towards the skeletal remains of a soldier resting against the wall. The skeleton has a .44 caliber Colt revolver in one hand and the rusted remains of a "wrist breaker" sword lying nearby his other hand. Prominent in the middle of the skeleton's skull is a bullet hole.

Blake rubs his chin in thought. "From the looks of this guy, there must have been some sort of dispute."

Carter moves closer to the remains of the gray-clad soldier. The remains of a red sash are wrapped around the soldier's waist, and some of the staff officer buttons still glisten from the gold gilt on them.

"Look. There is something around his neck." Carter reaches out and gently pulls a gold chain from around the soldier's neck. At the end of the chain is a key. "Another key. I wonder what this goes to."

"Let me see that key Carter." Rachel turns the key over several times examining it under her flashlight. "Look, this key is just like the one you found in Virginia except it has different numbers and letters."

*

A drift back in time by the adventurers would have revealed that the soldier was indeed killed from a dispute. A mutinous dispute had arisen from the soldier's harsh cruelty against his men. The dead soldier was the captain who long ago had the two Confederate privates shot on a dark rainy night.

The captain had gone through Henry's belongings in his saddlebag. Upon reading Henry's papers, he found a letter stamped with an exquisite seal with the words The Southern Confederacy Capitol on it. The letter described a group of buildings in the Amazon built in the style of Greek Architecture. The buildings were to be a new Capitol for the Confederacy. The Confederate leaders planned to move some of their assets to this new stronghold and distribute it as needed to the new Confederate States. The location of the assets were to be kept top secret and guarded by The Confederate Secret Service.

A note from Captain Henry said the buckle he wore must be forwarded to Jefferson Davis upon his death. His buckle with two others would provide clues to where the Confederate assets were stored. The two Rebel privates had really found clues to a treasure. The secret almost went with the men to their graves when they would not tell the captain where the buckle was that Henry had mentioned in his papers. The captain would not let the men's relatives near them until they had breathed their last breath of air.

The evil captain had found a name in Henry's papers of a man who had been a quartermaster of supplies at the Southern Confederacy Capitol. Toward the end of the war, the captain located the man. The quartermaster told the captain of his journey to the secret Confederate Capitol deep in the jungles of South America where he had loaded up boxes for a trip to Richmond, Virginia. The quartermaster had taken a vow of secrecy, but now with the war ending, he thought this might be a good opportunity to score some riches.

The quartermaster went on with the story to say that there were rumors that the boxes were laden with gold headed to the Confederate treasury. The boxes were mysterious in the amount of security that surrounded them, and no one was allowed to examine the contents of the boxes. The captain struck a deal with the quartermaster to split any wealth they found. With the quartermaster as a guide, he would lead a group of his fellow soldiers on a long difficult expedition into the jungle to try and locate any treasure that might still be at the secret Confederate supply depot.

*

In the present, Christie continues to snap pictures of the room and the soldier's body. "Hey guys, this area looks okay for us to stay for the night, but if we are staying here in the building, we need to move the soldier outside."

Blake looks over at the soldier and then back to his friends. "Well we can bury him. I spotted a small cemetery on the side of the building."

The men examine the body for any more treasure clues and possible booby traps. They wrap the body in a tarp and carry it outside for burial. The team gathers together and says a few words over the soldier's burial.

Rachel rubs her chin. "I feel like someone may have killed that man in self-defense, considering he had his pistol and sword in his hands and there are no other bodies around."

The temperature begins to drop as the last bits of soil are thrown on the soldier. The rain starts to come down. The group come to a final decision that, with the soldier's burial and a little cleanup of the inside of the building, setting up camp inside the structure is a great idea. The group decides to put up their tents inside the structure. The insects and crawly things would still be with them inside the structure, and the tents mesh would keep the bugs off of them.

After setting up the tents, the rain subsides a little. Blake and Carter decide to break out their metal detectors and headlamps. They walk outside to see if some treasure can be found. They recover eagle buttons and bullets in front of the structure. Carter, once again, makes a great recovery by finding a cache of fifteen gold coins.

Rachel, standing on the porch, looks out over the jungle. “This can’t be all there is to the mystery of the three belt buckles. Look at this place, it was designed to preserve the ability of the Confederacy to rise again. We are missing something, some clue that will unlock this mystery.”

“Right, when you look at the location and terrain of this position, it is fortress,” says Carter.

Rachel looks over at Carter. “Exactly, and look at the relics we saw back at the village. This place was being stocked with ammo and supplies so that the Confederacy could put an army and a government back into the field if they were defeated during the Civil War.”

Blake takes a seat on a rock wall. “We have to find the clue that they must have preserved here to lead us to the big treasure, a treasure large enough to fund a long-term takeover of the Federal government.”

Carter puts his fist into his palm, “A new government and army would have been only part of their mission. These were revolutionists who also would have wanted to fund the preservation of their social and political ideas."

Rachel continues to look for any clues and starts to study a raised area in the middle of the great chamber. "Something ceremonial was meant to be placed in the center of this chamber. These holes in the floor are for poles … maybe bed posts or a curtain to either hide something, or to keep out all of these infernal jungle insects."

Rachel with her hand on her chin continues. "This whole structure is a temple. The Freemasons must have built this place. They could have hid a treasure in the stone work but more likely they left us a clue that will lead us to their treasure."

Chapter 39

Blake ensures that the perimeter around the Southern Confederacy building is secure by placing state of the art security monitors at various distances in the jungle. Blake opens up his laptop and sets his monitors at a slightly less sensitive setting so smaller creatures will not trigger the sensors. If a panther had any intentions of creeping up to make dinner out of them, Blake would have a heads up. Blake is also concerned about the seclusion of their position.

The laptop back-up batteries can only last so long before they need to be recharged by the roll out solar panels he packed. The amount of sunlight coming in at this location was limited. If the laptop satellite connection and Rodrigo's satellite phone both went out, they would have no way of getting help if anyone attacked them. Even if an emergency call for help was sent out, Blake knew that it might be difficult for a rescue team to get to their present location quickly.

A campfire is going in the in the main circular room with the domed glass ceiling. Blake and Rachel are talking among themselves. Christie and Carter are also engaged in a conversation between themselves. During the course of their conversation, Carter leans over, kisses Christie and then the two embrace. Christie leans her head on Carter's chest. The group tired from the adventures of the day are ready to turn in for the evening. Carter glances over at Blake. Rachel has her head resting on Blake's shoulder.

Carter whispers over to Blake, "Hey Blake, if it's okay, can Christie and I take this tent to ourselves tonight?"

Blake flips his hand to Carter. "Of course man, me and Rachel will share this tent."

Later in their tent, Blake says to Rachel, "My mind keeps going back to the engraving on the Georgia buckle of Stonewall Jacksons last words, 'Let us cross over the river and rest under the shade of the tree.' I think you're right, we are missing something."

Rachel is lying up against Blake, his arms around her. "It's like we have been saying, this building must have been built as part of a staging area for a future front in a continuation of the American Civil War. They must have hidden some clue that would resurrect the Confederacy when the time was right."

Rachel gazes out of the tents nylon mesh and up at the Confederate state seal panels, studying what the significance might be of the panels. There was a state seal for each of the recognized Confederate States at the end of the Civil War. As Rachel caresses Blake's powerful forearm, she spots something out of place and unusual on one of the panels. Her attention shifts to the state seal of Alabama. "The Map on a Tree!"

The panel of the map of Alabama on a tree has tiny tick mark lines spaced out around its edges. Rachel now remembers that the back of one of the buckles also had small, almost unnoticeable, tick mark lines spaced out around its edge as well.

Sensing that maybe she has discovered another clue, she tells Blake, "I may have something. I know it's late, but it won't take but just a minute."

Rachel crawls out from under their blanket, gets her camera and photographs the great seal of the Alabama map on a tree, along with all the other state seals. "Hey, wake up y'all. I think I have found another clue. Blake! Get up! Do you see what I see?"

Blake sleepily looks out from their tent. "I think so."

Rachel holds her hands out towards Blake. "Check out where the river crosses the map on the tree? You don't see the obvious clue, do you?"

Blake's one eye, that always remained partially open while sleeping, looks up and out through the tent's nylon mesh. His gaze stops at a point on the wall of the circular room. "I see it now Rachel. The engraving on the back of the buckle is a clue to one of the state seals in this room?"

Rachel gracefully turns her long slender neck from Blake, towards where Blake is looking. Their eyes fall on the Alabama state seal which consists of a map on a tree with rivers running within the map.

Blake pops up out of his slumber. "Rachel, I want to knock a hole in that wall panel and see if there is anything behind there."

The rest of the group stumble out of their slumber and are informed of Blake's idea. The team agrees that it won't hurt anything to knock a small hole in the plaster of the Alabama map on a tree seal to see if anything could be hidden behind the wall.

Blake uses a hammer from one of the backpacks to knock a small hole in the great seal of Alabama. "There's something in here. It's a box!" Blake pulls the wooden box out of its hiding place. It has a keyhole. "Carter hand me the key you pulled off of our soldier friend. I bet it will open this box."

Carter pulls the old key out of his pocket. The key does not turn when inserted in the box. "Hey, I wonder if the Virginia key I found will fit. I brought it with us for good luck."

Blake uses the key that Carter found in Virginia and it easily opens the box with a sharp popping sound. Inside the box is a hand drawn map with hills and streams in it, along with cryptic characters at the bottom. Also in the box are two letters. The letters are from Walt.

One of the letters is titled: "To Sara, my beautiful lover and friend." The letter is addressed to Nassau, Bahamas. The other letter is to Andy McCarver.

The letter addressed to Andy McCarver reads:

Mills House
Charleston, S.C.

Dear Andy,

If you are reading this it means that I am deceased, as well as Henry. I hope you were able to locate the money that I earned as a blockade-runner without too much trouble. I apologize for making this journey so difficult, but absolute secrecy is a must. As I write this letter from Charleston, plans are underway to have the clues sent to wherever you are now reading this letter. It would be better for the General's Relic to be lost for all time rather than for it to fall into the wrong hands. You will need the key you used to open this box and Captain Henry's key in order to gather the remaining clues and locate the General's Relic. I know you will do what is right, Andy.

Your Friend and Comrade,
Captain Walt Henson
Deo Vindice

The letter to Walt's lover starts:

Mills House
Charleston, S.C.

Nassau, Bahamas

My beautiful Sara,

You are the only girl I have ever loved. Our time holding each other and dancing on the beach are memories I will cherish forever. Andy will provide some of my earnings to you for provisions. I think we both know and sense I will not return. A man's got to take a stand against tyranny. Unfortunately, our generation has had tyranny arise in the form of Yankee aggression. Please continue to love me and the memories we shared. I know we will see each other on the other side.

Love Forever,
Walt

Christie is the first one to speak, "What an amazing story."

Carter rolls his fingers back through his coarse, thick brown hair. "There really is a treasure, and now we have our first definite confirmation from a Confederate officer, that it is out there. The General's Relic, whatever that is. We might be sitting right on top of the treasure."

Blake holds the wooden box out to the team. "Hey guys, Walt isn't kidding about needing Captain Henry's key to open the next box. It's booby-trapped. Look at this lever. It is designed to cause a spark if the box is forced open. A spark igniting this vial of flammable liquids nestled right here would have destroyed the contents of the box. Very clever stuff."

Carter looks in the box and then rubs his chin. "I don't think the body we found here was Henry's. Henry wouldn't have left his buckle and gold coins along that creek in Alabama. He was on a mission. I think the mystery soldier was somehow connected to Henry's death.

Rachel shines her flashlight from the wooden box back to the letter. "Incredible! We are getting somewhere now. I think these clues are going to lead us back to the States. Walt's blockade running money was hidden in the Deep South, so the big treasure must also be hidden somewhere in the Confederacy. I will have to analyze the clues further, but this map may lead us to Virginia."

Carter, looking over Rachel's shoulder, says, "We just have to hope that a shopping mall hasn't claimed the next set of clues. Lots of construction has been going on in Virginia."

Chapter 40

Taking turns with the night vision goggles, Blake and Rodrigo watch throughout the night in case there's any trouble.

Rodrigo had mentioned Indian tribes in the area, but explains further, "These Indian tribes are afraid of strangers for good reasons. Big oil corporations have been known to send military units deep into the jungle. Heavy fighting in this decade has become more common here than outsiders would like to believe."

"The indigenous people in the thickest parts of the jungle aren't going to give up their ancestral homelands without a fight. Almost all of the tribes are wary of outsiders. Hiking out here in no man's land we need to worry about three things: tribes that won't let us onto their protected areas, military units appearing out of nowhere, and—the threat that worries us guides the most—drug traffickers. This deep in the jungle, a tour accidently walking into a drug-processing facility will result in certain death for the entire party."

Deep in the night, Blake keeps getting a feeling that something is not right. Blake always had a good sixth sense and he knew it would be wise to listen to it now. Blake's laptop beeped.

"Guys and gals, we've got company."

Blake could just make out the footsteps of the intruders. He also faintly hears that the men moving towards them have heavy accents, possibly European and Middle Eastern mixed together. It is almost dawn and Blake alerts the other members of the party that someone out in the jungle has been watching them and is now closing in on their position. Blake, with a great deal of experience in the art of stealth, recommends that the team quietly leave the Southern Confederacy Capitol Building and make their way out into the jungle for a getaway.

Carter in the early twilight, using a corner spy mirror Blake hands him, takes stock of who the bad guys might be. Carter sees a burst of gunfire erupt, then bits of stone pelt him from bullets hitting close by. The unknown assailants all open fire, forcing Carter and the rest of their party to take cover. Rachel reaches for her bag and pulls out a black 9mm semi-automatic pistol. Blake is quick to get into action as well and reaches in a bag to pull out the upper and lower receivers of his M4 Carbine, his favorite personal defense weapon.

Blake swiftly attaches the two rifle parts together to get into action. "Keep your heads down, we will make it out of here." Blake turns to Rachel. "I'm going to flank these guys, cover me."

Blake crawls out a side window unnoticed, as Rachel lays cover fire on the unseen enemy, rapidly firing her 9mm caliber pistol. Blake runs down a trail he had spotted when he was laying out the motion sensors.

Blake positions himself in a cropping of rocks and logs among the jungle brush. At this position with a night vision scope, in the twilight before dawn, the enemy is blazingly apparent. The enemy is dressed in professional camouflage uniforms. Blake begins to have flashbacks of the battles he and his mates had waged in the mountains of Afghanistan.

Sighting the night vision scope at the base of one of the enemy combatant's skull he pulls the trigger once and the bad guy slumps over. He is surprised at how many hostiles have surrounded the old Southern Confederacy Capitol.

There were probably twenty to thirty armed men raking fire onto his friends. In the corner of his non-shooting eye, Blake can see Rachel firing off rounds onto the enemy combatants. Blake proceeds to fire off another burst of 5.56 rifle rounds.

Now some of the bad guys were starting to return fire in his direction, the direction they had just heard him shoot from.

Blake hears voices from up on the ridge behind him. Terrified he has been flanked he turns and sees movement. Someone had just fired a weapon that was discernable to him as a 5.56 rifle with a silencer. Blake looks forward and sees two, then five enemy combatants fall within ten seconds. Blake sees that whoever the stranger is, he is on Blake's side in this shootout. Unfortunately, the bad guys figure out a really good sniper is picking them off from up on the ridge.

The enemy scrambles to get under whatever cover they can find and start firing wildly towards the ridge. The bad guys begin to panic as they become aware of being pinched between three positions shooting down on them.

Inside the well-fortified block marble Southern Confederacy Capitol Building, Rachel lays down a deadly accurate raking fire with her black 9mm auto pistol. Rachel's trained eye darts to one of the men bending down in the brush and readying something. Alarm bells start going off in her head. One of the enemy combatants has shouldered a rocket propelled grenade launcher and is pointing it in her direction.

Rachel yells out, "Everyone, get out now! Move!"

Rachel pushes Christie and Carter out the front door. Rodrigo and Sabio roll out of a side window. Bullets are ricocheting all around the front of the Southern Confederacy building from the automatic gunfire bursts of AK-47s. Blake stops firing.

He sees his friends spill out into the automatic gunfire just as a round from an RPG explodes and demolishes the front of the old structure. The massive explosion and fireball shatters the early morning dawn.

Blake stands up. Blake knows that without cover his friends only have seconds to live. Out of nowhere, bursts of shotgun blasts and rifle rounds start pouring into the enemy from the thick jungle, four hundred feet opposite of Blake.

Blake switches his weapon to full auto mode and rakes a fusillade of bullets down onto the fast retreating bad guys. As fast as it had started, the firing from the enemy stops.

Blake stops firing. He sees men coming out of the jungle. The small boy who had seen the adventurers earlier in the day had alerted the nearby village that armed men were following and watching a group of American tourists. The villagers, aware the Americans would most likely be robbed and murdered, had gathered together a group of men armed with military-style shotguns and hunting rifles to come to the rescue.

Christie asks the group, "Shouldn't we contact the authorities or police?"

Rodrigo who has just walked up and is holding a 12-gauge shotgun replies, "The police are afraid to come into many areas of the jungle that are largely controlled by the drug cartels. In this area, the villagers who just saved your lives are the police."

Blake asks, "Rodrigo, that's an old gun you have. Can I see and hold it?"

Rodrigo smiles. "I will show you."

Rodrigo holds up the Burgess 12-gauge, pops a latch, and shows how the gun folds in half to fit into his backpack. "This gun has been in my family for several generations. The story is that a group of Old West lawmen came into our village looking for an outlaw. I don't know who the outlaw was. The stories run wild. But the lawmen left my great grandfather this gun in return for helping catch the outlaw. I have kept it well oiled. It is valuable, as you probably know, and no one usually sees it. I guess you could say I also appreciate our past and history. Rough riders!" Rodrigo yells, as he holds the Burgess pump action triumphantly up towards the sky. "I figured it would come in handy someday. I normally don't bring it on a tour, but this area you wanted to hike can be very dangerous."

The villagers walk up to where the treasure hunters have gathered. The armed men are clean cut, wearing American-brand shirts, khaki shorts, and baseball caps.

Blake says to Rodrigo, "Please let them know how appreciative we are. They saved our lives!"

Rodrigo translates Blake's gratitude using the native indigenous language, and the villagers reply back through Rodrigo.

"They said you are welcome. They followed you and weren't sure what you were doing way out in the jungle, but could tell you were good people. They were worried you would find trouble. There are a lot of bad people that travel through here. You should be more careful."

The small lad walks up.

Carter asks, "What is your name?"

Rodrigo translates, "He said his name is Maximino, which means the greatest."

Carter hands out five of the gold coins to the boy as the boy's father watches. "You certainly are the greatest in our book. If it's okay with your father I want you to have these. They will keep your tribe supplied with food and goods for a long time."

The son hands his father the coins. The son smiles, then walks up, and hugs each member of the group.

Blake, Rachel, and the villagers spread out across the area where the firefight has occurred, checking behind trees, rocks, and bushes. Not a single body is found, but the group finds plenty of blood.

Rachel yells out, "I have found something that belonged to the soldiers." She holds up a bloody shirt by its collar. "This shirt has a black patch with the word 'Shadow' around the top edge and a large number seventeen in the center, with '*Nunquam Cede*' around the bottom edge of the patch, which is Latin for 'never surrender.'"

Blake walks over. "Only professional contractors could be this organized."

Blake estimates from the amount of blood spilt where the shirt is found and at other points on the battlefield, that two of the armed bandits had been killed and several more severely wounded. It was clear only a disciplined, well-trained group would have gathered their dead and wounded like this. The bothersome question was why a group of professional contractors would be after American treasure hunters in the Amazon Jungle?

The villagers are mystified as well. The villagers are certain the bandits were drug traffickers, looking to take a group of Americans hostage for ransom money.

The party loads up their gear to start their journey out of the jungle, with their team a little shaken up, but remaining confident after winning the battle, and glad to make new friends with the villagers.

Chapter 41

Sabio and Rodrigo approach the villagers.

Rodrigo asks, "What is the fastest safest passage out of the jungle?"

The villagers draw him a map of a direct river route to Manaus by boat. The villagers lead the group through their village and to the jungle river landing close by.

Rodrigo explains while walking, "The people here depend heavily on the nearby waterway to transport supplies to their village. The river is going to be the quickest way out of here if we can procure a boat."

Blake, now fully armed with his rifle and pistol, brings up the back to protect the group. As the treasure hunters get close to the river landing, Blake becomes nervous, fearing another attack. Through Rodrigo, the villagers let the group know that the owner of the boat and the people who control the landing are all about business. Once the landing is reached, the group notice there are several men standing guard at the landing, holding shotguns. The owner of the landing steps out. Rodrigo speaks to the man in Portuguese.

Rodrigo translates to the rest of the team. "The owner of the boat is not interested in letting us use his boat. He is concerned we might be carrying drugs."

Carter holds up a single gold coin. "Ask him if this will change his mind."

The boat owner's eyes widen and his demeanor changes, he walks over to Carter takes the coin and hands Carter the keys to the speedboat. The boat's owner, with a smile, talks to the group in Portuguese.

Rodrigo translates, "We can leave the keys with his cousin in Manaus. He said we can borrow his boat any time we like, with the gold coin he can replace his boat three times over, if needed."

The boat is loaded with the group's backpacks, as Blake keeps an eye out.

The businessman's speedboat does not start up. Carter adjusts the choke, then makes sure the engine is fully tilted down.

Christie yells, "Hey guys, a boat is approaching and it looks like the same crew from earlier."

Rachel shouts, "Lock and load!"

Blake jumps in, releases the choke, and pulls the throttle down. The boat sputters and backfires, then the engine comes alive. Everyone hangs on tight. Carter takes the wheel and pushes the throttle full forward. The boat surges muddy water from its propeller and pushes out into open water in a split second. Carter drives. Blake gets onto a back seat and slings his gun for a sighting prop and prepares to defend the group.

As soon as the strangers get into range of Blake's M4 carbine, he sees one of the men raise his weapon. Rodrigo radios ahead to the authorities in Manaus to be ready for trouble and to be prepared for an armed attack. Blake, looking through the scope mounted atop his combat rifle, fires his weapon on a three-burst setting. The bad guys spray bullets everywhere. Blake sees the water chop up close by from a few lucky shots, but continues to concentrate, controlling his breathing and firing shots with the waves of the boat. Two of the assaulting party is hit, and the raid upon the treasure hunters stops.

Blake asks, "Is everyone okay?"

Carter yells out, "I am hit in my left shoulder, but it's just a graze."

"Carter, you take care of that wound. I'll take over driving. I think these bad guys have had enough of getting shot to pieces. Rodrigo, you keep watch behind us."

The party speeds out of the inlet and into the main channel. As the group passes an adjourning inlet, a second boat, with men dressed in the same camouflage shirts, whip out of an inlet and give chase. The reckless boat captain swings sideways; the boat's crew manages to knock a few holes in the fiberglass hull of the treasure hunter's boat.

A bullet whizzes by Rodrigo, startling him. Rodrigo, now the point man, is determined he is going to stop the Shadow Seventeen soldiers once and for all. Rodrigo returns fire with his 12-gauge Burgess shotgun, loaded with slugs. The pump action loads shells into the antique shotgun between each shot. Rodrigo's aggressive shooting finds the Shadow Seventeen gas tanks, igniting the boat's fuel tanks.

The boat erupts in a massive fireball explosion, throwing its occupants high in the air. Blake looks back to see the boat on fire and bodies floating face down in the water.

The adventurers move out of the narrow inlet waterways and into a less-secluded section of the river system. The entire team is shaken. All of the tired explorers, on edge from the shootout, have one common thought and that's to get out of the jungle and back to the United States.

"Who were those people?" asks Christie.

Blake breaks down his rifle to lower and upper receivers for concealment and wipes his forehead with a towel. "I could hear them as they got close to our camp, they spoke with heavy accents that sounded like they were from the Middle East and Europe … professional mercenaries. I know the villagers think they were a gang of thieves, or drug runners, but I don't think so. They were too well organized, trained, and had uniforms. The best explanation is that someone knew we were going into the jungle and what we were looking for—and whoever it is almost got us killed."

Chapter 42

Back in Atlanta, at Christie and Rachel's Midtown apartment, the team have a chance to examine in detail the old map and clues retrieved from the ceremonial room in the now destroyed Southern Confederacy building. The map has streams and hills, but lacks specific landmarks to help identify where the treasure is located. Squared off at the bottom left and right of the map is a set of numbers, letters, and characters.

"I found a website where Shadow Seventeen advertise themselves as specializing in protective services. Saudi connections … European, big organization … and well funded. They can add near-assassins of treasure hunters to their resume."

After studying the map for a few minutes, Rachel realizes the key from Andy's yard will decipher a puzzle of numbers and letters at the bottom left of the map. "We have another set of coordinates." She walks over to a globe in the main room. As she looks at the globe, she states, "I've got a location." Everyone gathers around Rachel's laptop. "The latitude and longitude coordinates correspond to a church in Virginia."

Rachel plugs the name of the church into the computer and starts reading. "It says here that the church was founded in 1850 so that will put it in the right timeframe."

Rachel gets up and walks over to another laptop and opens it. "There is a second section on the bottom right of the map containing more encrypted characters. Several of these characters match characters on the dead soldier's key we found in the jungle, which in turn match up to letters on the opposite side of that key." Rachel taps out a few more keys on her laptop. "The character encryptions translate the location of something hidden in the outside brick walls of the church. It gives the exact brick to move."

Blake puts his hand on the back of Rachel's chair. "Way to go, Rachel. Now all we have to do is drive up to Virginia next weekend and pick up the next clue."

Rachel continues to read about the old church. "Here's another article on the church. It says here that efforts to preserve the old church have failed, and the church is scheduled for demolition on Wednesday."

Blake and Carter look at each other. Carter says, "The church will be demolished the day after tomorrow. I don't think we can get there in time to find the clue."

"I've got some good friends up at the Clarksville Air Base, and I might be able to get a military transport helicopter to give us a lift up to Virginia before that church is knocked down."

Carter raises his ball cap and rubs his head. "I don't think I can make it tomorrow. I've got a big case going to court tomorrow morning in Birmingham. I've got to be there. Can't quit my day job just yet."

Christie says, "I'm supposed to meet with a client tomorrow for a photo shoot."

Rachel smiles at Blake. "Well it looks like I'm your girl."

Chapter 43

Blake steps out on to the balcony to talk to his commander. Jim answers the phone. "Blake. How's life treating you?"

"Can't complain. I know it is short notice, but I wonder if I can ask a favor."

Jim had just finished getting his children settled in for the night. "Sure, anything you need. What have you been up to? I haven't heard from you in a while."

"Right now I am in Atlanta. You won't believe it, but a few friends and I just got back from a trip to the Amazon Jungle."

"That's not hard to believe. You and I tracked all over those jungles hunting bad guys. We had a lot of missions down there."

"This time it was for pleasure with a good dose of some unusual excitement for a civilian. We ran into a firefight with some very nasty military contractors."

"Doesn't surprise me, folks in our line of work always run into excitement."

Blake asks, "Can you hook me and a friend up with a ride to Virginia in one of the transport helicopters? We are working on a treasure hunt, and we need to check out some clues. Our best clue yet is scheduled to be bulldozed this week."

"Be prepared for the journey in a few hours. You know the drill, I'll have a military transport ready for you at the Marietta Dobbins Air Reserve Base. You can fly out first thing in the morning."

Blake and Rachel arrive at the base, check in at the guard gate with special security clearance, and are escorted out onto the tarmac. Blake spots the large military transport taking on additional fuel for the flight to Virginia. The crew of the CH-47 Chinook transport is waiting to meet Rachel and Blake.

Rachel is impressed. “You must know some important people.”

Blake laughs. “It goes with the territory. You’d be amazed at what goes on behind the scenes in this country and abroad.” He asks, “Have you been in one of these before?”

“No, I haven’t. I’m pretty excited.”

The CH-47 Chinook helicopter lifts off the ground zipping the crew and passengers up into a steep climb.

Blake holds Rachel’s hand. “Hang on. This is going to be a fast flight!”

Chapter 44

An hour and a half into the flight, the pilots begin a descent towards an area where large smoke piles are smoldering.

"Rachel, we may be too late. I don't see the church. I only see bulldozed land and smoldering piles of cleared timber."

Rachel shouts, "I see it over there! That hill was hiding it."

The pilots, on cue, head towards a cleared area that's been scraped off by the bulldozers.

"Look over there!" Blake points out two or three metal detectorists in the field below them.

The helicopter sets down in the cleared field. The blades blow debris from the site of the future shopping mall. The pilots shut down the engines. "We'll wait for you here. You know the drill if you need anything call us on the radio." Blake takes the two way military spec radio from the pilot and attaches it on his belt.

As they walk towards the church, Blake asks Rachel, "Do you think we'll find what we're looking for?"

Rachel, watching the wet mushy ground beneath them for debris, replies, "Yes, I do, and I think we're close to deciphering the treasure map. We are going to find the General's Relic."

Blake looks out over the field. "I love the smell of a freshly bulldozed field. It feels like you can touch the past. I wish I could join these guys for some relic hunting."

Rachel stops in her tracks. "Seriously, Blake?"

"Oh, did I say all of that out loud?"

Rachel walks straight to a specific corner of the church and leans over. She pulls out a piece of paper. "Let's see, five bricks over from the corner and two bricks up from the foundation." Rachel's long fingers brush over the old red brick wall. "This is it. It's this brick." Rachel pulls a compact toolkit out of a fanny pack she is wearing on her hip and grabs a miniature hammer and screwdriver.

"You're one well-prepared lady."

Rachel looks up toward Blake. "The Girl Scouts taught to always be prepared for any situation."

Blake cannot help but notice Rachel's beauty. They have chemistry, but he can't allow himself to get distracted.

Rachel pulls the brick loose. She then shines a flashlight into the hollow cavity. "I see a box. Here, hold the light."

Rachel brushes her hair out of her eyes and looks up at Blake. "Can you grab that stick behind you?"

"Here you go."

Rachel fishes the box out with the stick. The box is antique mahogany with a keyhole on the front. She stands up and brushes a century and a half of dust off the top of the box. A brass nameplate on the top reads: "Raphael Semmes, Captain of the *CSS Alabama*."

Blake holds the box. "Wow, just the nameplate is an impressive relic."

Rachel reaches in her pouch and pulls out a small plastic bag. "Henry's key that we found on the skeleton in the jungle! This is providence, Blake."

Rachel pulls the key out of the bag and inserts it in the front of the box. Rachel turns the key and the box opens with the same sharp popping sound as the box found in the Amazon, confirming that it is the same booby trapped design as the one in the jungle.

Rachel and Blake's eyes grow large over the sight before them. In the box is a round gold-plated Confederate encryption decoder with the letters "C.S.A." stamped in big red letters in the center of the device. Around the outside edges of the encryption decoder are letters and numbers that when the disk is turned is meant to correspond with letters on a separate edge of the decoder.

Chapter 45

Rachel picks up the encryption decoder. "What an exquisite find."

She hands the device over to Blake.

Blake holds the decoder just below eye-level. "This is beautiful. It looks like we are getting closer to finding whatever it is Walt and Henry worked so hard to hide."

With the Confederate decoder encryption device removed from the box, the two find an aged, brown parchment at the bottom of the box. Rachel unfolds the stiff paper. On the paper is written in Old English cursive:

The secret of the General's Relic lies within the Lady Sumter's cargo manifest.

God Bless the Southern Confederacy,

Raphael Semmes, Captain of the CSS Alabama

Rachel and Blake high-five each other. "Let's get back to Atlanta. We need to figure out where the Sumter's cargo manifest is archived."

They start the walk back to the Chinook with their treasure wrapped in Rachel's hooded sweatshirt.

Rachel is about to say something when she notices headlights coming down the dirt road in their direction. "Looks like we've got company!"

Blake turns his head towards the direction of Rachel's gaze. Three large black SUVs with tinted windows are bouncing over the muddy construction access road and are closing in on their position. Blake reaches for the two-way communications device attached to his belt and radios the waiting Chinook helicopter pilots. "Fire up the helicopter, we may have trouble on the way."

The large Chinook engines roar to life and the blades start turning.

Blake shouts, "Run, Rachel! We've got to get out of here!"

The bad guys spot the helicopter and close in fast on it. Men begin pouring out of the SUVs armed with Uzi machine guns and black tactical, folding stock AK-47s. The men begin firing on Blake and Rachel who run for their lives to the transport.

Blake hopes their aim is lousy as he hears a bullet whiz by his head. The blades of the Chinook are at full speed now. Bullets pop up dirt beside and in front of them. As Blake and Rachel board the chopper, bullet holes appear as rounds hit the hull of the helicopter. They leap aboard and the pilot lifts the bird up. Blake is ready to breathe a sigh of relief when a shoulder fired missile slams into the tail of the bird.

Blake yells, "Hang on, Rachel, we're hit!"

The big chopper rolls over hard towards its right side, going down fast. The pilots in the cockpit do everything possible to prevent their imminent deaths. The Chinook sets down hard on its side. The helicopter blades break up and tear huge chunks of dirt out of the ground. The pilots, unharmed, grab their firearms, clamber out, and rush to help Blake and Rachel get clear of the smoldering wreckage.

Blake looks out towards the bad guys after helping Rachel from the destroyed helicopter. Help has arrived from an unexpected source.

The relic hunters had run to their trucks, retrieved their guns, and, as the helicopter crashes, begun to lay down a withering line of fire on the Shadow Seventeen assailants. The detectorists are well armed. Two of the men are firing high-powered rifles, a Ruger mini 14, and a scoped .30-06 hunting rifle. The other fellow is firing and hitting the bad guys with a .380 pistol he had been carrying in his front pants pocket.

The three detectorists have a good defensive position and are spread out about twenty feet apart behind an old stone wall. The Shadow Seventeen group takes cover and is forced to keep their heads down from the accuracy of the relic hunters' rifles. The bad guys gather their wounded and load into their SUVs, driving out even faster than they had arrived. The old church is not too far from some subdivisions, someone was bound to call all of this shooting in soon, and then local law enforcement would become involved. Shadow Seventeen prided itself on their quick-strike gun battles and ability to vanish to the safe houses the organization had spread throughout the world.

The two pilots radio in the crash. Soon the military would arrive and recover the wreckage. The press would be told the helicopter had gone down due to some mechanical problems and the detectorists paid off to keep their story out of the papers. The Northern Virginia detectorists close to Washington with family in the military and intelligence community were thrilled to have a story that they were part of a shootout with terrorists.

Blake looks over at Rachel, in one quick moment she is falling to the ground. Blake sees that Rachel has a small gash across her forehead and that blood is trickling across her cheek. During the crash Rachel had hit her head. Blake knows that she needs immediate medical attention.

Chapter 46

Blake catches a ride with one of the relic hunters to rush Rachel to the nearest emergency room. After a doctor stitches up the cut and confirms it is a light concussion they leave the hospital. That same night Blake and Rachel check into a quaint bed and breakfast in Culpepper, Virginia. There Rachel gets a breakthrough in her research.

"Blake, come look at this! Based on what I'm seeing here, Mobile, Alabama will be the best place to search for the steamship's lost cargo manifest."

"Are you sure, Rachel?"

"Of course, I'm sure! There are a lot of ship records there and that is where Raphael Semmes lived after the war."

"Well then, we better notify Carter and Christie."

The entire team of adventurers makes plans to head to Mobile, Alabama. They decide to book their hotel in Gulf Shores, Alabama to enjoy the beach while conducting their research in Mobile.

Christie walks a little behind everyone else, per usual carrying too much luggage. "I'm glad that we decided to stay in Gulf Shores, instead of Mobile."

"Yeah, why not enjoy the ocean while we are conducting our research. This trip maybe you'll get a chance to show off what you're carrying in that luggage." Rachel laughs. "I've got a good feeling about tomorrow. There are a lot of records in Mobile related to blockade runners and cargo manifests."

That evening the four have tequila shots and beers after enjoying fresh grilled fish at a restaurant on the beach. They spend the evening talking and comparing research notes around a table. A warm fire is going next to them from heat torches. Once the sun goes down it is brisk and cool at night on the Gulf in late September.

*

The next day the group meets in the lobby before dawn to make the hour drive to Mobile. Rachel is sitting in a chair, enjoying her coffee, and studying a local map. She looks up. "Hey there, Carter."

Carter yawns, and rubs the back of his head. "Do you think they'll have what we need? In the past decade, I've noticed a trend of libraries getting rid of primary source books and replacing them with watered down history books. It's pretty shocking!"

Rachel squints her eyes at Carter. "Late night, huh? Got into the whiskey, I see. Here, let's get you some coffee. We need everyone sharp today. Oh! Here comes Blake and Christie. Rachel stands up and shoves a bunch of loose papers in her leather satchel. Well, team, I have a few specific libraries picked out where I think we can find more information about the blockade runners."

Blake fills a cup of coffee from the dispenser. "I've got a great feeling about today. We are going to find the mother lode treasure map."

"We'll hit all of the libraries on my list and then some!" Rachel throws her satchel across her shoulder and heads out the door. The rest of the group follows her to the SUV. On the drive to Mobile, the treasure hunters enjoy good conversation and scenery.

Upon arriving in Mobile, Alabama, the team parks their SUV and enters the first library on Rachel's list. They approach an older lady that's about to fall asleep.

"Excuse us, ma'am," Rachel politely says to the older lady. The lady continues to nod off. "Ma'am. Excuse us!"

"Oh! When did you arrive?" The older lady awakes somewhat startled.

"Um, we just walked in ma'am."

"Oh, yes, yes. Thank you. How may I help you?"

"We are interested in your archives," Rachel informs the librarian.

"Archives, what for? Are y'all from around here?"

"No ma'am. We are historians, and we are interested in seeing if your archives have any books on blockade running, specifically old cargo manifest logs. We are interested in anything related to Captain Raphael Semmes."

"I can take you to the room where we kept a lot of books and papers boxed up, but I don't know if you'll find anything back there now. We had a sale a while back to keep this library going and some of the older books were auctioned off."

The librarian joins the group around the other side of the counter and begins to escort them to the back.

"Do you know who those books were auctioned to?" Blake asks.

"Well, it's funny, a lady who lives near the Captain Semmes' house purchased the majority of the records."

"Really?"

"Yes, seems appropriate for them to be back there."

"What do you mean?" asks Rachel.

"There were several diaries and memoirs from soldiers who served under Captain Semmes during what I like to call, the War of Northern Aggression. The lady who purchased the books was interested in putting together a museum. The Baptist Church now owns the Raphael Semmes' house. They may give you a tour of the home if anyone is there today."

Rachel asks, "Do you have the address of the lady who purchased the Raphael Semmes archives?"

"Yes, I do. Let me get my address book out."

Rachel notices the lady has excellent handwriting. She thinks to herself that writing cursive could soon become a dying art.

"Here it is, the address and phone number. She said she was looking for anything related to Captain Raphael Semmes. You are more than welcome to browse around, but I think you will have more luck digging into the Captain Semmes papers we sold. There was a lot of material there."

Rachel and the group follow the librarian into the archives room. There wasn't much left. "I think we might better utilize our time by heading on over and seeing if we can get in touch with the person who purchased the Raphael Semmes' papers."

They leave the library and load up in their SUV. Blake types the address into the GPS. The treasure hunters take a scenic drive to the house where Captain Semmes lived until his death. They pull up to the address. Blake scans up and down the street looking for any sign of trouble. He then takes the lead and knocks on the door of the house. He thinks about his metal detecting hobby: knocking on doors, requesting permission. Getting permission to relic hunt could be tough.

Patience and practice had paid off in making it easier to get permission to hunt for artifacts. An elegant, well-dressed lady greets the team. Everything about her demeanor is pleasant.

"May I help you?" she says in a heavy Southern drawl.

Carter steps up beside Blake. "Yes, ma'am, sorry to bother you, but we are historians researching Captain Raphael Semmes."

"Yes, Captain Semmes gave many speeches in this house during his time in Mobile. I have had many folks knock on my door requesting a tour of this historical home."

"Oh, I'm sure. We're sorry to bother you. We've traveled a long way," says Blake.

"Well, come on in. I'll show you a few of the rooms. But please shut that door before my cat runs out."

The group notices a massive Maine coon about to dart out.

"Is that a cat? What do you feed him?" Carter asks.

Rachel gives Carter a quick sharp look and elbows him.

"He eats a lot. He's a good boy. Come on, Fluffy."

The team proceeds in and walks around, touring some of the front rooms.

"Not much has changed since the time Captain Semmes lived in this neighborhood. Raphael Semmes spent many social evenings in this front parlor and in the gardens in back of the house. He gave lectures here about the politics and issues of the day. As historians, I am sure you already know Raphael Semmes was very opinionated about his views on the War of Northern Aggression. Captain Semmes was also a strong proponent for States' rights."

"You sure have a nice place, ma'am. These photographs are really good. Did you take them yourself?" Christie asks, while looking at beautiful pictures that line the walls.

"Thank you. I love photography. It's been a hobby of mine for many years."

The lady pulls out some pictures and papers for the group to look at. They fumble through the pictures and articles. Rachel does not see any of the papers or books that were mentioned by the librarian. She realizes that they are wasting time.

"We were told you had purchased some diaries and memoirs related to Captain Semmes from the library. Do you still have those papers?" Rachel asks as she hands the old photographs back to the lady.

"I purchased those on behalf of my late husband."

"Do you still have them?"

"No, I got rid of those after my husband died."

"Got rid of them?" Carter asks.

"I donated them to the Maritime museum a few blocks away. My late husband had a dream of turning this place into a museum. I never had a passion for Civil War history like my husband did."

Rachel looks over at Blake, with a now-we-are-getting-somewhere look. "Well, we had better get over to that museum before the day gets away. Thank you so much for your hospitality." The team exits the historic home and loads up for the next stop.

Rachel bites her lip. “Surely the Maritime museum still has those records.”

While en route to the museum, the group eats sandwiches they’d prepared before they left the hotel. The four had anticipated a storm of researching and did not want to break the day up by sitting in a restaurant.

“I hope the day isn’t a bust!” Carter says with his mouthful.

Rachel looks at him. “No whining, Carter. We are on the right track!”

“I feel like it’s been a scavenger hunt deluxe so far.”

“It has been a little grueling,” Christie says after she finishes her sandwich.

Blake looks at the SUV’s dashboard GPS and then scans his rearview mirror. “Toughen up, team. Rachel is leading us down the right track.”

They arrive at the museum at 1:00 p.m. The curator of the museum is in the lobby and greets them as they walk in the door. “Good afternoon! Welcome to the best museum in Mobile! Are you interested in a tour?”

The curator is a lean fellow with a pencil thin mustache and round glasses.

“We are interested. Thank you!”

“It will be fifteen dollars a person.”

The group gives the curator the money and enters the museum. They begin moving around, viewing the artifacts in the numerous display cases.

“Wow, this is much better than I had anticipated!” says Rachel.

The four see many buckles, rifles, and uniforms from the American Civil War. The Captain Semmes display consists of his spyglass telescope, reading glasses, a Bible, and beautiful Confederate States Navy buttons attached to his frock coat that is on loan to the museum according to a sign in the case.

The curator comes in to check on the four. "Can I answer any questions for you?"

"We came to Mobile to research blockade runners. We started at the town library but heard some of the research material—diaries and memoirs—had made their way to your museum," Rachel informs the curator.

"I have tons of old diaries and memoirs. I am just shocked at what people get rid of. But I gladly take it off their hands."

"How about blockade running records?" asks Carter.

"We have tons of those records. Come with me to the research room."

The group follows the curator into a massive room with books from floor to ceiling. They notice several college students and an older man in the back corner sitting at a table with many antique-looking documents in front of him.

Carter starts to browse the shelves. "This is impressive, you have a ton of documents and books in here!" They all begin to pick old books off the shelves, flipping through them.

"Yes, we have so much that we haven't had time to go through it all. You may find what you're looking for here, but you'll have to discover it; no one has gone through half of these documents yet."

Thirty minutes into researching, Christie makes the discovery they have been hoping to find. "I have it. Check it out. According to the footnotes in these papers dated 1930, a library in Cuba houses a section that contains binders of blockade runner manifests. Specifically, the footnote mentions a cargo list from the *CSS Sumter*."

Carter leans over the table on his elbows. "Only one problem: Cuba's a communist country that's been under a tourist embargo for the last fifty-something years. I have heard of folks traveling there by going through Mexico but I don't think we can get there quickly."

The team shows the historical documents to the museum's curator and asks him if he has any ideas how they can get the information they are looking for.

The elderly gentleman replies, "Up until just recently, no Americans could travel directly to Cuba legally. The trend, I think, is that the embargo will slowly be lifted. You might be in luck. Only a few months ago, Cuba and America agreed to allow research visas for U.S. citizens."

The four wrap up for the day. Two others are in the research room at the end of the day working over an atlas and some maritime manuscripts. One of them is an older muscular fellow with a beard and the other is a beautiful brunette with a French accent, dark eyes, and olive skin. The team only notices the two with a cursory glance. Snuggled in a corner, the French girl, wearing a tight black skirt with white blouse and heels, points to a line in a book the older man is holding, looking at it with a furrowed brow, deep in thought.

Rachel leans forward from the backseat as they drive away from the museum. "That girl in there was a little over dressed for researching, don't ya think."

"What girl was that, Rachel?"

"Oh you know what girl, Carter!"

Carter looks back at Rachel. "I think she was from France. I caught a little of her accent, and her mannerisms, the way she moved her hands, seemed European."

"Carter, I'm impressed you could tell all of that without meeting someone," Christie points out.

Rachel rolls her eyes and looks out the window.

Chapter 47

The team drives back to Gulf Shores, sharing notes on the way. They get to their hotel rooms, shower, and get ready to watch the sunset and enjoy the evening, sitting on the restaurant deck in beautiful Gulf Shores, Alabama.

They are excited and ready to celebrate the day's research success. They order food, beer, and a round of tequila shots for a toast at a table close to the railing with a great view.

Carter points out toward the ocean. "Check out the yacht anchored over there. That's my retirement goal."

"Well then you better hope we find this treasure." Rachel smiles and raises her glass for a toast. "To a productive day of research."

Christie looks around and adds to the toast. "And to us being blessed with a miracle soon to get us to Cuba."

The adventurers raise their glasses, lick salt, and down their tequila shots for a toast, biting into lime wedges right after.

"Okay, I'm not sure how we are going to get to Cuba quickly. Blake, do you know anyone that might be able to help us get there, like tomorrow?" Rachel asks.

Blake shakes his head. "I don't think my military contacts will fly all of us there. It's sensitive due to the embargo. The way to get there is to fly through Canada or Mexico but I don't know if we can book a flight for tomorrow. I think we should make another trip a few weeks from now or next year depending on what everyone's vacation schedule looks like. We can also check out the research visa. I don't know anything about it but that might give us a direct flight to Cuba."

Carter's attention drifts out to the easy waves rolling up onto the beach. He sits his beer down, then leans forward in his chair. "Check it out. A Jet Ski is headed to the beach from that yacht over there." Carter sighs. "Must be nice to live on a boat of that size."

The team thinks nothing of the couple on the Jet Ski until they get to the beach. Blake and Carter then notice the girl looks familiar. The girl, now wearing a white bikini, is the same girl, minus her glasses, that was at the library. The girl walks by the group and gives Blake a smile.

"*Bon jour*, gentleman."

"*Bon jour*!" Carter says, grinning.

"Carter, put your tongue back in your mouth. Seriously." Rachel leans over, puts her hand under Carter's chin and closes his mouth.

The mysterious girl walks to the bar and orders a beer for her companion, an older fellow with white hair and a white beard. The man appears to be in his mid-fifties, but fit looking, wearing a loose yellow shirt and white cargo shorts. The girl also orders a round of beers for all four of the explorers and heads over to the table.

"Hey, she is coming over here," Carter whispers and nudges Blake.

"Beautiful sunset! Don't you agree?" The man says to the group as he approaches the table.

"Yes, it's quite a view," Carter says, while looking in the opposite direction towards the young lady.

“My name is Flint Mason, and this is my beautiful wife, Josephine.”

“Wife?” Carter says. “Sorry, did I say that out loud?”

Flint laughs. “Yes, I’m a lucky man.”

Josephine smiles. “I’m the lucky one!” She leans in and kisses Flint on the cheek. “You can call me Josie.” She puts the beers on the table.

“May we join you?” Flint asks.

Blake, Carter, Christie, and Rachel look around at each other.

“Sure, pull up some chairs,” Blake says, as Rachel kicks him under the table.

“I noticed you were at the Maritime museum,” Rachel says, she then takes a sip from her longneck bottle.

“Oh yeah! I remember seeing you two there,” Carter says.

Flint leans over with his elbows on the table and his hands clasped. “We are here researching blockade runners, like you.”

“How did you know we were here researching blockade runners?” Rachel asks.

Flint leans back in his chair. “First, let me tell you a little about myself. I am a treasure hunter, like you all. I am passionate about historical preservation. I am a descendent of a soldier who served on board the CSS Alabama Confederate States Steamer with Captain Raphael Semmes. I think you will find I have some information I can share that will interest you.”

Flint piques the group’s curiosity. They scoot their chairs closer to the table. He pulls out a clear plastic protector sleeve, tucked in a carry pouch on his belt under his shirt, which contains a yellowish aged piece of paper with old English style cursive writing on it. The paper is torn in half. "As you can see, I am searching for the other half of this document. It was written from the Southern Confederacy Capitol."

Blake and Carter could not help noticing, much to the annoyance of Rachel and Christie, the beauty of Flint's raven-haired wife. She looked to be about the same age as them, early thirties, late twenties perhaps. Flint, upon closer examination, had to be in his early fifties, but was in such great shape that he might be much older. Flint carried himself with confidence, his dark Caribbean tan complimenting his muscular physique.

Flint takes another big swig from his longneck bottle. "My document is one half of a clue to the treasure your group has been researching for some time. I have been researching the same treasure, and I suspect you may have the rest of the information or a clue that will lead us to it."

"Why should we trust you?" Rachel asks.

"Why not? You need information and you have already seen that libraries are getting rid of primary sources. Diaries and documents are getting shuffled around resulting in their destruction or being boxed away in some storage area. You can either continue your wild goose chase, or we can share what we know with each other and find the treasure. I have searched on and off for years, and I am no closer than when I started. We have found treasure, but I want to solve the mystery of this document my ancestor left me."

Blake clears his throat. “We did find a clue. It is a box with a brass name plate, with the words ‘Raphael Semmes, Captain of the CSS Alabama’ on it. Inside was a CSS decoder encryption device. We also found a piece of paper that said ‘The secret lies within the Lady Sumter’s cargo manifest. God bless the Southern Confederacy.’ We think that there could be a clue in the missing cargo manifest list that could shed some light or give us another clue on what so far has been the treasure hunt of a lifetime. Whatever is hidden must be of great importance for there to be this many intricate layers of clues.”

Flint leans back in his chair. “I agree. Have you learned of a ship’s manifest for the Sumter and where that would be located?”

Rachel answers, “Yes. From our visit and research at the museum we learned that there are archives boxed away in Cuba that could have records of blockade runners, ships manifest and cargo lists. Christie here, discovered a specific footnote that mentioned a cargo manifest for the Sumter.”

“Remarkable, that one young lady has discovered such simple information that we need to solve this mystery. The files must be in Cuba!”

“We suspect so,” Rachel says. “We just can’t figure out how to get there quickly to find out. Our vacation time is about up for the year.

Flint laughs. “Well that’s the easy part for me! I have the transportation to Cuba right there.”

“Lucky you, how about us?” Carter says with a frown.

"If you have passports, I'm willing to help my fellow historians out. We can all win from this little journey." Flint leans in towards the group.

"I don't know about this," Christie whispers to Rachel.

"You can check out the credentials for our salvage company on the Internet, here is my card. My company has assets, equipment, and personnel that can help you on your treasure hunt, and like I said before it has been a very personal quest to find this treasure due to having this clue passed down through my family. The clue was in a seaman's chest stuck neatly in the family Bible when I came into possession of it."

"When do you need to know our answer?" Rachel asks.

Captain Flint lights a cigar, takes a puff, then says, "I'm leaving tomorrow morning."

"In the morning! That soon?" says Carter.

"Well, you all have my card. I can promise you that if you decide to partner up with us, that when you meet the rest of my crew you will be very impressed. I have brought together a treasure hunting team that has the highest integrity and a completely professional work ethic. The mission statement of our company is we serve the people of western civilization by preserving the precious history that has been passed down by our ancestors. Give us a chance and I can promise you an adventure you will never forget. Please give me a call later tonight, and let me know your decision. We will be docked right off the coast on my ship the Francois De Grasse."

Flint and the beautiful Josie bid the party goodnight and head back to their ship on their Jet Ski.

“What do you all think?” Carter asks.

“He sounds legit. I mean this might be our only way to get there this year,” says Rachel.

“It’s true, I have been racking my brain on how to get us to Cuba on this vacation and this might be our best bet,” Blake tells the group.

“Well, we better get a good night’s sleep. Sounds like we’re heading to Cuba tomorrow!” Christie says, as she finishes her beer.

Chapter 48

The Cuban-bound explorers rise at sunrise and check out from their hotel.

Blake calls Flint. "We're in! How do we get out to your boat?"

"Meet us at the dock. Ring us and I'll send someone from my crew to shore."

The group arrives onboard the *De Grasse*, with several of the crew and captain there to greet them.

"Top of the morning to you! My first mate, Sergeant McHann, will guide you to your cabins. I would like for all of us to meet in the sky lounge as soon as you are settled in."

Blake, Rachel, Carter, and Christie head to Captain Flint's sky lounge meeting room once they've dropped their bags in their room. Sausage biscuits, mimosas, and bottled beer are made available to the guests.

Blake walks over to the windows of the sky lounge and looks out, "Check it out there is a helicopter that is approaching us."

Flint walks in with a warm welcoming smile. "I am thrilled to have your group onboard. A seventeen-person crew runs the *De Grasse*. The weather forecast calls for calm seas over the next few days. Never can tell though about this part of the world, as a storm can brew up with little or no warning." Captain Flint looks out towards the helicopter that is preparing for descent onto the helipad. "We have one more guest that is arriving. Here now, let's have a toast to treasure, adventure, and new friends."

Blake and Carter opt for the beers. Rachel and Christie have mimosas in hand. They raise their bottles and clink them together.

“Have a seat and we’ll get started." The captain passes around printouts. “I have here what I suggest as our itinerary for our Cuba excursion, places that can be visited in relative safety. These locations and tips are what I recommend from the times we have visited Cuba in the past. The food vendors and restaurants I have marked on the maps are reputable.”

Rachel studies the map. “This is very detailed.”

“Thank you. And be aware you will see a great deal of poverty. Children may ask you for money. In the evenings, the salsa bars are full of some great dancing and action. They are a blast. Cuba can be a fun place, just keep an eye on your surroundings and be prepared. It is a communist nation.”

Blake folds up his map and puts it in his pocket. “I think this is going be an awesome experience. I have only been on the base. I think we will be a little blown away by it. There is a great opportunity for the country to one day capitalize on American tourism again.”

“Exactly, Blake. It’s unfortunate that more people do not realize what Cuba offers. After so many years under an embargo, a lot of the Cuban infrastructure is in ruins. Americans on the mainland do not realize that you can travel here legally just not by a direct flight from the U.S.A..”

“I can’t wait to get there. I have always wanted to photograph Cuba,” Christie says.

“Oh, here comes my first mate. He has something to share with you that I think you will find interesting.”

Sergeant McHann, wearing a green camo cap, introduces himself. "We're glad that you're here. We sort of met each other before today. I was on the ridge laying rifle cover for you in the jungles of the Amazon. A fellow crewman and I shadowed your movements. It was tough. You guys walked a long ways into the jungle. When you got in trouble, we stepped in and helped out. Those villagers scared the heck out of that small army the way they came at them screaming. I thought it sounded like the Rebel yell! The bad guys ran right into my line of fire. Initially, we were watching y'all to see what you knew about the treasure. Please don't hold that against us. We talked about it and decided you guys are the real deal and are serious about treasure hunting."

"You've been following us? Why didn't you mention that earlier?" Rachel perks up and asks.

"I thought it might scare you off, and our intentions are good," says Captain Flint with outstretched hands.

Carter leans over and reaches for his beer on the table. "That's remarkable. Thank you, we were in a tight spot. Your shots took out several of their men. I thought we must have had a guardian angel watching over us."

Rachel gives Carter a sharp look.

"You're welcome. We were glad to be of service. We saw you were in danger and needed help. It doesn't hurt that we think you guys are on to a substantial treasure," says Sergeant McHann.

"But still, you've been following us? I'm sorry, but that kind of freaks me out," Rachel says, as she furrows her eyebrows, narrows her eyes, and puts a finger to her chin.

"Look, bottom line is we're after the same thing. We don't want to cause you any harm. We want to act as partners," says Captain Flint, as he crosses his arms.

"How did you get on our trail?" Rachel asks Flint.

Flint uncrosses his arms and rubs the back of his neck. "Honestly Rachel, we want to provide you all the security you need to gather the clues once we land in Cuba."

"Blake nudges Carter to look out the window towards the helicopter."

Carter turns to look out at a woman with red hair stepping out onto the landing pad. "Is that Pam? What is she doing here?"

Rachel looks over at Carter. "Who's Pam?"

Carter squirms uncomfortably, "Oh, it's just a friend."

Rachel squints her eyes at Carter, "Carter, what exactly is going on and how do you know this Pam person?"

Captain Flint opens the sky lounge door to the outside. "Welcome aboard. It's good to see you." Pam gives Captain Flint a slight hug and kiss on his cheek.

Pam is wearing a tight black short sleeve shirt and black pants. "Hi Carter, Blake."

Captain Flint makes introductions, "This is a dear friend of ours who provides us with … information from time to time.

"Yes, well. That's what I do, provide intelligence. I worked at MI6 British intelligence for a number of years, but now I work for a corporation providing security services." Pam turns to Carter. "No harm meant, Carter. I typed your buckle's motif into my company's database and got a hit. Captain Flint has a puzzle he has been working on for a number of years. I contacted Captain Flint to see if he had ever been able to solve what his mysterious letter meant. The letter as you know was written from the Southern Confederacy Capitol."

Chapter 49

After the Cuban officials check the boat in Cienfuegos, the team gathers their gear for the day and prepares to depart to find the library.

"Anyone else coming?" Carter asks.

"Just me, my boy!" says Flint with his chest up, breathing the fresh air. "The crew will watch the boat."

"How about Josie, or Pam?"

"Josie is not a morning person. She'll get up later and do some research and Pam will be out on the sun deck today catching up on some r and r. She will be flying out tomorrow to meet a client somewhere on the globe. Pam stays busy"

Rachel mumbles under her breath, "I'm sure she'll find time to grace us with her presence soon enough."

Even though the group knows to expect it, they're astonished to see so many classic American cars on the streets of Cuba. While they're mostly from the fifties, a few modern cars dot the roadways. Even so, the island's amenities are nowhere near what the group is accustomed to back in the States.

Flint puffs on his cigar, sweat rolling off of him. "Due to the embargo put into place in 1962, the Cuban people have become very resourceful. Imports of Soviet-era cars and new Russian engines keep the classic American cars running."

"Are we going to get a car to travel around in?" Christie asks.

"I think our best option is to travel on foot," says Flint.

"Are you sure? Here comes a taxi," Christie points at a yellow, rusty-looking vehicle. The vehicle turns on the corner next to the group and the door flies open, dangling from the hinges. "Hmm, maybe not."

"No ma'am. Our best bet is on foot, it is not far, only a few blocks."

The team is intrigued at the mixture of the various styles of Spanish and Cuban rhumba music. The constant sound of horned instruments and guitars fills the air. A music festival is also going on. The smell of rum and cigars lingers in the air. The music permeates throughout the bars and street corners, with the locals dancing and keeping beat to the rhythms. Many of the buildings are very old and in a state of utter decay. Some are painted every brilliant color of the rainbow, others beautiful and vibrant at one time in the past show paint peeling off.

Carter drops money in a street performer's guitar case. "This place could use some capitalism. I have never seen such poverty."

Flint wipes the perspiration from his face with a small towel. "Cuba cries out for modern upgrades. No new structures have been built in the last sixty-five years. The city stopped in its tracks in the 1950's when the communist revolutionaries took power. The people, as a whole, are kind, humble, and hospitable, but poverty is everywhere and the black market is a way of life. Another thing you will notice is the absence of technology, like smartphones, that people in the States are always gawking at while walking and driving around. Those items are scarce here."

"What do people do around here to make money?" asks Christie.

Flint lights up another cigar. "There really isn't a sense of 'making money.' There is only a sense of surviving. The rural ranchers in the countryside work very hard harvesting tobacco, sugar, rice, and, potatoes. Rural farmers in Cuba mostly use oxen pulled plows and organic techniques to work their crops due to shortages in fuel and pesticides. Most of the food is imported and rationed by the government."

"That's horrific," says Carter.

"That's just the way it is here. You are either rich or poor. There is no in between."

Blake, Rachel, Carter, Christie, and Flint reach the public library in Cienfuegos after walking for a few blocks. Rachel leads the way into the beautiful Italianate style building. "I am excited about this library, the Captain of the CSS Alabama and Sumter, Raphael Semmes referenced Cienfuegos in his letters. The Sumter captured eight US merchant ships in July 1861 off the southern coast of Cuba. Every one of those ships was taken to the Cienfuegos harbor. The Sumter then took on water and coal here."

"I'm impressed. You really have done your research. Cienfuegos has not changed much since 1861. It has retained many of its original buildings because it's in a bay and is protected from hurricanes."

They all enter the teacup archways of the library and walk over the marbled tile floor, past the patrons sitting at tables drinking coffee and reading. They approach the front desk.

Flint begins speaking to the librarian in Spanish. He translates to the team. "He said we can go ahead and check out the research room."

The librarian leads them to a locked room in one of the back corners.

The group enters into the room, and they see that there are tons of boxes stacked up. Like many research rooms there would be lots of documents waiting to be rediscovered after having not been touched for decades.

Carter looks around. "We'll never be able to get through all of this."

"We better get busy and see what we can find," Rachel says, as she flips the cover off one of the boxes.

Blake grabs a box. "Alright, team! Everyone grab a box and let's dig."

After about twenty minutes of searching, Blake looks up with a map in his hands, "I think I have found something. Check this out."

Blake shows the other explorers an old map identifying a tavern with a small St. Andrews flag mark next to it.

"I wonder if this landmark is still here on the island?" Blake continues, "Perhaps—"

"Wait, guys! Wow! Look at this!" Rachel pulls out an aged binder that has 'Cargo Manifest of the CSS Sumter' written on the front.

"X marks the spot! That's what I'm talking about," says Carter. They open the binder and start looking through the papers. "There it is, the other half of the paper," says Flint, rubbing his head, his eyes wide and a half smile on his face. "I can't believe it, after all of these years."

Chapter 50

Everyone gathers together on the yacht for dinner and a celebration. Fresh mahi-mahi and drinks are enjoyed. Rachel pulls out the torn half piece of paper found at the Cienfuegos library and matches it up with Flint's half. She uses the CSA decoder she found in Virginia to translate the encrypted letter.

"From what I can tell from satellite maps, the coordinates lead to a cove in Northern Spain near Santander, at a site where a fort once stood." Rachel points at her laptop.

Blake leans over. "Looks like the spot is abandoned, with only a few ruins there."

Carter looks over their shoulders. "It is very secluded. The closest structure is several miles away."

Rachel jumps up from her chair. "We gotta get there! I can't wait to check this place out."

Blake swirls his tequila on the rocks and looks at Rachel. "But what about the tavern from the map I found in the library?"

"Blake, we don't have time for that. The pieces are finally coming together. We need to get to Spain."

"All I'm asking for is a couple of hours. Who knows when we'll get back here?"

"I don't want us to get sidetracked."

Carter drums his fingers on the round marble table. "Looks like it's a good place to metal detect. Might find some treasure there, too."

"Shut up, Carter. We don't have time to metal detect in Cuba."

"Don't have time to metal detect? We can always make time to metal detect!" Blake and Carter laugh, but Rachel is furious.

"Hey, what's all this yelling about?" Flint comes in with a bottle of wine. "I think you all need a glass of wine to relax. This is a bottle that I have been saving for a special occasion such as this. I think this is one of the best days of my life."

Josie clears her throat.

"Well, next to marrying you, *mi amor*."

Josie begins whispering in French and nuzzling up to Flint.

"Okay, that's all great, but we're in a heated debate at the moment," says Carter.

"I can tell! I'm shocked, considering our great finds today."

"That's what we're fighting about. The coordinates lead us to Spain. I think we need to go now and the guys think we need to go to this random site they've found."

"Spain. Hmm … the coordinates lead there?"

"Yes! See." Rachel brings her laptop over to Flint.

"Excellent. We will go. But not yet."

"What?" Rachel shouts. "Why not?"

"There is a tropical storm moving north. We won't be impacted here, but we can't travel through it. Just too risky."

Rachel plops down in a chair and crosses her arms. "I guess then we have time to tour the tavern."

"Yes!" The guys high-five each other.

"Rachel, would you like a glass of wine?" Flint offers a glass to Rachel.

"Got anything stronger?"

"You know I do!" Flint laughs.

*

The next day, the team heads out to Blake's site, in a rented dual-wheel truck, to investigate the coordinates he uncovered.

Carter asks, "Blake, why didn't we rent a jeep instead."

Blake smiles. "I think we should think positive. I have a feeling we're going to find something really cool."

Blake's coordinates lead them near the El Nicho Park. "We're lucky the coordinates didn't land us in the park. Only guided tours are allowed in the park."

They drive into the El Nicho Valley on a dirt road, passing along a beautiful river and through a small rural town. Coming over a hilltop the team see their destination. They pull up to a Spanish colonial style house near the park's edge. They approach the old stone structure and walk in.

"Check it out, this place is still an actual tavern!" says Carter.

"American tourists. Come on in. We don't get many of you anymore. This tavern has been in business for over two hundred years. We were once a thriving business, with visitors from all over the world, but now we're the favorite local hangout."

Blake and Carter take a seat at the bar, as the girls standing behind them look around at the autographed pictures of Hollywood stars from before the revolution.

Blake turns his head towards the tavern owner. "Your English is very good."

"My dad was a great businessman, we did a lot of entertaining. All of the famous American stars came through these doors back in the day. My father was adamant about teaching me English. Little did he know, that we would be in the state we're in now. Anyway enough about my problems, can I get you something to drink?"

"Actually, we found an old map with this tavern on it. Next to the tavern is a symbol," Blake points to the symbol on the map. "Behind the tavern it has the words sugar plantation."

Blake hands the tavern owner the map. The tavern owner pulls out his reading glasses and studies the map for a second.

"I might have something you will be interested in seeing." The tavern owner leads Blake and the group upstairs. "My dad told me that American Civil War soldiers visited here and wrote on the upstairs walls." The owner enters an old room decorated in Queen Victoria style. "We rent this room out to the tourists that travel to the park nearby. It is a popular room."

He removes an old picture of a blockade steam runner with dual stacks titled CSS Robert E. Lee.

Christie kneels down to snap a photo of the picture. "This is a really cool picture. I haven't seen a print of it before."

The tavern owner stands aside revealing a Masonic emblem on the wall, along with writing out beside it. Beside the emblem are soldiers' names and the regiments they served in.

"This has been here for a long time as you can see. My wife wanted to paint over this, but I think it is important to preserve history."

Carter looks from the writing on the wall to the tavern's owner. "Absolutely! We need more people like you in America. History is important. Like Mark Twain said, 'History might not repeat itself exactly, but it sure will rhyme closely.'"

Blake explains the history to the tavern owner. "Havana, Cuba was a major trading post during the time of the America Civil War. Blockade-runners, like the one in the picture there, would run past the Union's blockade of the southern ports. Soldiers were likely stationed here at this plantation doing guard duty to protect something or someone. This writing here is a clue."

Blake reads aloud:

Follow by a day's ride the pony's doubtful trail. The trail of shallows and hill. The right way is contentious and later on will look to be golden indeed. The Tennessee Army Regiments are numerous and like the Spartans of old will be victorious over the North's War of Aggression. From this tavern I was here on 7/13/1861. I was born on 5/19/1835.

Rachel turns to the others. "This sure looks like a treasure clue to me."

Blake replies, "It is odd the soldier didn't leave his name but his birthdate."

Rachel pulls out her personal laptop from her backpack and sets up her satellite connection. After a minute of searching Rachel turns her laptop around. "Check this out, I have a soldier here that might be a match, a lieutenant William Dagger that served aboard multiple blockade runners. He has the same birthdate. Could he be the soldier who left this clue?"

"Either he is the soldier or that is one strong coincidence. Maybe he didn't sign it because of the war going on?" Carter says, while rubbing his head.

Blake asks the owner, as he swings his hand back and forth, "Can we look around with our metal detectors for signs of the soldiers?"

"I guess that will be alright. I would be interested in seeing what you find."

The owner takes them behind the house. There he leads them to a trail that goes off to a gorgeous swimming hole with crystal blue waters and a waterfall.

"We have found lead bullets on top of the ground here in this area."

Blake looks down, watching his step, and keeping an eye out for surface relics. "Those bullets are a good sign of military activity here."

Blake and Carter put their coils to the ground. Blake's first hole gives up a .58 caliber three-ringer bullet. Carter digs a coin, bottle top, and then digs an 1860's three-ringer bullet.

Rachel and Christie opt for the swimming hole. Rachel gets out of the water and sits on a rock for a minute enjoying the beauty of the lagoon.

Something catches her eye, an even carved line beneath some moss on a rock wall near the waterfall.

Brushing away some vines and old moss, she sees a Masonic symbol along with the all-seeing eye. Moving more of the vines away reveals a St. Andrews Cross.

Rachel yells to the team, “I found something, check out the symbols on this rock wall!”

The team pulls moss and vines from the rock. They find crevices and edges along the rock wall. With a little muscle, a portion of the rock wall opens out to them, revealing an entrance to a cave.

“Do you think this is safe to go in there?” Christie asks.

“No, it’s not safe, but we came here for an adventure, right?” Blake says, as he begins to lead them down a set of stairs cut into the rock.

Carter, right behind Blake, upon reaching the bottom of the stairs, begins running from one corner of the room to the other taking lids off of wooden boxes and crates. “Look! Gun powder, muskets lining the wall, crates of miniè balls. Hey, there is a chest over there!”

The team runs over to the small chest and opens it.

“Can you believe this?” Carter asks.

“I’ve never seen this much gold!” Blake picks up a few of the coins. “There must be over two hundred coins here. At over a thousand dollars a coin this is going to be a good haul.”

“Mission complete. Can we take the gold and go home?” Christie laughs, while picking up several of coins.

Carter turns to the team. “Hey there is another box over here!” He opens it up and discovers original Confederate uniforms with infantry cast “I” buttons sewed onto them.

"Look at this. Some of these uniforms are for officers and they have the down turned eagle staff officer's buttons."

Carter opens another box and discovers five stunning two-piece English made CS sword belt buckles with their CSA swords attached to the leather part of the belts. Blake, Carter, and the girls are stunned by their discovery.

Carter's flashlight falls onto some writing on the wall. "I have a feeling our adventures are just beginning. Take a look at who left us a message on the wall."

On the wall, the message reads:

Many have perished in our just cause. Please protect and preserve these supplies for a day when we most need them.

Commander of the Sumter
Raphael Semmes

"Unbelievable!" Rachel says, as a shiver goes through her.

"Y'all, we've got to get this treasure loaded onto the truck, pronto!" says Blake.

"I spotted a side road that we can use to get the truck closer."

"Good eye, Carter! You and Christie go get the truck. Rachel and I will stay here and guard the treasure!"

"10-4!" Carter says, then he and Christie dart up the hill to get the truck. They drive the truck down the side road closer to the treasure.

Blake walks out of the treasure cave. "Let's load it up!"

Driving out of the lagoon, Blake says to Carter, “Stop by the tavern, I want to show our respects to the owner.”

“Blake! We have got to get back to the ship now!”

“What’s the problem, Carter? We have plenty of treasure here. Let’s share some of it.”

Carter stops the truck and slams it into park, looking out his side window to see if anyone is watching them. “Blake I didn’t want to bring this up before but metal detecting is illegal in Cuba. Folks do it but …”

“Oh! Thanks, Carter, for telling me now that we have a load of treasure. Wait here. I will handle this.”

Blake shows the owner of the tavern the Civil War bullets and hands the tavern owner all of the remaining Cuban cash he has in his wallet. “I want you to have this. You have a great appreciation for history preservation. We appreciate you letting us explore with our metal detectors and we want to show you our gratitude. We are headed home tomorrow and won’t be needing our Cuban money.”

The tavern owner is appreciative and happy to receive the substantial amount of cash. They shake hands and Blake wave’s goodbye as he gets back into the truck. The group drives off towards their waiting ship with the Civil War relics under a tarp in the back.

Christie has the gold coins in her day bag.

Flint is pacing, waiting on them to arrive so they can prepare to ship off to Spain. “Y’all have been gone all day! Did you have any luck?”

“Like you wouldn’t believe,” says Blake.

They back the truck right up to Flint's yacht and put the larger boxes onto pallets. Flint uses the ship's small deck crane to load the relics onto the ship.

"Nice work. Glad we're on the same team." Flint activates the deck crane and raises the treasure onto his yacht.

Christie opens her day bag to show Flint the gold coins.

Flint leans over and his eyes grow wide. "We had better put these into some protective bins."

Rachel raises her eyebrows. "I think the coins are fine where we have them."

"Trust me. They need protection. If we get searched, nothing will be found." Flint smiles and winks at Rachel and Christie.

Rachel and Blake meet up later to celebrate in private. They take their cocktails to a table on the balcony outside of Rachel's cabin to enjoy the evening sunset. Blake has in his hand, two gold coins that he had picked out of the treasure chest. He hands one to Rachel. "Look at how these coins shine with the Caribbean sunset hitting them. They look like they were minted yesterday."

Rachel smiles. "Breathtaking. Your instincts were right to explore the tavern."

Rachel slides her hand on top of Blake's.

"Is it hard for you to admit I was right?" Blake caresses Rachel's hand.

"I know I can be bossy, but I can also be nice." Rachel purses her lips.

Blake reaches over and kisses Rachel. "How nice?" Blake's hand moves down Rachel's back.

Rachel runs her hands across Blake's chiseled muscular chest. "Let's go inside and I can show you."

In Rachel's cabin the two embrace. Blake kisses Rachel's neck. The moon glitters off of the ocean and the gold coins.

Chapter 51

The adventurers prepare to set sail to Spain. Captain Flint readies the boat and crew for a speedy journey.

Christie asks, "Spain is a long ways away. How long do you think it will take to get there?"

"On most boats, it can take one to two weeks."

Carter looks at Flint with both hands on the side of his head. "We don't have a couple of weeks to spare! I mean some of us have day jobs!"

"Not to worry, my boy. This is not just any boat. This is one of the fastest yachts in the world. My goal is to have you there in only a few days."

The group relaxes and enjoys the journey. Captain Flint averages 50 to 70 knots to get them to their destination in three days.

Morning arrives off the eastern coast of Spain. Everyone comes to the deck. The team is well rested and ready for the next adventure. The sun's rays stream through the shadows of the old lost fort that they had been studying for the last two days.

Carter stands with his hands on the boat's rail. His hooded parka keeps a slight mist off of him. "Flint's ship has brought us right to where the main part of the structure would have once stood. Only ruins now. No one would ever suspect a building of historical significance once stood here."

"We're going to find something really good here. I can feel it," says Rachel.

An inflatable landing craft is readied to take them to shore. Flint brings two armed men with him to join Carter, Blake, Christie, and Rachel. First mate Sergeant McHanns stays on board the yacht. The water glows a soft silverfish aqua blue. A tint caused by the particular algae growth in this part of the world. Soft spray clips off the group's faces and parkas as the landing craft carries them to shore. Blake carries his favorite pistol, his .45 caliber stainless steel 1911. Rachel carries her black 9 mm pistol due to its minimal recoil. The craft comes to a soft landing on the shell-covered beach. No one is around due to the isolation of the location.

Carter pulls the hood of his parka back. "Man, this place looks like a scene out of a sci-fi movie. These rock formations are incredible."

Christie looks over at Carter. "There are stories that dragons lived in these cliffs a long time ago!"

Moss hangs from the nearby trees and vines grow on the ruins of the large, rock hewed, fort walls.

Blake climbs over the uneven rocks. "This place has completely fallen down. I don't see how any clues could still be here after this amount of deterioration."

Rachel, looking down watching her step, says, "I am sure the captain of the CSS Alabama would leave us a clue that could survive a hundred years. The clues in the archives of the library in Cienfuegos were intact and relatively easy to find once you knew what you were looking for."

Blake makes out holes in the structure's walls where cannon shells had hit long ago. The explorers continue past the fallen debris and enter into a section of the fort where the archways and some rooms were still intact. They continue farther into the fort, walking through crumbling archways, probing the walkways and arches to make sure the structure is stable enough for visitors. Carter spots a small St. Andrews cross on one of the bricks on the wall in front of him. "Hey guys, I've found something." Carter wiggles a brick. "I think this brick will pull free from the wall," he says, and with that the brick slides out from the wall.

Rachel, standing behind him, says, "Careful there, Carter. We don't want this wall to collapse."

"I wouldn't have thought anything about that symbol if Blake hadn't made his discovery in Cuba."

Rachel looks at Carter in shock and dismay. "What, you would have missed that symbol. Really!"

Carter looks at Rachel and rolls his eyes, shaking his head, muttering.

Under the brick is a large round brass button. Carter looks over at Captain Flint. "Should we press the button?"

"It could be booby trapped somehow. I hate to blow us up if we're sitting on a powder magazine. But we've come this far and we need to see this through!" Captain Flint steps over and presses the button. A rolling sound starts to occur and a squared section of the floor in a corner of the room slides to the side and up under the wall.

Christie pumps her fist. "Yes! Now that's what I'm talking about! We're on a roll now. Two hidden chambers in one week."

Captain Flint holds his hand out. "Let's be careful. We don't know what might be down there."

Rachel moves forward. "I'll go first. I know what to look for if there are any booby traps.

Blake says, "You sure, Rachel?

"I've got this." Rachel descends down the stone steps into a room with brick-lined walls and wooden shelves. "Wow, this is a library. Look here, these books are very old."

Blake unrolls a parchment. "Check it out. Look at the date on this map. This map shows ancient shipping routes that date back to biblical times."

Old documents and records that are military in nature are also stacked on shelves in a section of the room. The records in that section all have war dates between 1861 and 1865.

Carter pulls a map out of a long brass cylindrical sleeve and unrolls it on the table. Carter and Blake stare at the map in front of them in disbelief. Blake points at the markings on the map. "Can you believe what we have discovered? These marks indicate Union and Confederate Civil War camps. Check it out. There are marks on here for camps and picket posts all over North Mississippi, North Alabama, Tennessee, and Georgia."

Carter holds the map down to keep it from rolling. "I had read there were maps like this and you heard rumors of them existing, but anytime we inquired about it at the library all we got was 'don't know anything about that.' I can't wait to get home and check out some of these sites."

Blake shines his light over to the bookshelf. "It looks like lots of war records were smuggled to this location after or during the war. Truly remarkable."

Chapter 52

The adventurers descend another flight of steps that take them down a low long stone and brick corridor. At the end of the corridor they come out into a large cavern. In the dark water below them, moored to a dock, is an old screw sloop-of-war.

"Are you seeing what I'm seeing?" Blake asks, as he shines his flashlight along the entire length of the ship. "Carter run around to the back of this ship and see if there is a name on its stern!"

Carter runs around to the back of the ship. He yells back to the group, "It's got boilers! Look at this big smoke stack! There is no name on the back of the boat." Carter then brushes by Blake, clambers over the old gangplank, and boards the ship.

"Carter, slow down, be careful, that wood might collapse in some places." Blake remains on the dock in case the deck is too weak to support both of their weight.

After examining the ship's wheel, Carter, trying to catch his breath, runs over to the ship's bulwark, leans over, and placing both hands on the rail, yells, "French!"

"What does it say in French?" Rachel asks while motioning her hands for Carter to get it out.

"*Aide toi et dieu t'aidera.* God helps those who help themselves." Carter takes a deep breath and smiles.

Blake rubs the side of his head, thinking. "Yes, that is what was engraved on ship 290's wheel. I think the *CSS Alabama* may have survived the Civil War and we're looking at it."

"How is that possible?" Rachel asks. "I remember on a website that they recovered the same inscription on one of the bronze steering wheels from the ship that sank during the war off the coast of Cherbourg, France."

Blake crosses the gangplank to join Carter. "Perhaps this is a sister ship? Maybe to help get the enemy off the track of the real *CSS Alabama*."

Carter puts his hand on the ship's wheel and turns his head as Blake boards the ship. "That is impossible! Isn't it? The history books say that the *CSS Alabama* was sunk in the 1864 battle with the *USS Kearsarge*. Like Rachel said, they have done excavations and have even found the ship's bell."

Blake, exploring with his flashlight, walks towards the ship's stern and Carter. He shines his light on the ship's bell. "And just like this bell, it did not have any markings on it."

Flint Mason crosses the gangplank with Rachel and Christie. His men stand guard on the dock.

After walking up to the bow of the ship and probing with his flashlight, he joins the rest of the explorers gathered around the ship's wheel close to the stern. "What if the Rebels had a dream of refitting a second *CSS Alabama*? They might have been trying to rearm the South after the end of the war and make another run at an independent Confederacy."

Carter walks over and leans on the ships rail. "But ... the South didn't foresee the screw sloops-of-war becoming outdated."

Flint puts both hands on the ship's wheel and gently tries to turn it a notch. "Exactly, Carter. Unfortunately, for the CSS Alabama, the iron sides that came about from the

1862 clash of the Monitor and the Merrimack, would soon make the wooden cruisers, like the CSS Alabama, obsolete." Flint gazes out across the deck of the beautiful vessel as the team's flashlights illuminate it.

"Maybe we should explore below deck to see if there are clues inside?" says Rachel.

"Do you think it's safe?" Christie asks.

"Probably not," says Carter, jumping up and down on the deck.

They spread out and begin to explore the ship.

Rachel finds her way deep into the ship and reaches the captain's quarters. "Everyone, come here! I've found something."

The group enters into a spacious cabin. Rachel is holding up an old round object.

"What is it?" Christie asks.

"It's a decoder. And not just any decoder, but another C.S.A. one."

"Let me see that." Carter takes the object from Rachel and uses the flashlight from his phone to examine it. "It is a second C.S.A. decoder. What does this mean?"

"It means we have found another clue we need to solve the mystery of the General's Relic."

Chapter 53

Each of the explorers holds the decoder examining it, then they continue exploring the captain's quarters.

Carter, standing near one of the windows in the captain's quarters with his flashlight, studies an elaborate old map on the wall. He hears a distant popping noise, like fireworks, from outside the cavern. "Hey guys, listen, do you hear that?"

Blake shouts, "Sounds like gunfire! Everyone get topside now!"

The team of adventurers runs back up the stairs. They stand on the cliff where they see, off in the distance, the sight of a .50 caliber machine gun mounted on a modern cabin boat, firing warning shots across the bow of the yacht.

"All my men have are a few AR15s! Those won't hold off that .50 caliber! We gotta help them!"

Blake looks over at Carter. "Remember those times hanging out with the reenactors, firing off those cannons?"

"Are you thinking we can get those cannons on the one-hundred-fifty-year-old battle cruiser to fire?"

"Any other suggestions?"

"It's worth a shot. Everyone back down to the cavern. It'll take all of us to make this happen."

Entering the cavern, Blake points to the outside wall. "I spotted a lever over there at the end of the dock I think will open an entranceway. Go hit that lever."

Carter runs to the lever and pulls it, but it does not budge. "It's not moving!"

"Figure out how to move it!" Blake yells back.

Carter spots a rusted metal rod close by used to rake coal. He grabs the object and hits the lever. The lever gives way and a rattling of chains occurs as a massive door is raised up, exposing an entranceway to the cavern. Dust, rocks, and debris start falling at the entrance.

Rachel looks out at the blazing sunlight shining into the cavern. "Who would of thought? The entrance to this cavern has been cleverly coated to look like a rock wall from the outside." Rachel leans over the dock. "No one was supposed to ever find this."

"Team, we need to focus on rescuing the crew!" Blake yells. "Captain Flint, you and your men get up there and prepare to throw the ropes off and man the helm. Look up at the ceiling, at the beams and pulleys. The dock is designed to catapult the ship out into the ocean where it can be brought to battle at a moment's notice. Rachel, come over here. We're going to activate these pulley devices, and springs."

Christie and Carter board the ship. Carter yells out, "Which cannon do you want to fire, Blake?"

"Seriously, Carter! The big one! Plus, everything else you can load, pronto!"

"That big one looks dangerous!"

"Do it, man! Get a man from Flint and get on it!"

Carter shouts, "Captain Flint, have your men move some of those rifled shells and case shot over to the forward-most two cannons! And when they are done, I need all hands on deck to load this big Blakely pivot gun!"

Rachel and Blake pull the levers along the wall to activate the springs and chains in the rails along the top of the cavern. Dust and debris fall from the rails above as the chains start to move.

The big sleek battle cruiser bows away from the dock, water gushes up in waves, as the ship lines up and exits its one-hundred-fifty-one-year-old hiding place like it is fired out of a slingshot. Carter swabs one cannon, loads it, and packs it, while Flint and his men do the same with the cannons across the bow. Everything is there to load the cannons, most importantly the friction primers and powder packs. Carter, experienced in firing cannons from his reenacting days, moves from cannon to cannon sighting them in on their fast approaching target that has not seen them, yet.

Captain Flint and his men pull the ropes attached to the primers on Carter's yell, "Fire!"

On firing, the captain of the enemy cruiser gets only a glimpse of the old battle cruiser bearing down on them. The first shot lands smack on the engine compartment creating a huge fireball explosion. The second shell lands and explodes in the middle of the boat, sending pieces of the enemy into the water. The men swab the cannons and keep up a brisk fire. Still in the fight, the machine gunner tries to swirl the .50 caliber around, before he goes down with the ship.

"He is aiming the .50 caliber at us!" Flint yells. "Get ready to fire the big one, Carter!"

Carter rushes forward to the big Blakely pivot cannon and pulls the cord, firing the hundred-pounder. The entire enemy vessel blows up, sending smoke and debris everywhere. The *CSS Alabama* continues to sail towards the burning wreckage of the enemy's ship.

"Whoa! How about that!" yells Carter, as he and the crew high-five each other.

"I'm glad the Blakely pivot gun actually fired," Carter says, as he scans the ocean to see if any there are any other enemy vessels.

"What would have happened if it hadn't have fired?" asks Christie.

"We would have been toast, just like on the day of the fight with the *USS Kearsarge*."

The gallant *CSS Alabama* drifts past the debris and burning oil left from the sunken cabin cruiser. Captain Flint radios his yacht crew to provide tow ropes for the victorious Confederate battleship.

Flint smiles. "I bet this old gal never thought she would see another smoke and fire battle. What an adventure!"

"It seems to be an endless adventure," Christie says, as she wipes the dust and gun smoke smudges from her face with a cloth.

Carter jumps down from the big gun, wiping away perspiration and gun smoke from his face. "Nothing wrong with a gunpowder facial."

"I don't know about that."

"Hang in there, Christie. The best is yet to come!" says Carter, as he hands her a bottle of water.

Chapter 54

Flint's yacht sends over the inflatable landing craft with ropes to anchor the mystery ship to the yacht to prevent it from drifting. Rachel and Blake join the others on the mysterious screw sloop-of-war. Most of Flint's crew returns to the De Grasse to keep a look out in case any more bad guys show up.

Flint Mason leans over the Confederate ship's railing to get a closer look at the hull. "There is no question that this boat is still sea worthy. We'll need to make a thorough inspection to see what repairs she needs."

Carter rests his hand on the carriage of the big Blakely Pivot gun. "After the repairs are made, can we sail her right back to the Southland?"

"Well, we've made it this far with her. We've took out some villains and saved my boat, and she is still floating!" Flint laughs and hits his hand against the old ship's hull.

"The reenactors and historians are going to go nuts upon seeing this beauty sail up. It will be a Hunley moment all over again. Pretty soon we will have the pride of the Confederate Navy restored and ready for a grand display."

Blake walks up to Flint and Carter while Rachel checks on Christie. "Wow! You guys really know how to blow some stuff up. Forrest himself couldn't have done any better. I am proud of the way you handled those guns, Carter."

Rachel walks up. "We must also remember that we still have to solve the final clues that the Confederates left for us and see where this journey will take us next."

Carter looks over with a stern look. "Rachel, can't you let us have this moment?"

Christie nudges her. "Rachel is all work and no play."

"Seriously, people, we need to stay on track."

Flint sends a request to the De Grasse that his men bring more towing ropes to secure the CSS Alabama to his yacht. "We're going to pull her in! Won't we be the talk of the town?"

Rachel flips a page over in her research journal making a note before her thought gets away. "We don't want to stir up too much chatter, we have a mission, and we don't want to be on the radar."

Carter laughs. "Too late for that, Rachel. Only a few hours ago, we were firing cannons from a hundred and fifty year old warship. That might stir up some chatter. Do we have anything to drink around here? We should celebrate!"

"Champagne?" Josie walks up with a bottle of champagne that has a good layer of dust on it.

Flint opens his arms, and smiles. "Josie, I thought you were still on the yacht."

She kisses her husband. "*J étais tellement pour toi*, Capitaine Flint." The two kiss again.

"Okay, are we going to open up that bottle of champagne?" Carter raises his eyebrows.

They pass around glasses, and Josie pours the champagne for everyone.

Flint raises his glass. "To the General's Relic!"

"To the General's Relic… I like the way that sounds!" Rachel raises her glass.

The group raises their glasses together and toast to solving the mystery of the General's Relic.

With the CSS Alabama in tow, the team head to the Spanish mainland after gathering any useful documents and maps at the fortress castle ruins. Once the CSS Alabama is docked Flint sets up security details to guard the ship. A crowd of people are snapping pictures and wondering how a Civil War battle cruiser has ended up at the docks. Thanks to the Internet, their discovery begins making headlines back in the States that same day. The group shower and then meet for drinks and food at a casual steak house. They discuss the next phase of the treasure hunt and any security issues they can think of. Blake and Rachel, holding hands, start their own conversation of the day's events.

"Blake, can you believe that the ship actually fought in a battle after all these years?"

"They don't make them like that anymore!" Blake laughs.

"I'm amazed at the preservation of the ship and at the engineering that went in to keeping it hidden it in that cavern for all those years."

"I'm wondering if we can fire the boilers up and see how fast it will go?"

Rachel looks towards Blake with a worried look. "I'm not sure, maybe, after the repairs are finished."

"I guess there is a possibility it could blow up? We'll have to let Captain Flint thoroughly examine the ship's sea worthiness."

Rachel looks out over the grassy flat lawn reaching down to the scenic pebble beach below. "We've come this far, we don't need any more unexpected roadblocks causing us trouble." She takes a drink of her red wine.

In a parking lot across from the steak house, a black SUV sits with more Shadow Seventeen men that are associated with their now deceased friends on the bottom of the Atlantic Ocean. They watch Blake and Rachel through their binoculars. "We have severely underestimated this team of amateur treasure hunters. Everything we throw at them, they kill and jump right back up. Our bosses are not going to like these failures. We're going to have to throw out an army of really tough contractors and mercenaries to take these guys out and wrap this mission up."

"Yea, let's get back to the safe house and order up some replacement men to nail this group down!" The black SUV rolls off, away from the audacious and bold crew of the newly revived CSS Alabama.

The next day starts the repairs on the ship. Blake and Carter look in the cabin for any more hidden relics and clues.

"Did you ever think that you would be here repairing the CSS Alabama?" Blake asks Carter, while carrying an old board to the other side of the ship.

"Gotta be doing something!" Carter laughs while screwing down a replacement board on a wall of the ship. "But seriously, no, I am stunned by all of this. Our research has paid off big time."

Blake swings his hammer down on a nail. "Honestly, I didn't think we would get this far."

"That's why we came here... what did you expect to happen?" Carter smiles. "Maybe you came here to find love, Blake, but I came here to get the treasure!"

Blake rolls his eyes at Carter and they continue to work on the ship.

More hidden compartments are found with small caches of gold and silver coins in them along with historically significant aged maps and documents. Each find produces more excitement, as they continue to study the caches of coins and papers. They proceed to document every item discovered to track its historical relevance and solve the mystery of the ship's providence.

"Are you boys having any luck excavating this old ship's secrets?" Rachel comes out with a few more documents.

"Yeah, we've found some clues that might be useful, but it will take a team of scientists to make a final determination of the ship's identity. This ship is such an exact replica of the CSS Alabama that I can't tell the difference between the two even with the original plans of the ship right here in front of me." Blake points to original drawing plans he had downloaded off the web of the ship 290 before it was christened the CSS Alabama. "The CSS Alabama did have some very specific repairs made after a major storm. It's also possible that the Confederacy secretly sailed both of the ships at the same time, although there is no record of that occurring. It is a real mystery."

Carter stands up from his work. "At the end of the day, it is going to be an awesome museum piece no matter what happens. It is a beautiful ship."

Rachel adjusts her sunglasses up on her nose. "I really need to get back to the States and dig into all of these clues. We have that second C.S.A. decoder. I need to use this one, along with the one that I have back at my condo, to figure out the location of the General's Relic."

"Do you think we're that close?" Carter asks.

"I need to get home. Truly, I think that we're that close, but I need to get back home to put everything together."

"I'll check with Flint to see if he can sail the CSS Alabama back to the States with the repairs that we have made so far."

"Fine," says Rachel, while looking at her smartphone. "I don't want to wait for days, sailing on the sea in Blake's new toy. Let's try to get to an airport so that we can get back home, immediately!"

"Works for me." Christie says, and smiles.

"Works for me, too," says Carter, as he sees Flint Mason walking towards them. "Captain Flint, we need to talk!"

Chapter 55

The tired treasure hunters are able to catch a flight from the Santander, Spain airport. They arrive home, exhausted and needing time to recharge. They also need to get back to their daily work schedules to earn funds to support their hobby. They all hope that soon, from their finds in Cuba and the potential finds to come, their hobby will provide the income they need to become full-time treasure hunters.

Upon returning home, Rachel is eager to put the two decoders together with the documents, maps, and buckles to see if they will produce the needed coordinates to find the General's Relic.

"This has got to give us something," Rachel whispers to herself as she starts to pencil in the codes in her journal. After a few hours of work, she stares at her paper in astonishment and picks up the phone to call Carter.

Carter wakes up from a nap and answers the phone without looking at the caller ID. "Hmm … hello."

"Northwest Alabama!"

"No, I'm in Birmingham. Rachel, is that you?"

"Carter! The treasure coordinates point to Northwest Alabama! The treasure has been right under our nose the entire time!"

"Are you sure?"

"Positive. Never been more positive of anything. You and Blake need to go explore the area to see what you can find as soon as possible. I can't get over there at the moment due to a work issue. But I will be there when I wrap things up. I am sending everything I've found in a secure email right now."

"Alright, sounds good." Carter hangs up and opens his laptop. He clicks on Rachel's email and opens it.

His eyes get wide as he examines the satellite maps Rachel sent. Carter dials Blake's number. "Hey man! Have you rested up enough?"

"I have been catching up on emails from work. What's up?"

"Rachel thinks she has the coordinates. Well, she is pretty certain, actually."

"Where do we need to go?"

"You won't believe this but Northwest Alabama. Right next to some of the fields we have been hunting for years."

"No way!"

"Seriously!"

"I am covered up with work for the rest of the week. Can we go on Saturday?"

"That sounds perfect! Let's meet up bright and early at our regular lot near the grocery store."

"See you there, man! Can't wait."

*

Blake and Carter meet up that Saturday to explore the latitude and longitude points that Rachel has provided them.

"We know this area so well. I find it hard to believe the treasure is hidden here, considering we've covered every inch of this area," Blake says, as he throws his gear into the back of Carter's jeep.

"I agree, but this land is still underdeveloped; we don't know what might have been hidden here a long time ago."

"We'll see. I hope Rachel is onto something."

To their surprise, the coordinates lead them to an outcropping of rocks on the edge of a cotton field near several cliffs.

Carter looks at Blake. "Here we are!"

"This can't be right. There ain't nothing here but boulders and cliffs. You know good and well we've already covered all of this terrain digging bullets. This place is as remote as it gets."

"Well that might mean something, Blake. I agree this is not an obvious spot to hide treasure. Maybe Walt and Henry picked this spot because it doesn't stand out. I trust Rachel's research, so let's get out and see what we can find."

They had both hunted for artifacts before along this very cliff. After a long while of walking around the base of the cliff and poking into crevices, the two are about to give up. It is growing dark and both of them have a long drive home.

"Let's call it," Blake yells over to Carter.

"Fine with me. Let's rest for a minute before hitting the road. You can't beat a country sunset like this." Carter pulls out a bottle of water and sits on the moss-covered ground.

It is an Indian summer day, making the breezeless woods a hot place to explore. Carter takes off his cap and pours some water on his head. "I thought Rachel had the right coordinates. She sounded so sure of herself on the phone."

Blake sits next to him. "Yeah, she is a sharp girl and nice looking. It's hard to find the full package these days."

"Are y'all getting serious?" Carter asks Blake, with a hint of jealousy in his voice.

"I don't know. It's hard to say with her being in Atlanta. I'm not good at long distance relationships."

"I don't think anyone can pull off long distance relationships for very long. One of you will have to give. Either Rachel will need to move to Nashville or you'll have to move to Atlanta."

"I love living in Tennessee. There are still so many relics here, and people in Middle Tennessee have a passion for Civil War history. Atlanta has become too large and citified. Nashville is growing, but it still has that small town vibe to it."

A burst of cold air hits Carter's arm from behind him. Carter glances over to Blake. "Did you feel that?"

"What?"

"I felt cold air on my arm just now, coming up from behind me."

The two move towards a bush up against the cliff base. Sure enough, cold air is moving out of a small opening from behind the bush.

Blake puts his hand in front of the small opening, feeling the cold air. "How did we miss this, man? We've walked all over this area today!"

"You know what I always say, a miss by an inch may as well be as big as the entire ocean."

The two take their shovels and soon make a small entrance just large enough for the two to squirm through. After getting some gear out of the jeep, they prepare to lower themselves down through the cave entrance.

Carter adjusts a lamp on his forehead. "It looks like we will be here for a little while longer."

Carter and Blake had explored a few caves when they were younger and had some knowledge of caving. The two descend into the cave with their flashlights and cave gear. The entrance to the cave leads to a narrow passage, a slit just large enough for the two to crawl down into. The space becomes increasingly tighter from ceiling to floor. After twenty minutes it becomes almost too small for them to continue.

Blake leading the way, calls back to Carter, "How are you doing? Should we keep going or go back? I'm not sure we'll be able to fit through here much longer. And we don't have the equipment to widen this path."

Carter replies, "We've come this far, man! We gotta get to the end of this."

They crawl through several more tight turns, then Blake yells back to Carter, "I see an opening ahead!"

Blake pops his head out of the opening and is looking down into a large room in a cave. The two climb down into the room and take stock of what they've found.

Carter shines his headlamp along the walls of the cave, and catches his breath. "Wow, this is massive!"

The room is approximately fifty feet wide and forty feet tall; either way they look, the cave stretches out down long dark tunnels.

Blake rubs sweat and dirt from his head and neck with an old rag. "It's been right under our noses all this time."

The two decide to follow the tunnel to the right. As they come around a corner, off in the distance, they spot two structures that seem out of place.

"What's that over there?" Carter points towards large objects in a corner of the tunnel.

"Looks like an old wagon. Maybe two of them. Let's get closer."

As they move closer, their eyes fall on two old, well-adorned wagons. "Blake, are you seeing what I'm seeing?"

"I can't believe this. The treasure must be in those wagons. Our Confederate friends worked hard hiding the clues to this cave. A treasure could stay hidden forever in these caverns."

Chapter 56

Blake and Carter jump into the back of one of the wagons.

"Look at these chests, Carter! This could be the jackpot!"

The chests have Civil War era locks on them. Blake breaks out an ax, determined to break off the locks.

Carter stops him. "Whoa … before you do that, remember we found a couple of keys. They might work on something besides just those boxes!"

Carter inserts a key into one of the locks and turns it. The lock falls open.

"Good call!" Blake says, watching as Carter removes the brass lock.

"Works! These keys weren't random finds! We were destined to find the treasure!"

They raise the lid of the main chest and gaze their eyes on a smaller cedar chest with a warning on the top that says: BEWARE DANGEROUS MATERIALS with a symbol of a skull and cross bones.

"Remember the diary entry that said the General's Relic could kill an entire army or city?"

On top of the chest, off to the right hand side of the warning lays a fully loaded and cocked .44 Colt revolver in its holster. Carter carefully pulls the Colt out of the holster, admiring the gun. "Blake, check it out, this gun is caked in grease and is in mint condition. Someone did a really good job of packing this gun in here."

"All the same, we'd better not open that container. Looks like the .44 was meant to be a final line of defense in case of a surprise hijacking of the General's Relic. Let's check out this chest over here."

Carter puts the gun back in its holster and closes the chest. He inserts the second key he found in the jungle into the next lock. The lock falls off and Carter opens the chest.

The other chest is full of gold coins, jewels, a neatly folded Rebel battle flag, and a Bible with markings and symbols in it. As Blake and Carter glance through the Bible, they see symbols, maps, and other clues in it. They realize it might lead to more hidden Confederate caches.

"Do you believe this?" Carter asks Blake.

"No, it is like a fairytale. Do you think this cache could be the lost gold of the Confederacy?"

"Yes, at least part of it. There is bound to be more gold hidden in places like this!"

The two begin to pick up the old coins and look through the treasure.

Carter shines his flashlight off down the tunnel. "How are we going to get this out of here?"

"We're going to need to find the original entrance. I don't think we can get these chests out the way that we came in." Blake begins flashing his light all around the cave. "I see another tunnel over there." They walk a little ways and stop.

There are two corridors that turn off from the one they had just come from. They examine the ground beneath them and can see tracks where the wagons were brought into the cave. The two come to a wall where the wagon wheel trail ends.

Blake shines his flashlight on the wall in front of them. "This is the original entrance. Walt and Henry must have sealed this up with a landslide. There might be a way out here. Give me a boost up and I'll check it out."

Carter puts his hands together as Blake places his right foot on Carter's hands lifting himself up. He finds a ledge for his left foot and shines the light upwards.

Blake jumps down. "There is a small opening to the outside up there."

Carter points towards the opening. "Can we exit here? I'm like you, I'm pretty certain we won't be able to get those big chests out the way we came in."

"There is no chance of using this exit tonight. These boulders are huge and there's no moving them." Blake looks down. "I do have an idea though. Let's try to get the entrance coordinates on our GPS, so when we come back, we will know where the entrance is from the outside."

"Good idea. We should be able to get a reading on the GPS since it seemed pretty clear outside. Hopefully no clouds have appeared since we've been in here."

The GPS is put up to the small opening in the cave, but they are unable to get a reading without getting the GPS system farther out in the open sky. The two return to the wagon, and after a minute or two of hacking with their ax they pull off a thin board from the old wagon. With rope from their backpack, they are able to devise a pole to extend the GPS system out so they can get a good reading.

"I sure hope this will help us avoid using the other entrance in the future."

"We'll see. But we gotta use the first entrance tonight to get out of here. Looks like the reading is good!" Blake saves the coordinates.

"Awesome! Let's head out! We'll try to take as much as we can with us."

"One last thing. Here, Carter, you get on my shoulders and throw this stick out. I'll tie this towel around the stick. It'll give us a solid lead on exactly where the entrance is when we come back."

The two prepare for the hike out. They begin to shove coins and treasure into their pockets and pouches. They load their bags up with as much treasure as they can carry.

"Wow, this isn't even a fraction of what's here," says Carter, as he pulls up his cargo pants and tightens his tension belt to support the weight of the coins.

"We'll get the rest soon enough," Blake says, as they walk towards the narrow passageway that they used to enter the large cave.

The two work hard, winding through the tight areas of the cave. They reach the surface and realize the treasure has weighed them down more than they thought it would.

Carter dusts himself off. "We made it out, faster than we made it in. Even with all of this weight! I don't know about you, but my adrenaline is pumping so hard I feel like I just ran a marathon!"

"Yeah, we can call this a treasure high, you know, like the runner's high."

It's getting dark and the two keep their headlamps on the ground, watching their steps, while walking back to the jeep. They keep checking their pockets to make sure they hadn't lost any of the treasure.

They crank up the jeep and head back to the parking lot to get Blake's vehicle.

“You know Blake, We should probably give that Bible, pistol, and battle flag to a museum.”

“Why do you say that?”

“It looked pretty spectacular to me. I don’t know if it should be in a private collection. Seems like people need to be able to enjoy it. Especially the flag.”

“Don’t you think that might raise some questions?”

“Like what?”

“Like, where did you find these items? What else was found there?”

“We can handle those questions. I just feel led to get those artifacts into the right hands. Plus, there is so much treasure there.”

Blake lays his head back on the seat. “Fine, Carter, works for me.”

Chapter 57

Carter pulls up to Blake's truck in the parking lot.

"I'll call Rachel on the drive home. She's not going to believe what we've found," Blake says to Carter, as he unloads his gear.

"Sounds good! You know, we can have that cave entrance opened in a few hours with a backhoe."

"Let's rent a backhoe for next weekend. Maybe Rachel and Christie can be here for that since this has been a team effort."

Carter nods. "I agree. See you next weekend, Blake! Drive back safely."

Blake reaches the interstate and dials Rachel's number.

"Hi, sorry I missed you. Leave a message after the beep."

"Rachel, its Blake. I have some exciting news to share! Call me when you can! Bye." Blake hangs up and thinks it's odd that Rachel didn't answer. He figured that she would be on pins and needles all day waiting to hear back from them. Maybe Carter went ahead and called her, he thinks to himself.

Blake gets about twenty minutes from his house and picks up his phone. "Let's try Rachel again." He dials her number and a stranger with a heavy accent answers the phone.

"Hello."

Blake clears his throat. "Um, I'm trying to reach Rachel. I must have dialed the wrong number."

"Blake, no, this is the correct number."

Blake's eyes widen, his pulse quickens, and he gets a bad feeling in his stomach. "Who is this? Put Rachel on the phone!"

"Rachel is okay. And the other girl, too."

"The other girl! You have Christie! Let me talk with them now!"

"No. Not until you give me the treasure."

"What treasure?"

"Don't play games with me, Blake. I have the coordinates here, the ones Rachel gave you. I have been tracking your team throughout your hunt. I know you have found the deadly General's Relic. I want you to show me the exact entrance to the cave."

"The entrance is buried. It can't be moved without heavy equipment."

"We will blow the entrance with explosives if necessary. Listen carefully to me I have been searching for this relic for many years, and I'm not going to let some novice hobbyists take it away from me."

"Look, you're making a big mistake. Let the girls go or you are going to be sorry."

"Blake, I'm not someone to threaten. You should look up the name Salvatore Vale and see for yourself who you are dealing with. Bring me the General's Relic or you are going to be sorry!"

Blake hears the line go dead on the other end.

Blake dials Carter. "Carter, the girls are in trouble!"

"What are you talking about?"

"I called Rachel, and a guy with a heavy accent answered her phone. He said he has Christie and Rachel. He wants us to bring him the General's Relic if we want them back."

"Then let's get it to him, the girls are more important than the treasure!"

"Carter, I don't negotiate with villains."

"Blake! He has Christie and Rachel!"

"I know, but there is no guarantee he will release them once he has the General's Relic. We need to think this through. I don't want to call the police just yet either."

"Blake, we gotta do something and soon!"

"Hang tight, I'll call you back with a plan."

Carter gets a call from Rachel's cell phone and anxiously answers the phone, knowing it must be the bad guy calling him.

"Carter, I am sure by now you know why I am calling and that I have your friends."

"You better not harm them, do you understand?"

"Hush and listen. No harm will come to the girls as long as you turn over the treasure and the General's Relic. Most importantly, don't get the police involved. If you call them—"

"I want to talk to Rachel or Christie. Put them on the phone!"

"Listen up and calm down. You give me the information I want and I'll give you the girls."

"The General's Relic is in a box buried under a mountain of dirt and rock in a cave in Northwest Alabama. You won't find it even if you have the coordinates. The cave is impossible to find unless you know exactly where to look."

"Fine. Meet me in Birmingham and escort us to the treasure," the villain says in a snide voice.

"Let the girls loose, and I will take you to the treasure!"

"No treasure, no girrr—"

"Hello, hello! Are you there?" Going through a bad area Carter loses the signal of the Shadow Seventeen leader.

"This is bad!" he mumbles to himself.

Carter fumbles with his phone and dials Blake's number. Blake answers after one ring.

"The guys we had a run in with in the jungle have Rachel and Christie!"

"I'm not surprised. People like this guy are ruthless, and they're driven to get what they want."

"Blake! You are not surprised! Man, I'm freaking out! I was on the phone with him and the signal dropped. They have told me not to contact the police, and I've got to call them back in just a minute or so."

"Carter, stay calm. Do exactly as these guys tell you to do, and we will get the girls back. I know some people who deal with these types of situations on a regular basis. Play along with the bad guys, and don't let them know that we've got a plan."

"Stay calm? I don't know how to do that right now, but if you have a plan, I will go with it. They want to meet me in Birmingham tonight and then they want me to take them to the treasure cave."

"Listen to me closely. I can track your smartphone's location as long as they don't turn off the phone. Let's stick with his plan of taking them to the treasure tomorrow. That way even if I lose track of you we will know ahead of time where the bad guys will be. We'll lure them out in the open where we can deal with them effectively."

"Are you sure it will work?"

"It'll work. My contacts in the military and law enforcement will be all over this. Look, don't worry about the how. We are going to get this scum off the streets for good this time. Trust me!"

Chapter 58

Carter gets a call.

A grizzled voice growls, "Carter, we had some bad reception on the line. Are you ready to take me to the treasure?"

"Yes, yes, I am ready."

"Now listen carefully, Carter, you are to follow my directions to our location and you are not to contact anyone. We will kill your friends if we see anybody but you."

Carter drives another forty-five minutes and follows the villain's directions. Carter pulls up to a small brick house in a simple, suburban neighborhood in Birmingham.

Carter walks up to a house and knocks on the door. A man dressed in a black shirt wearing a brown leather jacket opens the door and gives Carter a hard look. He motions his hand for Carter to enter. Carter walks in but looks to the right and notices the neighbor next door peeking under his blinds as Carter enters the house.

"Carter, I'm so—" Christie rushes towards him.

"Shut up! And sit down!" A man dressed in all black lunges towards Christie.

Sitting in the back corner of the room another man speaks up. "Glad you made it, Carter. We'll need to search you and I'll hold your phone until we have the General's Relic."

"Yeah, I am ready to fulfill my end of the bargain. Are you?"

"Absolutely." The villain gets up and walks over to a table with four chairs around it. A lamp on the table is the only light in the room.

"Sit down, relax for a minute. Would you like a drink?"

"Sure, got any whiskey?"

"Whiskey, yes, like a true Southerner."

Salvatore Vale had been in the business of dark operations for many years. As the leader of Shadow Seventeen, Salvatore was hoping that his work on this treasure hunting expedition would result in a big final payout.

Salvatore hands Carter a glass of whiskey and asserts himself. "We have a little time to fill you in on what led me to you. You see, I came upon this story buried in amongst thousands of documents in an old musty library in England. I stumbled upon some papers containing an intriguing story of lost gold and a document titled top secret with a previously unknown Confederate seal attached."

"Don't look surprised, Carter. I'm quite the researcher, like you and your team. The document I discovered, described a terrible weapon capable of inflicting massive casualties. The document also gave me a set of clues about a group of cavalrymen in the Confederate Secret Service that were the caretakers of the weapon and gold reserves. I spent years tracking the clues down across the globe. And, what do you know, a team of amateur American treasure hunters beat me to it? And then one of you shot me and killed one of my lieutenants!"

Carter's eyes widen.

"Yes, that's right! Do you recognize me now?"

"Look, you fired at us!"

"Doesn't matter now, does it? I lost a good man that day and I almost bled to death."

"That wasn't our fault. We were protecting ourselves."

"Well, look how well that's done for you. Anyway, let's get some rest this evening and tomorrow you will take us to the treasure. Then we will all part ways and get back to our lives."

Carter, Rachel, and Christie are led to a small room in the middle of the house without windows. They watch the door close and hear it lock.

Carter whispers to Rachel, "Is there any way to escape?"

"Carter, they have AK-47s and black rifles," Rachel whispers back.

"And there are a lot of them." Christie says with a fearful look.

"Did they hurt y'all?"

"No, just roughed us up a little during the kidnapping. We're fine."

"That's a relief. Blake is on our track. Don't you worry! We're going to get out of this mess soon."

Chapter 59

The door unlocks and swings open, but Rachel, Christie, and Carter have no way of knowing what time it is.

"Rise and shine! We're heading out."

Carter tells his keepers that the main entrance to the cave that houses the treasure is buried beneath a ton of rubble at the base of a hillside in the edge of a cotton field in the Tennessee Valley. "Blake and I were going to rent a backhoe to open up the main cave entrance. You will never be able to locate the entrance to the cave without us showing you where it is. Let the girls go, and I will take you to exactly where the General's Relic is. At that point you will have the weapon and treasure in your possession."

Salvatore takes a sip from his coffee mug and slowly places it on the table. He looks up at Carter. "No, I've had enough trouble with finding the treasure and weapon. I will keep all of the security around me I can get. We have will blow the cave open with explosives."

Salvatore sits down, props his elbows on the table, and points to Carter. "I don't want harm to come to anyone if it can be helped, but make no mistake about it, we will stop at nothing to get this weapon. Even if it means that one or all of you must die, then so be it. If you take us to the cave entrance and help me get the General's Relic, I will release you and your friends and no harm will come to any of you."

"I said I will take you there. I am willing to stick to the bargain. Can we get some coffee and breakfast?"

The group looks around at each other.

"You sure are brazen, young Carter."

"I'm no good to you hungry. We need energy to get you to the treasure."

"Pour these Americans some coffee and make them some toast."

Christie says, "Toast, we had toast yesterday. Are you trying to starve us? We want some biscuits for breakfast, something hardier than toast."

Carter looks hard at Salvatore. "You heard her, pick us up some chicken, sausage, and egg biscuits, along with some hash browns, and we will take you to the treasure."

"Okay, you two, over there! Go pick up the biscuits for these pampered Americans."

Chapter 60

The Shadow Seventeen henchmen return with breakfast for Christie, Rachel, and Carter.

Salvatore sets their food and drinks down near them. "There you go. Eat up and let's hit the road."

The Shadow Seventeen villains proceed to load their victims into the SUV.

Carter whispers to Rachel and Christie, "Everything is going to be okay. Don't worry. Blake is close by."

"What's that?" Salvatore asks.

"Nothing."

"Keep it that way," Salvatore says while motioning with his 9 mm for the three not to talk.

As they get closer, Carter guides the bad guys to the long lost treasure and the General's Relic.

The sky is a hazy, autumn day. The leaves are changing to their brilliant fall colors.

"Those jackets look familiar. The patches on them are the same ones they were wearing on their shirts in the jungle," says Christie.

"Yes, they seem to be a well-coordinated militia group," Rachel mumbles.

These men all have pistols strapped to their sides under their jackets. Several are wearing tactical ski masks. As the three SUVs enter the cotton field, the ride gets bumpy. The snow-white cotton fields stretch out as far as the eye can see.

Salvatore speaks up, "No one would ever guess that an ancient weapon of death was hidden here."

Carter hangs on to the vehicle's safety handle. "Just around the next turn, close to the railroad tracks. We will have to park and walk a little ways."

They park the SUVs on a dirt road, behind some trees, on the other side of the railroad track. They get out of the vehicles and proceed through a dense patch of woods. After a few minutes of hiking, the ground becomes more elevated and boulders start to surround them.

Carter keeps his eyes on the ground, watching his footing. "Up ahead is a thirty-foot cliff with boulders strewn around at the base of it. The entrance we used is a tight squeeze. I'll show you where we found the main entrance that is sealed up."

Rachel gives Carter a look of aggravation after he reveals there is an easier way to the treasure. Carter shrugs.

Carter brings the group to a halt. "Here is where we believe the main entrance used to be. This brush is covering the entrance. Blake and I used the other entrance a few hundred feet from here, but like I said, that passageway is very difficult. We pushed a stick with a white towel tied to it out of a small opening here to mark the original main entrance."

Salvatore points toward the brush. "Okay, you men get in there and plant the explosives up against the entrance. Everyone else get behind the boulders over there."

The Shadow Seventeen leader sets off C4 explosives, ripping open a jagged hole, throwing rocks, dirt, and leaves through the pines. As the smoke and dust from the explosion clears, the henchmen walk over to the cave's entrance to assess the damage. A jagged entrance about six feet tall and five feet wide has been blown open, exposing the long buried cave's main entrance.

Salvatore motions for Carter, Rachel, and Christie to follow him into the cave's entrance.

Unbeknownst to any in the group, Blake is now in tactical mode and has assembled a military quick strike force of elite soldiers from a Special Forces' division he has served with on many past missions.

Chapter 61

Blake contacted his comrades from the military and explained the situation. The intelligence community had been trying for some time to gather enough evidence to arrest Salvatore Vale. The company commander fast tracks clearance from his superiors to implement an operation due to the importance placed on capturing the leader of the Shadow Seventeen dark operations unit. The soldiers are flown in from various parts of the country by helicopters and jets.

For aerial reconnaissance, Blake calls his friend Sandra. “Sandra, this is Blake.”

Sandra pauses a second. “How’s it going, Blake? I was sure I would have heard from you sooner.”

“Listen, I know. I’m sorry about not calling. Things have been nuts—and I went from Spain to Cuba for clues to a treasure. I am mixed up with a bunch of bad guys and need your help. Can you fly a reconnaissance drone above some ruthless villains and provide me with their positions?”

“Sure, you bet, but it will cost you an evening on the town and a few glasses of chardonnay.”

“You got it. I will plug into the live feed once you email me the connection. I really meant to call sooner…”

“On the way to you now, Blake. Be careful. I am looking forward to that chardonnay.”

“One more little thing. Pam showed up on our trip to Cuba. No big deal but I thought you should know.”

“Oh, was she in a good mood? She works for me occasionally and is an incredible operative.”

"It's all good. She said she is helping us with our treasure hunt."

"It seems like she has taken a liking to your team. With her it goes 'no better friend no worse enemy.' Stay on her good side."

*

The Special Forces team gathers together in a parking lot between two tactical sheriffs' buses to plan the attack. The team discusses the topography of the assault using a map that Blake would normally use to find relic-hunting spots. They determine that a twelve-man team can get close enough to the Shadow Seventeen group to eliminate them and rescue the hostages.

Blake knows the area well and also knows that even a Special Forces team might have trouble approaching across a wide open cotton field without being seen.

Blake points to a railroad track on the map. "We can use the train tracks. We will ride the railcars right up to the cave's entrance. There is a low spot right here where we can hop off the cars and advance along the edge of the fields most of the way without any chance of being spotted. We'll be right on top of them before they know it."

Blake's commander has contacted the FBI and local law enforcement officials who supply the buses and logistical support. The sheriff's department helps the team in commandeering a train.

Blake checks his ammunition in his 1911 pistol and M4 rifle. "Let's get going! The train depot is only a few minutes away."

The assault group load up in SUVs provided by the local sheriff's department and proceed to the train depot.

It takes the Special Forces team about ten minutes to reach the train yard. They see the train conductor standing next to the engine and approach him.

"Sir, we have a life and death hostage situation." Blake points at a place on the map and hands it to the conductor. "We need your help to take us to this point on the railroad tracks and let us exit a train car."

"Oh, that's all. I wasn't quite sure what you all needed." The conductor takes his handkerchief and wipes the sweat from his forehead. "Thought there might be an explosive onboard. Just never know with all of the crazy things going on these days."

"Sir, you're absolutely right. So, can you take us?"

"Sure, glad to do my duty! Hop onboard."

The rescue team performs one last weapons check, as the conductor gets the train ready.

"I spoke with the train's operator, and he is more than happy to help out to rescue the hostages."

Once the team is onboard, the conductor asks Blake, "Did you know that this train travels along the same rails that were used during the Civil War?"

"Oh yeah, that's what led all of us here!"

The conductor holds his lamp up to head level and looks at Blake with one corner of his lip turned up, like he is trying to figure out what the heck Blake is talking about.

"It's a long story. But let's catch up sometime." Blake hands him his card and then turns to the team. "Men, gird your loins! On my command we will hop out of this railroad car and into battle!"

One of the men in the assault group asks, "What did he say about girding … you're what?"

"You heard him right. Gird your loins. We're in for a brisk fight. I've been on many missions with Blake, and he likes to quote from history, brings us good luck!"

It is a cold autumn evening. A slight fog shrouds the evening air.

With darkness falling fast the train approaches the area where the cave is. Blake turns on his helmet mounted night vision monocular to scan the area. "Look, right over there are the two Shadow Seventeen SUVs." Blake points behind some trees beside the cotton field.

"Are you sure it's them and not some deer hunters?" one of the members of the team asks.

"I'm certain those are the same black SUV's with tinted windows from the firefight we had at an old church in Virginia."

Sandra feeds Blake information on numbers and positions through his earpiece and on his smartphone.

At the designated spot, Blake gives a hand signal and the rescue team jumps out of the railcar. They slip along the edge of the cotton field and enter it, getting close to their designated target by using a hill in the middle of the field for concealment.

One of the bad guys sees a patch of cotton move. Thinking it isn't a deer moving around, he opens fire on full auto with his AK-47. The firefight erupts with the Special Forces team returning fire, laying down three-round bursts from their M4 carbines, holding their ground between the rows of cotton.

The men of Shadow Seventeen spray automatic fire from their AK-47's all over the field, throwing cotton up in the air until it seems to be snowing. One of the bullets from the Shadow Seventeen unit grazes the arm of one of the men of the Special Forces team. The rescue team remains calm but quickly realize they have lost the element of surprise. Another soldier takes a hit in his calf and goes down in pain. He keeps firing.

Blake yells out, "Fall back to cover. Fall back!" Blake grabs the wounded man by the back of his jacket and drags him to cover behind a small hill. The soldier keeps firing his M4 out at the Shadow Seventeen men while being dragged. "We've lost our element of surprise. They've fallen back behind boulders in those woods. Everyone spread out. We'll have to flank them."

Up near the cave's entrance no one noticed a figure dressed in black fatigues and a hooded face mask quickly moving into the cave's entrance. The unseen soldier had been hidden for several hours near the cave's entrance under leaves.

Blake and the men move out to get a better position.

Chapter 62

Salvatore swings his head, panicked. "Did you hear that?"

"Sounds like shots to me," Carter smirks.

"You two, go up to the entrance and find out what's going on!" Salvatore points to the men.

"But, sir, that leaves only you here."

"I can handle them. Get up there now!"

The ninja-like warrior upon entering the cave pulls out an FN five-seven pistol with silencer and puts on a night vision monocle over one eye. Moving quickly down the cave two bad guys come around the corner. Two shots from the silenced pistol and they are disposed of.

The shadowy figure sees that the room ahead is well lit up with LED lanterns and pauses to put away the night vision monocle. Coming around the corner Salvatore Vale has Rachel in front of him with a gun to her head.

"Stop! Don't come any closer! Drop your weapon or I will shoot."

Pam lowers her pistol to the ground.

Salvatore orders the black clad person to pull off their tactical ski mask. Pam's red hair falls out when she removes the hood.

"Ah, I recognize you! MI6's finest. Don't blink an eye or this girl dies."

"Actually, I am semi-retired from MI6 now. Got tired of dealing with scum like you Salvatore." Pam keeps Salvatore talking. When the time is right she intends to pull out her concealed Sig Sauer P238 pistol and kill Salvatore. "What do you want?"

"You know exactly what I want. The General's Relic belongs to me." Salvatore Vale presses his weapon up against Rachel's head. "If you come any closer, I will shoot her!"

Pam holds her hands out. "Take it easy. Let me know how we can resolve this, peacefully."

Salvatore grits his teeth. "I want a helicopter to come here, right outside the cave entrance. I want it to be ready to take me out of here safely."

Salvatore points to Carter with his gun, holding Rachel in a tight grip with his other arm. "I want you to open that chest now. I want to see the General's Relic."

Carter walks over to the chest with the key in his hand. Carter remembers the old Colt pistol lying atop the skull and crossbones chest. He thinks to himself that the Colt revolver has been protected from moisture all these years, and maybe it will fire. He knows that he might only have one chance to save his friends.

Carter opens the chest. In a quick fluid movement, Carter has the old Colt out of its holster. Rachel viciously slams her elbow into Salvatore's ribcage as he fires his gun. The round misses Carter, knocking a hole in the side of the wagon. Carter aims the powerful Civil War pistol at Salvatore's shocked face and squeezes the trigger.

The 1860 army Colt revolver thunders off its round, dropping Salvatore dead with a .44 bullet through his left eye socket. His head jerks back, then he falls onto his face, ending the threat.

Chapter 63

Carter drops the Colt .44 and rushes forward to catch Rachel.

"Are you okay?" Carter brushes Rachel's hair from her face.

"I'm fine."

Pam picks up her pistol. "Great shot, Carter!"

Carter looks up and over at Pam. "Thanks, We really owe you. You saved our lives."

"Nothing to it. You fired the kill shot." She gives Salvatore a kick to make sure he is dead. "The world will be a lot safer without this guy around." Pam armed with her powerful FN Five-seven pistol turns her attention to the caves corridor to keep an eye out for any more bad guys that might reenter the cave. She has her military spec radio search for the channels being used by the rescuers outside. "Blake, this is Pam. I am inside the cave. Salvatore Vale is dead and the hostages are rescued."

Blake radios in to the local law enforcement and they announce over a loud speaker to the Shadow Seventeen men that Salvatore is dead. Some of Blake's men come in behind the bad guys near the cave's entrance and order them to drop their weapons. The remaining Shadow Seventeen men surrender. Overhead a police helicopter hovers shining its search light onto the area.

Christie sits down and looks up at Rachel. "I've had my fill of adventures for a while. Y'all really take them to the extreme."

"So what are we going to do with the General's Relic?" asks Carter.

A sheriff's deputy approaches. "We'd better take that dangerous-looking box back to headquarters. You can do what you like with the treasure, but I can't let you leave with that box."

Carter raises his eyebrows and smiles. "Fine with me. What say we load this gold up, y'all?"

Pam looks over at Carter. "Don't forget about Captain Flint and his team. They deserve some of this bounty also."

Blake walks up. "There is plenty here for everyone." He points one figure in the air, swirls it, and looks over at his treasure hunting friends, "You heard the sheriff's deputy, let's load up this gold before they change their mind. They can keep the General's Relic!"